MW00491887

MURDER BEYOND THE PALE

A JESSE O'HARA NOVEL

WENDY CHURCH

POLIS BOOKS

The following is a work of fiction. Names, characters, places, events and incidents are either the product of the author's imagination or used in an entirely fictitious manner. Any resemblance to actual persons, living or dead, is entirely coincidental.

Copyright © 2023 by Wendy Church
Cover and jacket design by 2Faced Design

ISBN 978-1-957957-34-0
eISBN: 978-1-957957-49-4

Library of Congress Control Number: available upon request

First hardcover edition November 2023 by Polis Books, LLC
62 Ottowa Road South
Marlboro, NJ 07746
www.PolisBooks.com

For Rudy

PROLOGUE

It was December, and I was shirtless. I should have been cold. But I felt comfortably warm, possibly from the large quantity of alcohol I'd put away in the last hour.

Sitting under the stars, drinking my favorite whiskey, made it an almost perfect night, marred only by the dampness seeping into my jeans from the wet ground. That, and the barrage of bullets whizzing just above my head. Every now and then one of them would plow into the wall on the other side of me, chipping the stone, and a piece would ricochet into my head. I was bleeding now from a dozen small cuts. Nothing serious yet, as far as I could tell. And the warm blood slowly dripping down my face and neck was oddly soothing. I was grateful to this wall for taking all of those bullets for me. Made centuries ago by Irish farmers, the low limestone structure was the only thing separating me from four angry men with guns.

I took another drink from the bottle in my hand. Jameson 18 Years. *Damn. So smooth.*

I could taste fruit, honey, caramel, a touch of spice and vanilla, and just enough burn to make sure you knew you were drinking whiskey. I savored the long finish.

It was a shame I wouldn't be able to drink it all.

I pulled off one boot and sock, then took one last, long sip and stuffed the sock into the mouth of the bottle. I lit the end of it on fire and threw it over the wall, in the direction of my attackers.

The gratifying sound of glass shattering on pavement was followed by a flash of light and then heat.

The bullets stopped.

They'd start up again shortly, I knew. I'd kept the men with guns away for over an hour, but it wouldn't be long now.

I reached into the case for the last bottle.

ONE

"I'm seeing Dad next week. Do you want me to take a message to him?" my sister said.

"Sure." I drummed my fingers on the countertop while I waited through her lengthy pause.

"You know I'm not going to say, 'Fuck you,' to our father, right?"

"Oh. Well then, no message. Thanks."

We were on the phone, but I was familiar with Shannon's sigh and the face that went with it. "You know, he's changed a lot."

"I'm sure he has." I lowered my voice and rasped an ominous-sounding, "Prison changes a man."

"He's been sober for over a decade now. He's completely different."

"It's not like he's had a choice." I knew prisoners could get their hands on alcohol and other contraband, but my dad had never been that resourceful.

"You should go for a visit. He really wants to see you."

This conversation again. I picked up the Jameson bottle on the kitchen counter and poured a healthy amount into an only slightly dirty glass, then opened the freezer and dropped in a couple of ice cubes. "I have seen him," I said, taking a deep sip.

"Showing up at his parole hearings and arguing *against* early release doesn't count as visitation."

"He'll be out soon enough anyway." I took another drink, the ice cubes clinking against the glass. Over the years, I'd gone to every one of his parole hearings, offering comprehensive arguments for keeping him in prison. As far as I was concerned, his fifteen-year sentence was too light.

"Are you drinking *already*? Tell me that's not alcohol. It's eleven in the morning."

"It's eleven thirty somewhere."

She sighed again, a different one that I recognized as the precursor to the end of our discussion. Surprising me, she said, "Can you stay on for a few minutes? Seamus has something he wants to talk to you about."

"Sure." I waited while she passed the phone over, again contemplating the awesome alliteration of Seamus and Shannon's married union.

"Hi, Jesse. How are you?"

"Hey, Seamus. Fine, you?"

He paused. "I need your help."

That was new. Seamus and Shannon had been married for three years, and during that time, I'd never heard him utter those words. He was a hardworking, stand-up guy, and I'd been relieved when they announced their engagement. Shannon had only been thirteen when Mom died and Dad went off to prison, so she'd been sent to live with our grandmother in Cleveland. I always worried about where she'd end up. The track record of kids with alcoholic fathers wasn't great. In my view, she'd gotten the worst end of the family stick, and by all accounts, she should have been the more damaged offspring. But Gram had done a great job with her, and Shannon ended up really solid. She would likely be having kids soon, who would also no doubt be more well-adjusted than me. An admittedly low bar.

"What's up?" I replied.

"You know my brother, Michael?"

"The one who lives in Ireland?"

"Yes, in Sligo, western Ireland. His daughter, my niece, Cait... she's missing."

I searched my brain to recall the last family gathering and my half-hearted participation in its mind-numbing small talk. "Didn't she go off to college this year?"

"She did. In Galway, at NUI, the National University of Ireland. She was supposed to come home for Christmas break. She never showed up."

"That doesn't sound all that strange for a college kid. If it's her first year, she's probably just running around with friends."

"That's what the police told them. But, normally, she talks to her mom every day, and Rose hasn't heard from her in a week. They've been calling and texting her...there's nothing. They're really worried."

"Have they contacted the university?"

"Yes. She's not on campus."

"Does she have a boyfriend?" Lots of young women on their first time away from home get caught up with a guy. I wasn't sure what it was like in Ireland, but I assumed college kids were pretty much the same everywhere.

"There's a boy in Sligo she's close to. But he hasn't seen or heard from her either."

This didn't sound good, but I wasn't sure why he was telling me this.

"Shannon tells me you're an investigator."

And there it is. "You know I'm a *financial* investigator and expert witness, right?" Or, at least, *was.* After my last, now world-famous courtroom gaff, my expert witness business was dead, another in a long line of career corpses I'd accumulated by the age of thirty. I'd dropped one F-bomb too many in front of the wrong people.

"But you helped solve that bombing case in Spain last year, didn't you? You caught a terrorist?"

It had been in all the papers. My friend Sam had gifted me a luxury cruise around Spain, one that happened to include a terrorist in the process of trying to blow up an industrial gas plant in Bilbao. We'd caught the bomber and prevented a catastrophe. Given my aversion to being trapped on a boat, or anywhere, with lots of people, that had been the highlight of the trip for me.

"Yes. But this is a missing person's case. I don't have any experience with that."

"Jesse, you're really smart. And we all know about your... special abilities. The police haven't found anything, and my brother doesn't know what else to do." I heard his voice catch. "You have family in Ireland, don't you? You could use the trip to visit them."

I'd traveled pretty extensively after college but somehow missed Ireland, which was strange, as both sides of my family were from there, two of the four grandparents having come over on the figurative boat. My family had deep Irish roots, and I looked it. Straight, almost black hair to my shoulders, pale skin, blue eyes, a deep and abiding love of whiskey...I would fit right in. And the Guinness and Jameson plant tours *were* on my bucket list.

"I'll pay you, and pay for the trip."

I'd always wanted to go to Ireland. And I could write it off on my taxes, should I actually earn enough this year to pay any. And maybe there was something to this investigation thing. I was one for one so far...

"Please, Jesse, this is killing Michael."

It *would* be an easy trip. I'd discover that his niece went away for a few weeks to explore her sexuality, get her to call her mom, and then tour my ancestral home, a land filled with ancient megaliths and other very cool historical artifacts. Not to mention that Ireland now sported a growing number of world-class chefs and had recently experienced a renaissance in their food scene. Yeah, this could be a thing.

"Okay, I'll check it out. Tell Michael I'll let him know when I'm coming in."

He exhaled loudly. "Thanks, Jesse. I've met Cait. She's got a great head on her. I really think there's something wrong."

We said goodbye and hung up. Apparently, Shannon had no parting words for me.

I finished my drink and walked out of the small house, into the yard. I'd been staying at Sam's the last few days, a large estate in the Edgewood neighborhood of Chicago. Her place resembled a retreat center, with a main house flanked by a number of smaller ones, like little vacation homes, including the one I'd been staying in. Even though I had my own place, I often stayed at Sam's. The big, empty house I'd shared with my family seemed lifeless now, and I slept better here.

I went to the big house to look for her. Her pack of rescue dogs greeted me at the door, tails wagging. I'd never known her to have fewer than five dogs at one time, along with an indeterminate number of cats. I scratched each of their heads, the price of admission into the house. The pack followed me up the winding staircase, where I found Sam painting in her second-floor studio. As I stepped into the room, I heard a low growl.

Chaz, the sixth rescue dog, was on the floor, sitting on a pile of soft, flannel blankets, all nestled on top of a memory foam mattress several times bigger than he was. He was a Chinese Crested breed, also known as the Jeopardy answer to, "What is the ugliest carbon-based life-form in the universe?" And it wasn't just the way he looked. His personality was as fucked up as his face. At least around me.

He didn't get up when I came in, but his eyes narrowed and his thin gray lips quivered as he bared his crooked teeth. I gave him the finger.

I stood behind Sam and watched her paint for a moment. She was really good.

"Want to go to Ireland?"

She put the brush down on the palette and picked up a small towel to wipe her hands while she turned to me. "Any special occasion?"

"My brother-in-law's family in Sligo needs some help. They think their daughter is missing. He thinks I have mad skills and wants me to help look for her."

"You *do* have mad skills."

It was true, I did have some mad skills. Mostly related to a near-photographic memory and an ability to know when people were lying to me, which seemed constant in daily life and why I preferred to avoid them for the most part. I also had a PhD, was maniacally goal oriented, pathologically curious, and a little bit of an asshole, all of which made me perfect for a career in investigative forensic accounting and its lucrative side business, expert witnessing. I'd been really good at it and starting to make real money in high-stakes corporate malfeasance cases. Then I'd blown it by losing my cool on the witness stand, telling the court that the high-profile defendant was "as useful as a baby building a space shuttle." My sense of humor and skill with simile weren't assets on the witness stand, and I'd been unemployed since.

At the moment, I was still searching for my next career, and it wasn't immediately obvious what would best take advantage of my unique skillset and general misanthropy.

"We'd need to leave soon. If she's really missing, every day will count." I knew this for a fact, having watched every episode of *Law and Order*, *Law and Order: UK*, *Law and Order: SVU*, and *Law and Order: Criminal Intent*. Most people who went missing were either found soon or not at all.

Sam raised an eyebrow. "If?"

"She's been away at college and didn't come home for the Christmas break. It may be that she just decided she likes being an adult and is doing her own thing. I don't think it's going to take very long. She's probably running around with a boyfriend. We can meet with the family, look around, find out where she is, and then see the sites."

"I'm guessing by *sites* you mean the breweries and distilleries?"

"You know it. And the megaliths. The country is filled with monuments that are thousands of years old. You know I love that stuff."

"I haven't been to Ireland in years...it would be nice to check out the art scene," she said, looking out window.

"Well, we're going to be starting in Sligo. I'm not sure what kind of scene they'll have there. It's a small town, across the Island from Dublin."

"They have the Model Art Gallery."

I wasn't surprised Sam knew about a fucking gallery in Sligo. She'd spent a number of years in English boarding schools, which in addition to acting as a springboard for travel, also left her with a faint and very pleasant English accent.

She looked over at the dog bed. "I really would love to go. But I'm not sure I should leave Chaz right now. He's depressed."

"Why? Did he finally look in a mirror?"

She leaned down to scratch him under the chin. "It's just a side effect of the chemo. You know, I don't understand why the two of you don't get along."

"I don't know either. Most dogs love me. Maybe he was dropped on his face as a puppy. That would explain a lot."

Sam picked him up, ignoring my comment. "What about Gideon? Do you think he could take care of him?"

"Normally, yeah, but he's in the middle of a big project at work." Gideon was a former boyfriend of mine. Our romantic relationship had hit a snag when he realized he was gay, but we'd remained close friends. One of two for me.

She looked at the canine Toxic Avenger fondly. "Maybe I can get Tatiana to watch him."

Tatiana Borisova was the young Russian woman we'd met on the cruise the year before. Sam had informally adopted her after Tatiana's father was captured trying to blow up the gas plant. He'd been blackmailed to do it, but he still had to spend some time in prison. The woman who'd blackmailed him was Svetlana Ivaschenko, the CEO of Russia's largest oil company. She'd gotten away after we uncovered her plot and was still at large, and we were worried for Tatiana's safety if she went back to Russia. I was worried for my own too, which accounted for the other reason I often stayed at Sam's place. She had a state-of-the-art security system that made it easier for me to sleep at night.

Sam put Chaz gently back down on his bed. "It shouldn't be too difficult for Tatiana to watch him. He's past the worst of it now; the doctors say he's in remission. There's no more cancer in his body."

It probably left voluntarily. Even cancer has standards. "Can you ask her? And I'll see if Gideon will check in on them while we're gone."

"Okay. When do you want to leave?"

"Let's try for tomorrow. If Cait's really missing, then time is important."

But I wasn't too worried. I remembered my first year in college, and if my folks had called the cops every time I didn't contact them for a week, they would have had the police station on speed dial. That is, if I'd had any parents around when I went to college.

I was excited. I was finally going to the home of my ancestors. We'd get there, wrap things up quickly, then hit the country for some archaeology and drinking. Not necessarily in that order.

TWO

We took the redeye the next night from Chicago to Dublin. The last time I'd been on a plane was a few months ago when I went to San Sebastien to see Ander. He was a federal law enforcement officer I'd met while he was working undercover on the cruise we'd taken. He was smart, great looking, and a terrific guy, and I really liked him. But it wasn't going anywhere. He wasn't going to move to Chicago, and I wasn't going to move to the Basque Country, and I didn't think transatlantic booty calls would make a great foundation for a long-term relationship.

As usual, Sam had upgraded us to first class, another benefit to having my best friend be over-the-top wealthy. Her family was old money. Her grandparents were from Spain, but left with their fortune during the Franco years. They'd settled in a suburb near Chicago where her mom was born. As many rich kids did when coming of age, her mom had traveled the world. She'd met a man in Jamaica during that trip, one that was cut short by the arrival of Sam.

As the first grandchild, Sam had been raised in the lap of luxury, but despite her privileged background, she didn't have the sense of entitlement that often went along with that. She oozed genuine warmth and compassion, was almost always happy, and as a result had a large and constantly growing circle of friends. In other words, the polar opposite of me. Sam approached people with interest and curiosity. My frame of mind with people started at apprehension and, depending on my first impression, could escalate quickly to barely concealed hostility, often followed by escalating verbal abuse. The two of us averaged out to a normal person.

Our strong friendship was the result of unique circumstances. I'd met her in college, late one night in a near-empty campus building. She was being assaulted by a group of men, and I'd interrupted the attack by cleverly getting the shit beat out of me long enough to distract them. She'd escaped, and I'd gotten away mostly intact. The four-inch scar on my forehead was the only remaining physical artifact of the event, but the trauma we'd experienced together had created a singular bond between us.

The sky was clear, and we could see the coastline as the plane lowered for landing at Dublin Airport. The Emerald Isle was aptly named. Dublin was by far Ireland's biggest city at almost a million and a half people, but there was still green everywhere, including patches of it in the heart of the city. Outside of the city boundaries, all I could see were green fields lightly crisscrossed by small highways. Sligo was on the other side of the island, and while the Knock Airport was closer to Sligo than Dublin, there were no direct flights into Knock from Chicago. But the drive across the island would take less than three hours, and we needed a car anyway. I wasn't sure where the investigation would lead, and I might have to go to the university in Galway at some point.

First class meant being first off the plane, and we made it through customs and the car rental desk quickly. We weren't scheduled to be in Sligo until three and had more time than I'd planned for us to get there, so I made an executive decision. Leaving the airport, I headed south.

Looking out the window, Sam asked, "Isn't Sligo the other way?"

"We have time for one stop."

I drove into the center of Dublin, eventually leaving the modern city's large roads for cobblestone, and parked the car. We walked a couple of blocks, turning onto a narrow street. After a short way, I stopped and looked up at a green sign.

Bow Street. ESTD 1780. Dublin. The site of the original Jameson Distillery.

My drink of choice was a beer and a shot. Specifically, Guinness and Jameson. This was the birthplace of Jameson. Even though the distillery had moved to Cork many years ago, this was where it had all started.

I stood in reverent silence. This was a sacred place, the holiest of grails. Looking up, I wondered if this was how other people felt when they visited the Sistine Chapel or the Parthenon. I resisted the urge to drop to my knees and kiss the sidewalk.

"Are you crying?" Sam asked incredulously.

"No."

We walked into the building, and Sam waited patiently while I looked around the space, which included high ceilings, wooden bars and tables, and a spectacular chandelier made entirely of Jameson bottles. I wondered if I could get one of those.

"Too bad we don't have time for a tour," she said, looking at a brochure. "It includes a comparative whiskey tasting."

"We can come back." I knew for a fact we'd be back. It wouldn't be a good idea to show up in Sligo with whiskey on my breath. But this was a chance to get an early start on my Ireland bucket list. Item number four was to buy my favorite whiskey directly from the source. I picked up a case of Jameson and splurged by throwing in a few bottles of the higher end Jameson 18 Years.

When we got to the car, I put the case in the back seat, laying it gently on our coats and securing it carefully with the seatbelt.

I gave Sam the keys. I usually liked to drive, but I wanted a chance to look around the countryside, my first view of the home of my ancestors. She headed out slowly over the surface streets and back to the highway.

We took the M4 and then the N4 that cut west across the

island, the most direct route to Sligo. The view from the plane had been an accurate preview. Once we left the outskirts of Dublin, it was a largely pastoral swath of green fields frequently bounded by low stone walls whose primary purpose appeared to be keeping sheep from wandering into the roads. The walls were everywhere, miles of them, snaking around the countryside in every direction.

It was cold and the rain was coming down in a light mist. This normally would have been a serene, peaceful road trip. But as usual, with Sam driving, it was impossible to relax. Speed limits to her were quaint suggestions, and we were screaming down the narrow two-lane freeways, passing everything in a blur and barely avoiding banging into the walls that sometimes came right up to the road. At their largest point, the highways were four lanes across, but in many places, they narrowed to two. And while periodically we encountered slow-moving trucks that were backing up traffic and should have slowed us down, they had the opposite effect on Sam. She relished the opportunity to pass them. It gave her an excuse to drive faster.

"You're a maniac," I said, exhaling a breath I'd been holding as she flew down the wrong side of the road to pass a small pickup.

"I'm a great driver."

"If by *great* you mean that you haven't killed anyone yet, then yes, you're *great*. Can you please slow down? We're not in that big of a hurry."

She slowed down briefly, but sped up again after a few miles.

I gave up and tightened my grip on the doorhandle. For the next two and half hours I focused on not thinking about dying in a fiery car crash. We crossed into County Sligo from County Roscommon and I started to relax. After another half hour or so we'd be in Sligo and she'd be forced to stop for lights.

Traffic had been light, but as we passed through a little town called Collooney, it came almost to a halt. Up ahead of us were flashing lights. Normally, I found traffic jams highly irritating, but in this case breathed a sigh of relief when Sam had to slow down. I loosened my grip on the doorhandle.

We moved slowly, stopping and starting until we were adjacent to the commotion. There were several white cars and vans parked along the side of the road with yellow and blue stripes and Garda written on them. Uniformed officers stood outside of the cars, looking into an undeveloped marshy area.

"Can you pull over?" I said, peering out the window.

Sam drove the car over to the side and came to a stop just ahead of the garda vehicles on the grassy strip alongside the road. I got out and walked back to where they were setting up police tape.

A garda walked over and put a hand up. Officer Murphy, by his name tag. "Ma'am, please step away."

"What's going on?" I tried to look over his shoulder.

A group of six gardaí and a couple of guys in suits stood huddled around something on the mucky ground. They were peering into the brush. Two other men in suits were standing within the perimeter being set up by the tape, along with one guy wearing one of those white paper suits that didn't leave any contamination.

Officer Murphy looked up the road, ignoring my question. "Ma'am, is that your car? Please return to it and continue on."

"Can you just tell me what's in there?"

His voice took on an officious tone. "Ma'am, if you don't return to your car, I'm going to have to give you a citation." He motioned to one of the other cops, who started to walk toward us.

I didn't want to spend my first day there in Irish jail, so went back to our car and got in.

"Well?" said Sam.

"I don't know. There's some kind of crime scene in the marsh. But I couldn't see anything, and they're not talking."

Sam unbuckled her seatbelt and got out. She walked over to Officer Murphy, now standing with the group of officers. I couldn't hear them, but I could see their body language. All five of them turned to her, leaning forward slightly. She was smiling, and they looked like they were competing to see who could tell her the most.

No surprise there. In addition to her magnetic personality, Sam was world-class beautiful, her stunning looks stopping most people in their tracks. Her lush brown hair framed high cheek-bones; large, deep brown eyes; olive skin; and the world's most winning smile. It was a deadly combination for anyone trying to keep a secret.

A few minutes later, she came back to the car, but not before every one of the gardaí had given her his personal card.

"We're at the edge of the Slieveward Bog. They've just pulled a body out."

"A bog body?"

I'd read about those. Ireland was covered in bogs, a type of wetland, but with a unique composition that was more acidic than other kinds of swamps. The particular chemistry of bogs acted like a kind of natural embalming, and they'd found bodies in them that were literally thousands of years old. In some cases, the bodies were so well preserved that they could tell what they'd eaten for their last meal. They'd found one a few years ago in a small village about fifty miles west of Dublin. A two-thousand-year-old man who was in such great shape they could see the manicure on his nails.

"Actually, they found *two* bodies."

"Wow...the anthropologists will have a field day with that one. No pun intended."

"The thing is, they're not old. They're recent."

"How recent?"

She hesitated. "Very."

I started to get a sinking feeling. "Was either one a woman?"

"They don't know yet."

I didn't say what we were both thinking. This could be the shortest missing persons investigation in history.

We got back on the road. The traffic cleared up quickly once we got past the bog. Even with the delay, thanks to Sam's lead foot we'd made it to Sligo in just under two and a half hours.

My plan had been to stop at Cait's home, talk to her parents, and then visit the local police—gardaí—to find out where they were with their investigation and see what we could learn. If that didn't get us anywhere, and if Cait didn't turn up in the meantime, we'd go to the university in Galway tomorrow.

Added to that plan now was to find out whose bodies they'd pulled out of the bog.

THREE

The Gallaghers' house was a little southeast of the town center, in the middle of a residential neighborhood not too far from the Sligo Racecourse. The lot was large; as far as I could tell, the biggest in the neighborhood. Low, manicured hedges framed the yard in front of the tidy house. Around the back was a green barn surrounded by pasture, in which a couple of horses idly ate grass.

The long driveway from the street to the house was visible from the front window, and by the time we parked, a small woman was standing on the front porch. She was short and a little stout. Her dark hair was flecked with gray and held up in a bun. She was wearing an apron and wiping her hands with a kitchen towel.

As we got out of the car, she walked toward us, her brow furrowed and her hands clasped tightly in front of her. "Dr. O'Hara?"

"Yes, Mrs. Gallagher?"

"Please call me Rose." She looked at Sam.

"This is Sam. She'll be helping me look for your daughter."

Rose came to each of us, her blue eyes shining as she took our hands in both of hers and shook them gently. "Thank you. Thank you. Please come in."

We followed her up the carefully groomed path to the door and went in. She closed the door behind us and led us into a living room. The room was high-ceilinged and dominated by a massive fireplace, in front of which were a couch and coffee table resting on a thick rug. Adjacent was a dining room with a large table surrounded by chairs, and the walls were covered with paintings and photographs of horses. The house was modern other than the fireplace, which looked extremely old. I could have seen the same one in *Outlander*. Its substantial mantel was crowded with framed pictures, almost all of the same four people. Three boys and one girl.

I picked up one of the photos with just the girl. "Is this Cait?"

Rose looked over my shoulder and nodded, then touched the photo gently. "That's our girl." Up close, I could see Rose's eyes were red, and she was drawn and tired.

"How old is she?" I said, handing the picture to Sam.

"Nineteen, just. The baby of the family. We took that photo a few months ago, before she went off to university."

In the picture, Cait was standing in front of the house with some luggage, smiling broadly and holding up a small banner with NUI, Galway in bold white letters. She had long, slightly wavy red hair that framed her face, flawless white skin, and striking green eyes. She was pretty. Maybe not in Sam's league, but no slouch either.

I put the picture back on the mantel. "Is this her first year away at school?"

Rose nodded, then reached into her apron pocket, pulled out a well-worn rosary, and ran her fingers along it.

"What is she studying?'

"She's started her courses in the Business and Law College. She's very smart, our Cait..." She broke off, her voice wavering as she fingered the rosary again.

Rose picked up more pictures one by one and showed them to me, pointing out Cait in each frame. Cait with her brothers as a baby; Cait as a toddler; Cait on her dad's shoulders at the beach; Cait on a horse. She looked happy, really joyful, in each picture. Each time she picked up a frame, Rose would touch Cait's face.

I felt a wave of pity. Even if Cait was on a lark, her mom was worried to death. It was her only girl. I was about to say something sympathetic, when she put the last picture down and turned around. I saw her face change in an instant from sadness to stormy.

"*Brian!*" Rose's thunderous shout came out of nowhere and Sam and I startled. I heard the slight tinkle of mantelpiece tchotchkes shaking.

A young man appeared at the top of the stairs.

"Get off your duff and bring in the extra chair."

Brian came down the stairs and went off into an adjoining room.

"That's my layabout son Brian." Rose pulled down one of the pictures, looked at it lovingly, then gave it to me. "That's himself with John and Colin. They'll all be joining us for dinner."

The picture showed the three boys at a beach, standing in front of the surf. Colin and John were clearly twins, both dark haired and dark eyed. Brian looked more like Cait, with reddish hair and the same intense green eyes.

Sam and I had a hotel room in town and hadn't planned to come back to the house, but it didn't seem like Rose was the kind to take no for an answer. I looked over Rose's head and raised my eyebrows at Sam. She gave a little nod.

Rose gestured for Sam to take the couch, and she sat down. Brian came in with the chair and put it down next to the couch.

"Jesus, Mary, and Joseph in a van, Brian! Bring the *nice* chair!"

Brian picked up the chair and left, returning a few moments later with the Nice Chair. Rose gestured to me, and I sat down on it. It was nice.

Brian stood behind his mother, resting a hand on her shoulder. She reached up behind her and put her hand on his, and he covered it with his other one. She tilted her head and leaned her cheek into it, briefly closing her eyes.

"Mrs. Gallagher—"

"Rose."

"Rose. Can you tell me about Cait? Why do you think she's missing and not just with friends?"

Rose looked around, then her face set into the same look she'd had before she yelled at Brian to bring the chair. This time I was prepared.

"*Brian!* Are ye *daft*? Bring out the tea!"

Brian gave me a small smile and a wink and left for the kitchen.

"Cait is a nice girl. She tells us everything. She wouldn't tell us she's coming home and then not come." She ran her fingers again along the rosary.

"Could she be with a boyfriend?"

"Her and Paddy were spending time here before she went off to university. He lives down the street. They've known each other since they were wanes. He hasn't heard from her either. If ye want to talk to him now, he'll be at the pub with Mik."

"Mik?"

"Cait's da. They're close since his own passed."

"And you've spoken with the police here? Er, the gardaí?"

"The gardaí say they looked into it, but they don't have much contact with those in Galway. The Galway ones took a report, but I think they believe she's just a wild child. They say that young ones often runabout at college and that I shouldn't worry. I know my Cait. She wouldn't runabout."

"Does she have any other friends in Sligo? Girlfriends?"

"Aye, she's loads of friends. Most went to university too and are just back. We've asked around, but they've not heard from her." She reached into the pocket in her apron and pulled out a card. "This is the Sligo detective who has her case. He's the one who talked to the friends." She handed me the card, then looked down at her lap and ran her fingers over her rosary again. "I know she's in trouble, Dr. O'Hara. She's a good girl. It's not like her to just disappear."

"Please call me Jesse, Rose."

Sam asked, "Rose, does Cait have any special places she likes to go? Clubs? Or groups here she spends time with?"

Rose looked down at her lap, saying quietly, "She's not a nighttime girl, if that's what yer askin'. She likes the outdoors. She's hiked most of the trails around Sligo many times..." Her voice trailed off, and she closed her eyes again. She was anguished and unlikely to tell me much more at the moment.

I looked at my watch. It was close to four, and I wasn't sure how late the garda station would be open. "Rose, I need to head over to the station. Before I go, do you mind if I take a look in Cait's room?"

"Yes, of course. Her room is at the top of the stairs, first door on your right. Don't mind Fergus."

I got up off the couch and headed toward the stairs, leaving Sam behind. I knew she would use the time to see what else Rose would tell her. I went up the stairs and found Cait's room. The room was small, with a bed in the corner underneath a window, a vanity and desk alongside one wall, and a closet next to a large bookshelf on the other. The bed was made and looked like it hadn't been slept in other than for the large and very old golden retriever laying on it now.

"Fergus?"

He opened his eyes and his tail wagged weakly once on the bedcover. I guessed he was Cait's dog, doing what all dogs did when their main person went away to college. Actively missing her in a way that only dogs could.

The desk was covered with neat stacks of papers and books. There were a few small, framed pictures of the family. I opened the closet. It was filled with clothes that were functional and nice. A couple of button-down blouses, a light jacket, and some turtle-necks. Nothing that screamed *party girl*.

The large wooden bookcase was overflowing with books stacked on top of each other, along with a few resting on the floor in piles that hadn't yet found their way to a shelf. I scanned the titles: James Joyce, Shakespeare's complete works, various volumes on Irish history and mythology. And, of course,

Yeats, one of Sligo's famous sons. All of the books looked well worn.

I moved to the dresser, on which was a mirror and a jewelry box that held a necklace with a cross, a few rings, and a rosary. Interesting that she hadn't taken the rosary with her.

What I wasn't seeing was as notable as what I was—no entertainment or teen magazines, no posters of famous singers or movie stars, no ceramic figurines, no knickknacks of any kind. Nothing frivolous.

Kids often went nuts when they got away from home the first time and were faced with a new world of options. But it was hard to reconcile that image with what I was seeing in Cait's room. Everything in this room spoke to an intelligent, serious young woman, not the kind to go clubbing, get wasted, and go home with someone for an extended period of time. In other words, not like me at that age.

I gave Fergus a scratch on the head and left the room, wanting to leave plenty of time for the visit to the garda station.

Rose was staring blankly out the window, as if waiting for her daughter to walk up at any moment. She turned when I came into the room. "Where are your bags?"

"They're in the car. We booked a room at the Glasshouse."

"Nonsense. You're looking for our girl, the least we can do is put you up in our house. You'll stay with us for the duration. Please treat it as your own."

Sam nodded to me behind Rose's back. Done deal, I guess. We'd be staying with the Gallaghers.

Rose reached into the pocket of her apron and pulled out a key. "So ye can come and go as ye please. Dinner is at six." She handed me the key, then frowned. "*Brian!* Bring the girls' bags in from the car and put them in the rooms."

"Can I help you with dinner, Rose?" Sam said.

"That would be lovely of you." But she didn't move, continuing to stare out the window.

We were interrupted by a loud *bang* and then the clattering of a door. A brown blur dashed into the living room, raced among the chairs, did small circles around each of us, leaped on top of the couch, jumped from there to the Nice Chair, and then bounced off to run back out to the kitchen. We heard another *bang* and clattering.

"What the hell was that?" I said, looking toward the kitchen.

"Don't mind him. That's Wee Petey. He's our small dog." Wee Petey's entrance seemed to break Rose out of her trance, and she turned from the window and headed into the kitchen.

Sam gave me a little wave and joined her.

Brian followed me out the door and we walked together to the car. "So, you've done this before, yeah? Find people?" he asked.

"I'm, uh..." I didn't want to tell him that I'd actually never done this before. "I've done a lot of investigations."

He seemed satisfied with that and took our bags out of the car. He waved goodbye as I pulled out of the driveway. I waved back, smiling way more confidently than I felt.

I'd been operating under the assumption that Cait was doing the Christmas holiday her way, a getaway with some friends or catching some serious alone time with a boyfriend. But while what is in your bedroom in your parents' house isn't necessarily reflective of a complete personality, I was good at reading clues, and this kid wasn't a flake. The notion that something bad had happened to her was looking more plausible.

I was starting to get a bad feeling about this. My bucket list might have to wait.

FOUR

I t took me all of two minutes to drive to the garda station. It was on Pearse Road, near the confluence of three streets that looked like some of Sligo's major thoroughfares: Pearse, Chapel, and Old Market. I parked a few blocks away and walked over.

I liked the look of the town. The buildings in the area were a mix of new and really old, the kind of old you don't see in the US. My short walk took me by Sligo Abbey, a thirteenth-century monastery and one of Sligo's most famous landmarks. A single tower anchored the roofless structure, surrounded by very thick stone walls with parapets. It was hard to believe something that old was still standing. I was looking forward to exploring it and the rest of the town once we tracked down Cait. The garda station was just down and across from the Sligo Courthouse, a stone castle-looking thing with round archways. Further up the street was a pub on the corner, and not far from that a number of shops and restaurants. Modern apartments were comfortably situated among the businesses and old buildings. The sidewalks and shops were bustling with lots of people out and about.

The garda station was small and old, limestone bricks framing three floors of windows. I walked through the entryway that jutted out into the sidewalk and then into a small lobby. There were a couple of chairs and a bench, and a presumably locked door leading into the inner workings of Sligo's finest. Behind a window at a counter sat a thirty-something uniformed officer, slender and prematurely balding, sporting a frail brown mustache.

I leaned over the counter and explained who I was and who I wanted to see. Officer O'Fenton, according to his nametag, looked up briefly and then back down, telling me in a deep but oddly effete voice to take a seat, someone would be with me shortly.

Fifteen minutes later, I was still waiting. A number of uniformed officers had gone in and out of the locked door since I'd gotten there, but no one for me. I got up to check in again, but as I was just standing up, Officer O'Fenton said politely, without looking up, "Someone will be with you shortly."

I sat back down.

Thirty minutes later, I decided I'd had enough. It was after five, and I was worried they'd leave me there until they closed. I stood up again just as a small group of officers came from the back, into the reception area. I used the group to shield me from O'Fenton and slid through the closing door after the last one came through.

The sanctum sanctorum of Sligo's law enforcement consisted primarily of a large open room crowded with desks, ringed by a few offices and conference rooms. Two hallways led off the main area, presumably to whatever jail or holding cells they had and likely bathrooms and a kitchen. And while the whole place looked like it had undergone recent renovations, it was by no means modern. New computers sat on old wooden desks, and a recent paintjob hadn't entirely covered up the cracks in the walls and ceiling. There were twenty-five people, all but three of them men, in the main area. Half were in uniforms, the other half in suits. I scanned the room and found what I was looking for. A nameplate on a desk covered in folders and empty food wrappers displayed Inspector Calbach Mullarkey.

I approached his desk and said in my most respectful voice, "Inspector Mullarkey?" It was hard to keep a straight face, and I resisted the urge to ask if his colleagues Officer Tomfoolery and Sergeant Shenanigans were around.

Mullarkey was middle aged, with graying hair, a large red nose, and watery, pale blue eyes. He started to look up with an exaggerated sigh as if I was distracting him from some incredibly important work, but as his gaze fell on me, he did a double take. I noticed a faint smell of whiskey.

"Uh...yes?"

"You're the one working on the Cait Gallagher case?" I asked.

"Yes. Who are you?" He looked over at the door. "How did you get in here?"

"Jesse O'Hara. I walked in."

"Well, Miss O'Hara—"

"It's *Doctor* O'Hara. I'm here on behalf of the Gallaghers." I didn't usually pull out the *doctor* bit, but I was taking an instant dislike to this guy and wanted to establish some credibility right away.

"Of course, Dr. O'Hara. I'm sorry you had to come over. I could have told you over the phone that we have no new information, as I've shared with Mrs. Gallagher. But the case is active, and we'll let her know if we find anything out about Cara—"

"It's Cait. Her name is Cait."

"In any case, you can tell the Gallaghers we'll let them know if anything turns up." He looked back down at his desk, signaling that our discussion was over.

I took a quick look at his desk and around the room, putting my near photographic memory to use.

"You're not working on this case at all. There's no mention on the open cases board." I nodded to the white board on the wall next to the door, which included thirty-two rows of information related to various investigations, and none of them Cait's. "And it's not among the files on your desk." There were stacks of folders on his desk, all labeled with numbers and names, also none of them Cait's. "So, Chief Wiggum, let's start over. What information do you have on Cait Gallagher's disappearance?"

He looked up, eyes wide, like he'd been caught doing something he shouldn't. Or in this case, *not* doing something. "Um...as I've told Mrs. Gallagher, I can assure you, we're doing what we can. The disappearance happened in Galway, which is outside our jurisdiction. But—"

"If by *what you can* you mean *fuck all*, then yes, you are definitely doing what you can."

He scoffed. "Please watch your language. And you know nothing of police wor—"

"I know you're lying. The case isn't active, you've done nothing, and you've been lying to this poor woman and her family by telling them you're actually doing anything. And you're lying to me right now." I really, really hated it when people lied to me. I grew up with an inveterate liar and, at this point in my life, had zero tolerance for it. I could feel my miniscule pool of patience circling the drain. "It's one thing to pass off work because of jurisdiction. It's another to openly lie to a woman who may very well have lost her only daughter and make her believe you're looking for her."

"Miss O'Hara, I—"

"It's *Doctor* O'Hara, you lazy, lying fuck." It normally took me at least a little while to start dropping F-bombs, but I'd been deeply and immediately affected by Rose Gallagher's pain, and this case was already personal to me. So much so that my deep well of anger that sat dependably just below the surface rose to the top.

He stared at me, his face reddening. He wasn't used to being talked to this way by people and probably especially by women.

"Why mislead the parents into thinking you're doing something?" I raised my voice. "And are you *drunk*? Give me what you have, right now, or I'm going to your boss." I reached down to his desk and started moving papers around and grabbing folders.

"Stop that!" He quickly opened one of the desk drawers and pulled out a slim file with Gallagher on the tab, then opened it and pretended to look over it. "You see, Dr. O'Hara—"

I grabbed the folder out of his hands and opened it.

He stood up quickly, crumbs flying off his lap, his substantial belly now resting on his desk. "You can't take that! It's official gardaí property!"

I ignored him and looked at the single page that made up the totality of the file. They'd interviewed the boyfriend, a few local girlfriends, and made one fucking phone call to the NUI Galway security office.

Closing the file, I looked down at Mullarkey. "Great work, Sherlock. I'm sure you'll have this case cracked in no time. Do you at least know if either of the bodies they pulled out of the bog today could be Cait?"

"No. They are both male." He reached for the folder, which I pulled just out of his reach.

"See, you can be useful. You know, if this gig doesn't work out for you, I'll bet there's a mall somewhere that could use a cop."

He lunged and grabbed the folder from my hand, but I'd seen enough. Which was fortunate, because three uniformed officers had come through the door and were purposefully moving toward us.

I was escorted out of the room and out of the station with an admonition not to come back. Not the first time I'd been thrown out of a police station. But it was no problem since there was nothing there anyway.

My next stop was to see Cait's dad Mik and the boyfriend at the pub, which was good timing as I was ready for a drink.

Their pub, Murphy's, was not far from the station, so I left my car where it was and walked over. Murphy's was old, a plaque on the brick wall indicating it had been established in 1898. The entranceway sat between two large windows in the front. Placards in the windows advertised Trad Music Every Night.

An adjacent door down the block marked the entrance to an associated package store—"off licence"—that was packed to the gills with bottles. Both the pub and the connected package store sat below one floor of apartments. Above the door was a small blue sign notifying passersby of CCTV camera operation.

I'd watched a lot of crime dramas and was familiar with the prevalence of CCTV in the UK and Ireland. Virtually everything out in public was caught on camera, and when TV police started their investigations into crimes, the first thing the boss would tell everyone to do would be to "pull the CCTV footage." I couldn't imagine Americans allowing their every move to be filmed, but, man, did it make catching criminals easier. I guess that made up for the fact that British and Irish cops didn't usually carry guns, even though the criminals often did. If they needed firepower, they had to get special permission or call in an armed response unit. So maybe it was a wash, cameras instead of guns, although I always cringed when watching unarmed cops chasing after armed bad guys.

I opened the heavy wooden door to the pub and walked in.

The place was almost full but fairly quiet. Most of the seats at the bar were taken, as were most of the tables and a long wooden bench under the front window. A big TV above the bar was showing a local game. Something involving wooden sticks and a ball, and lots of guys smacking into each other. Looked fun.

A small blackboard had handwritten prices for various ages of Redbreast whiskey, a brand I'd never heard of. I always ordered Jameson when I went out, but now that I was here, I thought it might be time to expand my horizons. And the fact that they had seven different labels of Redbreast was a good sign. Behind the counter were four beer taps, two of them Guinness. My mouth watered.

I'd never met Mik, but he was easy to pick out from the pictures I'd seen on Rose's mantel. I spotted him at the end of the bar, head down and both of his hands wrapped around a pint next to a small shot of something caramel-colored. There was an empty stool next to him with a half-finished pint on the bar in front of it.

I walked across the bar and stopped next to him. "Mr. Gallagher?"

Without looking up, he mumbled, "Aye?"

"I'm Jesse O'Hara from Chicago."

He didn't respond, still staring into his drink.

"Uh, Seamus's sister-in-law? The one who's looking for Cait?"

He looked up at me with unfocused eyes, then put his beer down and stood up unsteadily. "Dr. O'Hara? Oh, you've come." He put his arms around me, hugging tightly.

The bartender walked over and raised his eyebrows at me. Over Mik's embrace I ordered a Guinness, my first in Ireland. I wondered if it would be different than what I got in the US.

Almost certainly. I could hardly stand the suspense.

"Mr. Gallagher—"

He stepped back and said, "Please, call me Mik," then motioned to the empty stool next to him.

I sat down. "Mik, what can you tell me about the investigation into Cait's disappearance?"

He covered a small belch with his hand and sat back down slowly. "I can tell you they're not doing a god damn thing. They think she just ran off." He took the shot from the bar and put it away in one gulp, following it with a long sip of his beer.

"Where do you think she is?"

"I don't know. I just know she wouldn't go away without telling us."

As we were talking, a young man walked over and stood between us. Mik looked up and then back down to his beer. "Dr. O'Hara, this is Paddy Feeney, Cait's one. Paddy, Dr. O'Hara." He was slurring, and I wondered how many drinks he'd had today.

More than me, that was for sure. I looked up again at the glacially slow pour of my Guinness.

Paddy took my hand in both of his and shook it energetically. "You're the American investigator. Thank God you're here."

He was a bit shorter than me, about five seven, and skinny, with an unnaturally large head; pale, watery green eyes; and bright red hair that was long but somehow managed to stand straight up in parts. His overall look was "Weasley brother on a bad hair day." He found another stool and dragged it over between us, reaching around me to grab his beer. It passed briefly in front of my nose, long enough for me to smell it. I watched him take a drink, the foamy top giving him the signature beer mustache.

Where the hell is my beer? I looked over at the taps and saw the dark and creamy liquid slowly filling up the glass.

"You were Cait's boyfriend before she left for college?"

"Am. I *am* her boyfriend."

"Okay, when was the last time you saw her?"

"Four weeks ago. I went down for the weekend."

"What did you do while you were there?"

He looked away. "Not much. We talked."

Girlfriend went away to college, he visited her after months away, and they spent their time talking? Didn't sound like any long-distance reunion I'd ever heard of. "What did you talk about?"

"Oh, you know. Lots of things."

"Like what?"

"Uh, school, and, em...holiday."

"How long did you stay?"

He took a long drink, and I looked over again at the taps, finding my beer was still being held hostage by the sadistic bartender. It was three-quarters full, and he was now watching it rest.

"Just the day."

I raised my eyebrows at him.

"I, em, needed to get back." He wasn't looking me in the eyes.

What kind of relationship was it where the boyfriend would make a two-hour drive and not stay the night? He was definitely hiding something. "Do you have any idea what happened to her?" I asked.

"No. We agreed I would pick her up at the bus station this last Friday night. She wasn't on the bus." His voice caught; he was choking up.

He took another sip of his beer. Even if he was keeping something from me, it was clear he was pretty devastated by Cait's disappearance. Maybe he was making up the part about just talking to avoid mentioning shtupping her in front of her father.

I'd need to get him away from Mik at some point to see if he'd open up.

I pressed him. "Could she have gotten off earlier? Taken a different stop? Or taken an earlier bus?"

"No, no...we were really clear that she was coming in at six and I was going to pick her up."

"Does she have any other, er, friends in Sligo that might have picked her up?" I said, thinking maybe she had something on the side in Sligo. It wouldn't be hard to believe. This guy didn't seem like much of a catch.

"Like who?"

Not to put too fine a point on it, I said, "Was she dating anyone else?" *Where the hell is my beer?*

As I looked over again, the bartender tipped the glass back and pulled on the tap to finish it off. It wouldn't be long now.

"*No.*"

He was getting a little huffy, so I backed off. But there was something going on with him. That, and nine times out of ten, when a woman went missing, it was usually related to the boyfriend. I would come back to him later.

The full glass under the tap looked ready to drink, a slim, perfect head on top of luscious, creamy dark brown liquid. I watched the bartender pick it up and walk to the other side of the bar, putting it down in front of someone else. He walked back to the tap, placed another glass beneath it, and started the process all over again. There were two taps, but I guessed the process demanded that he do one at a time.

Staring into his pint, Mik said, "You'll find her, won't you, Dr. O'Hara?"

"It's Jesse, Mik, and I'll do my best." I wasn't in the habit of promising things I couldn't deliver. Starting an investigation into a missing girl a week after she disappeared wasn't a recipe for success.

I glanced at my watch. Rose had said dinner was at six, and it was getting close to that now. I had the feeling I didn't want to be late to one of her dinners.

"We should probably head back to the house," I said, looking sadly at my near-finished Guinness pour, which was just now coming to a head. *Damn.* Well, it wasn't like this was the only pub in Ireland that sold Guinness. There would be other opportunities.

Mik finished the last of his beer in one large gulp and stood up shakily. He was in no shape to get behind the wheel of a car, so Paddy offered to drive him back. Mik leaned on him, and they shuffled out of the bar. I followed behind, and we split up when we got out the door.

On the way into town earlier, the area had been lively. But now it was like the town had shut down. All of the shops were closed, the alleys between them dim and gloomy. The sun had set and the streets were dark, except for the small patches of light from the occasional streetlight that showed off a gently falling mist. With no one else on the street, it was dead quiet. Where before the town had looked cool, vibrant, and inviting, now it was empty and kind of spooky. I was glad my car was only a few blocks away.

I'd walked a couple of blocks when I started to get a tingly feeling on the back of my neck. Probably nerves, frayed, no doubt, from the tantalizingly close proximity to my first Guinness in Ireland. Still, I sped up a little, past the Abbey and across the street, and turned down the road to my car. The tingling of my Spidey-Sense followed me around the corner.

I'd ignored that sense in the past to my peril, so I stopped and abruptly turned around.

No one was there.

Must be jet lag. I was just creeping myself out. Nevertheless, I hurried past the remaining closed shops until I got to my car. Fortunately, I'd left it underneath one of the streetlamps. I stood in the center of a circle of light, letting out a small sigh of relief as I pulled out my key.

As I was unlocking the door, I heard footsteps. I looked up to see a shape behind me reflected in the car window. It was a man wearing a hooded sweatshirt.

Where the hell did he come from?

I tensed, ready to throw an elbow at whoever he was, a well-honed, hair-trigger reaction to anyone touching me without invitation.

"Dr. O'Hara?"

I stopped my elbow shot and turned around slowly. The man was putting up both hands in a defensive posture and backing up a step. "I'm sorry, I didn't mean to scare you. You're—" He stopped mid-sentence and stared at my face. "You're...uh...Jesse O'Hara, aren't you? You're looking for Cait Gallagher?" He was looking at me strangely.

Not ready to let my guard down yet, I replied, "Who are you?" Then I glanced around, looking for anyone who might respond to a distress call.

The street was deserted. Where the hell was everyone? Probably in the pub, drinking Guinness.

"I might be able to help you."

I noticed he hadn't answered my question. "How do you know who I am?"

"It's a small town." He smiled, relaxed now, although still staring at me in a strange way. But he wasn't giving off a rapey or mugger vibe, and I unclenched my fists.

It didn't hurt that he was drop-dead gorgeous. Shoulder length black hair curled from underneath his hood, framing powerful blue eyes that flashed out from under dark, thick eyebrows. Hard to tell his age...early thirties, maybe.

"My name's Liam. Liam Gilmartin." He held out his hand.

I ignored it. No matter what he looked like, I wasn't ready to give him an easy way to grab me.

He dropped his hand. "The local gardaí aren't going to find her. They're barely looking."

No kidding. "How do you know? Are you working with them?"

"Like I said, it's a small town." Again, avoiding my question.

"Do you know Cait? When did you last see her?"

"I think you'll find what you're looking for in Galway. Go to the university."

We were going there anyway the next day. I shrugged. "No shit, Sherlock. Look, do you know where Cait is or not? If not, you're wasting my time."

"Contact campus security. They'll help you with whatever you need." He reached into his pocket and pulled out a slip of paper. "Here's a number where you can leave a message for me. Call me if you find out anything, or if you run into any problems."

"What's your relationship to Cait?"

"I'm just someone who wants her found."

I waited for him to say more, but he just stared at me. I finally reached out and took the paper from him. "Who *are* you?"

He turned around and walked back into the mist.

FIVE

When I got back to the Gallaghers, Mik was already home and Rose had invited Paddy to stay for dinner. I knew this as it involved her yelling at Brian to set an extra place for him. As far as I could tell, the foghorn roar was reserved only for Brian.

I popped my head into the kitchen to see if I could help with dinner. Sam was already there with Rose, moving among pots and dishes, stirring and adding things. It was no surprise that she'd already gotten access to Rose's kitchen and dinner process. Sam was handing her a plate when Rose stopped and dropped her head to her chest. Sam put the plate down and put her arms around her as Rose started to sob. Sam hugged her tightly and looked at me over her heaving shoulders, shaking her head a little. I nodded and backed out of the kitchen.

I went upstairs to my room and called Gideon.

He answered on the third ring. "Hey, you! How's Ireland?"

"Green as advertised, and so far Guinness-free. I've got a small thing for you. Can you see what you can find on a Liam Gilmartin, in Sligo?"

Gideon worked in the Chicago PD's Special Investigations Unit, in the section focused on crimes against children. He was on the technology end of things, using his unparalleled hacking skills to expose pedophile rings. Since the rings were often international in nature, much of his work went beyond the US and his access to data and information was extensive. More importantly, he was willing, to a point, to research and share information with me. He'd been a great help in my previous career as a financial investigator and really came through when we'd nailed the cruise ship terrorist earlier in the year. Other advantages of Gideon included an extensive library of Yiddish insults and an upbeat personality that completely neutralized mine.

"Happy to. What about him?"

"I don't know. He approached me today, kind of out of nowhere. He claimed to know where I can find information about Cait but wouldn't tell my anything else. I have no idea who he is."

"Hmmm. I'll do what I can. Can you give me anything else to go on?"

"Uh, he's got blue eyes and is about six foot two, probably in his thirties. He's really good looking, if that helps. He looks like a beefier Colin O'Donoghue."

"Who?"

"Colin O'Donoghue. You know, the guy who played Captain Hook in *Once Upon a Time*."

"No one watches that show but you."

"Someone's watching it. They lasted seven seasons."

He laughed. "Whatever. Should be a snap. How many Liam Gilmartins could there be in Sligo? The town only has fifty thousand people."

"Thanks. Any news on the Svetlana front?"

Svetlana had made it clear that she blamed me for ruining her plans to bomb the gas plant in Bilbao, and even though she lived in Russia, she was a billionaire, and I didn't think it would be too hard for her to get whatever revenge on me she wanted to take. She'd sent me a package after escaping the cruise ship—a bottle of her favorite vodka, Crystal Head. I wasn't sure if she liked it because of the taste, or because it came in an ornate disturbingly skull-shaped glass bottle. Either way, I'd taken it as a warning. She and her dead husband had well-known ties to Russia's FSB and were rumored to be involved in a number of assassinations that had paved the way for their rise to power and wealth. I had no trouble believing the rumors. After meeting her, I knew she was capable of anything.

Was she still thinking about me? I didn't know, but I hoped not. I hoped she was fully absorbed in running her empire and didn't have time for the likes of me. But we'd interfered with her carefully laid plans, and she didn't strike me as the kind of woman who would let something like that go without repercussions. So, in addition to my own daily Google checks on Svetlana and her company, Rusgaprom, I'd asked Gideon to monitor her. It was far more likely that he would uncover anything than I would.

"She hasn't left Russia since the cruise. She did take over a Greek oil company, Janus Oil, last week. I'm sure that's keeping her busy."

"Is that it?"

"Uh, no..."

"What?"

"She sent you another bottle of Crystal Head, to your house."

So she *was* still thinking about me. *Great.* "Was there any card or note?"

"No. What do you want me to do?"

"I think it's best that you not go back to the house, just in case." He'd been picking up my mail, but at this point, who knew what she might do to the house, or anyone in it.

"Okay. Mind if I open the bottle?"

"Sure, knock yourself out."

We hung up, and I went to the bathroom to wash up for dinner.

When I went back downstairs, the table was set and all three boys, Paddy, and Mik were in their seats. I took an empty chair next to Paddy and made my introductions to John and Colin. They were—like many of the men in Ireland, I was learning—

smoking hot. Both were tall and well built, with longish wavy dark hair and dark eyes.

I heard a *bang* as Wee Petey came through the dog door in the kitchen and made his entrance to dinner. He did his indoor parkour thing around the living room, then dashed over to Mik, stopped, and sat up, staring at him.

Now that he'd stopped for a minute, I could see he only had three legs. One of his back legs was missing. He also had one brown eye and one blue eye that seemed to bulge out, and he was really fat. He looked like a large brown sausage. I couldn't imagine how he could run so fast, or at all, carrying all of that weight around on his three stumpy legs.

Mik ignored him, so Petey let out a single loud bark.

"Calm down, ye miniscule bastard. You'll get yours shortly."

Petey curled up underneath Mik's chair and closed his eyes.

Rose and Sam came out of the kitchen carrying trays with steaming bowls of food that they set on the table. It was enough to feed a small country.

Rose looked at the table and scowled. I knew what was coming. "Jesus in a gymnasium! *Brian!* Bring in the wine!"

Brian left the table for the kitchen and returned with two bottles and a corkscrew. He opened both bottles and went around the table filling up glasses. There was a wine glass in front of everyone except Rose, who was drinking a small glass of beer. It was dark, and I could smell it.

Guinness. Sweet, delicious Guinness.

In response to my look, she said, "I drink one glass of the black stuff a day for my health."

Sounded good to me, and if one was good, several might be better. I wished I had one, but not wanting to be rude, I accepted the wine.

Everyone bowed their heads, and Mik mumbled through a quick grace, one that included a respectful request to God to bring Cait safely home. Everyone dug in.

"Ah, Ma, ya made the Guinness pie!" said John.

Guinness pie for dinner? Maybe I should move here. These are my people.

The savory pie consisted of a buttery, flakey crust, inside of which were tender pieces of stewed meat in a rich brown gravy, accompanied by an inoffensive amount of vegetables. I could taste parsley and thyme and definitely the Guinness, which gave it an unctuous deepness. I ate it quickly, because it was the closest I'd gotten to Guinness since I'd gotten here.

The pie was accompanied by a very large bowl of mashed potatoes, fish cakes with tartar sauce, and a bowl of peas. Also on the table were a round loaf of soda bread and butter. The bread was dense and crumbly and warm, although unremarkable, until I layered it with some of the butter.

Irish butter...I'd never tasted anything like it. *Wow.*

As if everyone had agreed, we kept the conversation light and steered clear of the elephant in the room—the missing Cait.

John and Colin looked tired. I guessed that with their dad incapacitated by a combination of grief, and whiskey, they were carrying the bulk of the working load. But it didn't stop them from putting the food away. What had looked like enough food to feed an army was disappearing quickly.

The boys said little during dinner, other than John mentioning that, "The potatoes are grand, ma," followed by Colin's, "Aye, floury," through a mouthful of food.

I thought it might be helpful to draw the family out a bit, so I asked John, who so far seemed the more talkative of the twins, "What do you do?"

"We work in the family business, Sligo Equine."

"You sell horses?"

"In a manner of speaking." He reached for another scoop of potatoes. "It's a stallion semen farm."

I reached for my wine glass and took a long sip to cover up a small choking cough. A million questions went through my mind at once, followed by images, and immediately after that, a realization that I might not want to know the exact details of what they did during the day to work up such an appetite.

No, I couldn't help myself. *A semen farm. They spend the day jerking off horses.*

I had so many questions. How did one do that? And how long did it take? Did a horse have to be in the mood? Did they wear special gloves? Watching John reach for more food, I hoped they wore gloves. Did they talk to the horses while they did it? Was it a bonding experience, between horse and jerker? Did they even refer to themselves as *jerkers*? Or something else? It was Ireland, after all...maybe *wankers*?

No, that didn't sound right. Stick with jerker.

Did just one jerker do one horse, or did horses prefer multiple partners? Might it take two jerkers at the same time to do one horse? How did they collect the...effluent? And how often could a horse perform? Horses seemed pretty virile...was it multiple times a day? No wonder these guys were tired.

I thought about my friends who wanted children and had turned to artificial insemination for various reasons. Some had gone the "frozen sperm of the month club" route, which was very expensive and often with disappointing, or at least painfully slow, results. I also knew people who went the more rustic, fresh direction. One friend of mine literally had her cousin jerk off into a shot glass and then they'd done the application with her partner and a kitchen baster right afterward. That one had worked the first time, as had subsequent efforts. They had four kids now, all courtesy of a few quick bathroom wanks and a kitchen utensil.

Sam was staring at me with wide eyes, knowing exactly what I was thinking. Her face was frozen in a look I recognized as her pre-mortification look, which came out when she expected I would say something inappropriate. It got a lot of use when we were out together. But I surprised her and let it go. For now. I had an investigation to run.

I took another long sip of wine to compose myself and, with some difficulty, forced myself to stop thinking about horse jerking. "Hey, I was wondering, do any of you know a Liam Gilmartin?" I asked, looking around the table.

"There are the Connor Gilmartins, Eamon and Olivia," said John.

"And Sinead and Brady Gilmartin," Mik added.

"Finn Gilmartin lives just down the street," said Brian.

"Then there's Jack, Molly, and Shane Gilmartin," Rose said. "But I'm not aware of any Liams."

They all shook their heads.

Gilmartin seemed to be a popular name. But interesting that there was no Liam in the bunch. That might make it easier for Gideon to track him down.

"Does it have something to do with Cait?" Rose asked, hope creeping into her voice.

Shit, I'd have to be careful. I didn't want to get her hopes up. "No, just someone I ran into."

At the mention of Cait, the conversation seemed to die. Mik poured himself more wine, and the boys focused on their food, what little was left of it.

Sam knew when to come to the rescue. "What's that picture, Rose?" she said, pointing to a large framed photograph on the wall. It was a mountain with a small figure on top of it.

"That's Cait on Knocknarea Mountain. She loves that place." Her face brightened. "It's the site of Queen Maeve's tomb."

"Queen Maeve?"

"Maeve was—" Rose was interrupted when Paddy suddenly pushed his chair back and stood up.

"I should go." He didn't look well.

Paddy had picked at his food but not actually eaten much, and had said even less during the meal. He'd also gotten up a few times to go to the bathroom, making me wonder if he was sick.

Rose stood up with him. "Are you sure you'll not be staying, Paddy?"

"No, thank you."

Mik got up and walked him to the door.

Sam said, "Rose, you were saying about Queen Maeve?"

She sat back down. "Yes. Em, Maeve the Warrior Queen is the

center of Ireland's most famous epic tale, the Táin Bó Cúailnge —"

"The what?" I asked.

"The Cattle Raid of Cooley. Táin Bó Cuailnge is its Gaelic name.

"The story tells that Maeve was attempting to increase her own wealth to be equal to that of her husband, Ailill. The only difference between them was a single bull. To become as wealthy as her husband, Maeve arranged to acquire a bull from a man in the town of Cooley, in the northern province of Ulster. The deal fell through, so she brought her great army to Cooley to capture the bull. The battle lasted many days, and her army was defeated. But she managed to capture the bull and bring him back to Connacht."

"Sounds like a lot of trouble to go through to get a bull," I said.

Rose laughed, which was good to see. "The story is long and more detailed, of course. Regardless, Maeve is a symbol of independence, courage, and strength, and a great leader. Her name also translates as *intoxicating*. She was said to be quite beautiful."

"So she's buried on Knocknarea?"

"Like all important ancient warriors in Ireland, it is said that the queen was buried upright, with her spear in her hand, facing her enemies in Ulster. Her burial place is marked with a cairn on the summit of Knocknarea. There are many very old, important historical sites in Connacht, but this is the most sacred. And it's only a short ways from our house."

A famous warrior's tomb. I liked the sound of that. I would definitely make the trip.

"Was Maeve real?" I couldn't believe I'd never heard of her.

"No one knows for sure. She may have lived around the time of Christ, as a real queen. It is said she ruled Connacht for over sixty years."

"She sounds formidable. No wonder Cait admires her," said Sam.

"Aye...Cait's a bit like the queen herself. And she's proud of the fact that Ireland's national epic has a woman at the center of it."

Mik had returned to the dining room and was leaning over a wooden hutch that held the family's liquid assets. Pulling out a bottle of Jameson and some small glasses, he said, "Would anyone like a drink?"

I wasn't sure how much he usually drank in a day, and Rose didn't look too happy, but I wasn't about to turn down Irish whiskey. I nodded.

"Maeve had five husbands," Rose added as she was picking up plates from the table.

"Five? That must have been a lot of work."

"Yes, I suspect it was," she said, looking sideways at Mik.

He poured healthy shots into the glasses and passed them around to each of us.

He lifted his. "Sláinte."

We all drank, and he quickly poured us all another, putting his away immediately.

"Do you ever drink Redbreast?" I asked, looking into the hutch at the other bottles.

Mik nodded. "Aye. But rarely. It's a little rich for us."

"What about Bushmills?"

He put his empty glass down hard on the table. "We'll not be serving that protestant shite in this house." He poured himself another shot.

I could see where this was going, and while I was usually up for a whiskey drinkalong, we had a lot of work to do tomorrow and I didn't want to be completely hung over. It was still early, but I was feeling some jet lag.

I put away my shot, and looking longingly at the bottle, said, "Thanks very much for dinner. We should probably tuck in, we have a long day ahead of us."

"Rose, would you like some help cleaning up?" Sam asked.

"No, thank you, dear. *Brian!*" She headed off to the kitchen, Brian following behind her with a stack of plates and leaving Mik and the twins drinking at the table.

Sam went upstairs, and I went out to the car. When I came back, she was in the hallway just coming out of the bathroom.

She nodded to the case of whiskey in my arms. "Please don't tell me you're going to sleep with that."

"I didn't want to leave it out there in case the temperature dropped too far. Extreme temperature changes are bad for alcohol." And I wanted to look at my bottles. "What room are you in?"

"Brian's. Rose moved him to the couch."

We said our goodnights and headed to our rooms. After going down for his dinner and a short trip outside, Fergus had resumed his vigil on Cait's bed.

I opened the box of whiskey I'd brought into the room, cutting through the tape with my fixed blade, three-inch Worden DATU boot knife. Since the attack against Sam and me at the university, I'd rarely gone anywhere without it. It was worth checking my luggage to bring it with me. It wasn't exactly a lethal weapon, but I felt better having something on me. Sam had had a similar reaction to the attack, her resultant accessory a Berretta 9mm handgun that she'd become quite accomplished with over the years and carried in her purse. I didn't carry a purse, my only other accessories a lighter and a small set of lockpicks that frequently came in handy.

There were twelve bottles in the case. I'd bought seven regular Jameson and splurged on five of the pricier Jameson 18 Years, that had spent its time aging in both bourbon and sherry casks.

I reached in to take one out and look at it. Peering in I noticed one different bottle and pulled it out instead.

One of the bottles of regular Jameson had been substituted with Jameson Vintage Rarest Reserve. *Holy shit.* The Vintage Reserve was the highest end of the Jameson line and normally retailed for $300. But it was extremely scarce and in reality you couldn't get your hand on a bottle in the US for less than $1,500. I'd seen it on sale for as much as $4,000.

How did that get in there? I didn't remember buying it.

In any case, I'd have to save it for a special occasion. Like a Wednesday. I put the bottle back carefully in the case.

I didn't want to disturb Fergus and didn't feel right about getting into the covers of a missing, possibly dead girl's bed, so I laid down on top of the covers next to him with my clothes on and fell asleep.

Six

We wanted to get going early, so met at the top of the stairs just before dawn. I had the case of whiskey in my hands.

Sam nodded to the case. "Are you going to take that everywhere you go?"

"Well, I wasn't, until I learned there was a bottle of Vintage Reserve in here." I looked over at her while we walked down the stairs. "You wouldn't know anything about that, would you?"

She smiled. "I thought it would be a nice surprise."

Damn, I loved this girl.

Rose was already up, and when she saw us, she waved us to the table. "Coffee or tea, ladies?"

"Coffee for me, thank you," I replied.

"I'd love some tea," said Sam.

Rose returned with our cups and then again carrying plates stacked with food. Scrambled eggs, sausage links, large pieces of what looked like thick bacon, slices of fried tomatoes, and baked beans. There was a basket of freshly baked scones on the table and small bowls of fruit. Apparently, every meal had to include enough food to supply a full-scale relief effort.

I didn't usually like to eat much in the morning, but didn't want to be rude, so I plowed into the food. Sam, as usual, had a healthy appetite, not that you could tell by looking at her. Somehow, she managed to stay perfectly slim. Unlike me. I relied on daily workouts to resist my genetic heritage, one that included a steady line of corpulent women going back as far as photographs were a thing.

We made a good dent in the food and then said our goodbyes, both receiving warm, strong hugs from Rose.

Before we left, I walked over to the mantel. "May I borrow this?" I said, picking up one of the recent pictures of Cait.

"Of course." Rose took the back off the frame, carefully took the picture out, and handed it to me, but not before touching Cait's face.

"I'll take good care of it."

We left the house, and Sam pulled the keys out of her coat.

I grabbed them from her. "I'll drive, thanks. I'd like to make it out of Ireland alive." I carefully put the case in the back seat, and started to get in the driver's seat, then stepped back out. There was a piece of paper on the windshield, stuck between the wipers.

The note was crudely written in pencil: *FUCK OFF AND GO HOME.*

I handed it to Sam. "Someone doesn't want us here."

"Like who? Do you think this is related to Cait? Or just someone who doesn't like Americans?"

I got back in the car and started it up angrily. "I don't know. We haven't been here that long. The only people who know we're here are the Gallaghers, and Paddy, and the gardaí." And Liam.

"That was fast. Usually, it takes you at least a couple of days to make people want to threaten you."

"It doesn't matter. I'm not going to be scared off." The worst thing someone could do if they wanted me to go home was tell me to go home. I crumpled up the note and threw it in the back seat. If anything, the note made me more committed to finding Cait.

I pulled out of the Gallaghers' neighborhood and headed west, bypassing the N4 to Galway. We were soon driving on very narrow, barely two-lane roads, in between green fields.

"Are you taking the scenic route?" Sam asked.

"We're taking a quick detour."

After a few more minutes we pulled up in front of the Carrowmore Megalithic Complex. We had time to tick another item off of my Ireland bucket list.

In response to Sam's raised eyebrows, I said, "It's on my list."

"It looks closed," Sam said.

"I know, but we can still look around. We have time. It will only take us ninety minutes or so to get to Galway." I was starting to get used to how close everything was here.

There was a bar blocking the entrance to the parking lot, so I parked in the street just outside of it. The lot was adjacent to a visitor's center that looked like a converted house. We walked through the parking lot into an open grassy area that spanned several acres.

"It doesn't look like much," Sam said.

She was right. At first glance, it didn't look like anything, just a bare, gently undulating grass field with large stones lying around in various locations. But I loved archaeology and had done my research before we arrived. Carrowmore was actually a world-famous complex that included many of the features of the ancient times. And it wasn't just the oldest megalithic cemetery in Ireland, but one of the oldest in Europe.

"You're looking at the remnants of ancient tombs, Sam. Some of these are over five thousand years old." I pointed to a low cylinder of rocks that looked like the top had been sheared off. "Take a look at this. It's a burial tomb from thousands of years ago. And it's still in great shape."

We walked toward the mound.

"I think we can go into it," I said excitedly.

We went through a rock-lined entryway that led up a slight incline into the structure. Inside, open to the sky, was a chamber bounded by walls of stacked, softball-sized rocks, shorn up with chicken wire. A flat table-like structure stood off to the side, made out of another very large slab of stone.

"One of the things that's so cool about Irish megaliths is that they're constantly discovering new ones and new features within ones that they've known about for years. Lots of the structures are underground and hidden until someone actually walks over them." The idea that there were still things to discover in Ireland that were thousands of years old was amazing to me.

We walked back outside.

"Across the road"—I pointed toward our car—"are the remains of a ringfort. They're all over Ireland. At this point there's not much left of them other than circles on the ground."

"Like alien crop circles?"

"Smaller than those. The ringforts are the sites of old settlements. That's where they find a lot of the underground features. They're called souterrains. No one's sure what the souterrains were for, maybe pantries, maybe the prehistoric version of a safe house."

I looked around. It was thrilling to see things that were not just centuries, but millennia old. Compared to Ireland and most of Europe, the US really was the new world.

"This is so cool. We may have to extend our trip. There's so much to see here. You know that County Sligo alone has over ninety different—"

"*Hello, ladies.* The site is closed." I turned to see a middle-aged woman calling to us from the parking lot. "We open at ten."

"Okay. We were just leaving." I took one more last look around before heading back to car. I would definitely need to go back and explore some more later.

The woman stood in the parking lot and watched us until we drove away.

We drove out of the city on the N17 to Galway. On the map it looked like a major highway, but most of the time it was another two- or three-lane road. We drove for an hour, surrounded by fields, fences, and farmhouses, and occasionally passed through towns.

"This really worked out well. Once we find Cait, we'll be close to a lot of the things on my Ireland bucket List."

"Isn't the Middleton Distillery in Cork?"

"Yeah, we'll hit that on the way back to Dublin. But there are other really amazing ancient sites in western Ireland. Knocknarea, the place that Rose said was one of Cait's favorites? It's one of them, and it's only a few minutes from their house."

We drove for another half hour, and once we started seeing signs for Galway, Sam moved us into debrief mode. "What did you learn from the gardaí yesterday?"

"They're doing fuck all, and the guy in charge of looking for her is a lazy, lying drunk. I did learn that the bodies they pulled out of the bog were both male. And we might have another resource. Some guy who seems to know something about Cait."

"Was it Liam Gilmartin? The one you were asking about at dinner?"

"Yeah. He followed me to my car after I met with Mik in the pub."

"What? He followed you?"

"It's okay. He just said to go to NUI Galway and talk to the security guys there." I left out the part about him sneaking up on me.

"We're already doing that."

"I know. But he seemed pretty confident that she was there. And he gave me his number. At least, I think it was his number. He said to call him if we learned anything. Maybe it's nothing, but maybe he can be a resource. I guess we'll find out."

"Who do you think he is?"

"I have no idea, but Gideon's on it." If anyone could track down Liam Gilmartin, it was Gideon. Even if there were ten thousand Liam Gilmartins in Sligo. "Did you learn anything yesterday from Rose?"

She shrugged. "Probably nothing you don't already know. She's devasted but trying to keep it together for her family. Mik drinks all the time, and the boys are picking up all of the family work. Thank God for Brian." Sam had been looking out the window, but now turned to look at me. "I don't know, Jesse...I'm starting to think that Cait's not out on a lark."

I sighed. "Yeah, me too."

We didn't say what we were both thinking. She'd been gone over a week at this point, and if she'd actually been taken by someone, the chances that we'd find her alive were getting slimmer.

"Did you learn anything at the pub?"

"Mik was too drunk to be any help. Paddy's hiding something. I'm not sure what. It could be he just didn't want to talk about spending the night with Cait with her dad sitting there. And he's clearly broken up about her being missing. It's obvious he cares about her, a lot. But..."

Sam raised her eyebrows expectantly.

"Doesn't it seem like Cait's a little out of Paddy's league? I mean, I've never met her, but she's attractive, apparently smart, starting her adult life at the university. And he's kind of...twitchy."

"Maybe he's really nice? Or smarter than he appears?" Sam was always looking for the best in people. It was part of what made her so attractive to everyone, why everyone wanted to be around her, and why she had a large group of friends and acquaintances. "And he doesn't seem like the violent type."

"True." He didn't seem aggressive, or even energetic enough to do anything to someone. "But I don't know. He didn't seem all that smart. Let's face it, she's a ten and he's a three, on a good day."

We left it at that as I pulled into the university. The security office was near the center of the campus, on Distillery Road, which I took as a sign from God that we were on the right track. We parked and walked into the small building.

I was a little surprised that the guard on duty, Kelly, had not only heard from Liam, but was expecting us and seemed highly motivated by the call to help us. Apparently, Liam was the real deal. Kelly took us straight to Cait's apartment, part of a new section of on-campus housing. He knocked on the door on the ground floor, and after hearing no answer, let us into her unit.

"Do you know who her roommates are? And whether or not they've gone home for the break?" I asked.

"I can get their contact information for you." He left us in the unit to look around while he went out to the hallway to make a call.

Cait's apartment was a compact space with a small kitchen, living room, and two bedrooms. I identified her room by the family pictures on her dresser. Her bedroom was small, with a single bed, desk, closet, and a bookshelf. The desk was neat, but like her room at home, covered in stacks of books and papers. The crowded bookshelf included some more recent volumes than those in her home bedroom: *Girls Like Us: Fighting for a World Where Girls Are Not for Sale*; *A Memoir, Disposable People: New Slavery in the Global Economy*; and *Human Trafficking Around the World: Hidden in Plain Sight*. Tucked into the latter were a couple of brochures. One was from an organization called Ruhama that read, *Supporting women affected by prostitution*. The other advertised an anti-human trafficking conference in Dublin, scheduled for the second week in December.

Was this where she was? I made a mental note to look into the conference.

Among the books were volumes on international policy and crime. Her mom had said she was in the College of Business and Law, and all of this looked consonant with that. She was studying criminology, maybe with an emphasis on the trafficking of women.

The security guy came back into the unit. Looking at his notebook, he said, "Her roommates are Caoimhe Doyle and Fiona Byrne. We've spoken to Fiona, who had left for home before Cait and didn't know anything. She did say that Cait was best friends with Caoimhe. We've not spoken to Caoimhe yet. We believe she's still in Galway, but she won't return our calls. Here's her name and number." He ripped the page out of his notebook and handed it to me. "Is there anything else you need?" He seemed eager to please.

I shook my head and thanked him, then made one last cursory check of the other bedrooms and didn't see anything of note, other than that there was no cell phone, purse, or wallet anywhere in the apartment. Cait had definitely left with all of her stuff. Kelly waited by the door and locked it behind us as we left.

We thanked Kelly and walked outside, and I pulled out my phone to call Cait's friend.

"What the hell is this?" I said, looking at the page with the phone number.

Sam took the notepaper out of my hand. "That's how you spell Caoimhe."

"*Kweevah* is Caoimhe? You're kidding."

"No. It's an Irish Gaelic name."

"Is Gaelic code for, 'the letters have no relationship to the sounds they make'?" This was beyond languages like Polish; at least for those you could ask Vanna for a vowel. This was utter madness.

"Gaelic was Ireland's language until the eighteenth century. There are parts of the country where it's all they speak, and collectively they're called the Gaeltacht. The Irish were actually the ones who exported Gaelic to Scotland and other places. And believe it or not, there are hundreds of thousands of Gaelic speakers in Canada."

"How the hell do you know that?"

Sam spoke a lot of languages, an artifact of the various boarding schools she'd attended in Europe, but I'd never heard of anything in Ireland. I'd known her for years, but she still surprised me every day.

I called Caoimhe, and she answered her phone, which made me wonder how hard the security staff had actually tried to get a hold of her. She was just getting ready to start her shift at a club and asked us to meet her during her break at three. We agreed to meet her there.

It was twelve thirty, and we had some time to kill. I had an idea. "Do you think some of the professors are still around?"

"Maybe, why?"

"Just a feeling." I pulled up the university website on my phone and scrolled through the faculty list. "C'mon."

We walked through the campus to a modern-looking building

that housed the professor I was looking for. Much of the campus was made up of very old stone architecture. The College of Business, Public Policy and Law was newer, made up of several relatively recent structures, including the one we were heading to.

We entered the building, and I scanned the main floor directory, then we took the elevator up to the third floor. Sam followed me down the hallway and past a number of offices until we came to the one I wanted.

Dr. H. Jarlath, Head of Criminal Studies was stenciled on the door's glazed window. I knocked and heard a friendly, "Come in."

A forty-something-year-old man was standing by a metal cabinet, putting away files. The office was large, with windows overlooking green fields bordered by trees. Scattered papers covered a large metal desk in the center of the room.

"May I help you?" he said, looking up from the files.

"Are you Dr. Jarlath?"

"I am."

"I'm Jesse O'Hara, and this is Sam Hernandez. We're looking for Cait Gallagher. We're here on behalf of her family." No reason to beat around the bush.

"Cait? Is something wrong?" His accent sounded English, the kind that sounded like he'd spent his childhood playing croquet on the *Downton Abby* estate.

"She's missing. Do you know her?"

"Yes, she's in my introduction to criminology class."

Introductory classes typically involved hundreds of students. I couldn't imagine any of my professors in college knowing my name as a freshman after only one quarter. "Do you know all of your first-year students, Doctor Jarlath?"

"No." He laughed. "But Cait makes quite the impression. She's an outstanding student, and unlike many freshers, she seems to have figured out her major. She's already planning out her course of study and has been coming to me for academic planning advice."

"You study human trafficking?"

"No. My focus is broader. I look at comparative aspects of the links between organized crime and paramilitaries."

"Paramilitaries?"

He closed the file cabinet, walked over to his desk, and sat down, motioning us to take seats on the opposite side. "You're American, but you've probably heard of the IRA, yes?"

"Yes, of course. But I thought all of that was over?"

"The Good Friday Agreement in 1998 ended formal hostilities, yes. But there are still armed and organized groups on both sides of the conflict operating in Northern Ireland and, to a lesser extent, here in the Republic. These are referred to as paramilitaries, paras in shorthand. On the Republican side—the one that wants a united Ireland—you have the IRA, which you've heard of, but also a variety of splinter groups, including the New IRA; the Provisional IRA; RAAD, Republican Action Against Drugs; and the Continuity IRA. These groups are constantly splitting and merging. On the other side—the unionist side, those who support staying with the UK—you have the UDA, the Ulster Defence Association; the UVF, Ulster Volunteer Force; and the LVF, Loyalist Volunteer Force. From the outside, these groups appear to have minor differences in philosophy or approach. But there's a lot of infighting, and internal battles are always the fiercest."

"Kind of like the People's Front of Judea versus the Judean People's Front?" I quipped.

He looked at me blankly.

"Never mind. Please go on." *What kind of English guy doesn't watch Monty Python?* My opinion of him immediately plummeted.

"Of course, there are also plenty of people who aren't truly adherent to any political ideology, and use it as an excuse to make money through criminal enterprise. Regardless of motivation, the paras are responsible for much of the crime in Ireland, particularly smuggling operations near the border. The other half to the crime problem here is organized gang activity, which includes large, family-centered organizations as well as an increasing number of smaller, more decentralized groups. I look at the intersection of the gangs and the paramilitaries, and my recent focus is on geographic patterns of comparative operating procedures."

That sounded sufficiently obscure to warrant university research. 'Learn more and more about less and less until you know everything about nothing,' was how I described PhDs, including my own, which was a real snoozer—"Detecting and Quantifying Fraudulent Accounting Methods: Spatial and Temporal Markers in a Corporate Context."

"I had no idea Ireland was so dangerous," Sam said.

He smiled. Despite his accent, he seemed like a pleasant guy. "It's not. Our crime rate is one of the lowest in the EU and significantly lower than you have in the US. But one of our major issues is drugs, and the drug-related crime we have is largely perpetrated by these two factions. Here, take a look at these." He handed me some sets of stapled papers titled "Cooperative Crime: Irish Gangs and Paramilitaries" and "Cross-Border Drug Vectors in Ireland."

This guy was prolific. The articles were two of many that were scattered on his desk with his name on the author line. He'd written extensively about Irish crime, gangs, and drugs.

I folded the papers and put them in my pocket. "So Cait has been working with you on this gang/paramilitary crime thing?"

"We were just starting. She'd originally been focused on human trafficking, which is unfortunately also a serious problem in Ireland. It's not my area of study, so I'd been connecting her with colleagues at other schools who do more with that. But just recently she's been talking to me about changing her emphasis to paramilitaries and gangs."

This was interesting and a little surprising. Sligo was a small town across the island from Ireland's only real metropolitan city, where you would think most of the crime would be happening. Why would Cait take an interest in gangs and paramilitaries?

Sam was thinking along the same lines I was. "Do you have any idea why she would decide to do that?"

He looked thoughtful. "You know, I'm not sure. It's not uncommon for freshers to do some exploration and change their minds a number of times before they settle on one area of study. In Cait's case, though, it seemed more deliberate. She's not the kind of person to do things on a whim."

Something was off about this guy, but I wasn't sure what. "When was the last time you saw Cait?"

He opened a date book on his desk and turned some pages. "She stopped in to say goodbye on the last day of finals. I assumed she was going home." He frowned. "She's really missing?"

"She never made it back to Sligo." I took one of his cards from the holder on his desk and wrote my cell phone number on it. "If you hear anything or think of anything that seems relevant, can you give me a call?"

"Of course. I'll help in any way I can."

We left him looking troubled and walked back out to the elevator.

I held up the articles he'd given me and flipped through them on the ride down. "Well, that was a bust. But at least I've got some bedtime reading." They were filled with charts and maps and looked sufficiently dense to help me get to sleep.

"So maybe she's not at the conference in Dublin?" said Sam.

"Probably not. But we should still check it out."

"I wonder why she switched her focus?" Like me, Sam hadn't found his answer satisfactory.

"He said that first-year students often switch multiple times before settling. But I'm not buying that."

"Nor am I."

I looked at my watch. It was one o'clock. We still had some time before meeting with Caoimhe. "Where do you want to stop for lunch?"

Sam patted her stomach. "*Oof.* You're kidding. I'm stuffed. How can you be hungry?"

Usually, it was Sam who had the bottomless stomach, but this time I felt ready for another heart attack on a plate. "It's in my blood. This is the food of my people. C'mon, there are always places to eat near a university."

We walked around the campus and across one of the

bordering streets that was loaded with restaurants and fast food. Lots of choices, but I knew what I wanted—item eight on my Ireland bucket list. We stopped at a chipper for fish and chips.

I wasn't a huge fish and chips fan and generally limited the amount of fried food in my diet. But I knew this was one of the things that was really different in Ireland, and it didn't disappoint. The piping hot fried white fish and fries were served in newspaper, the fish flaky and tender and the fries crisp, and there was none of the cloying, rancid aftertaste that happened with less than fresh frying oil.

"This is amazing," I said through a mouthful of fries coated with a liberal amount of tartar sauce.

"Definitely. But I could do without the peas," she said, poking at the small pile of mushy peas that accompanied the meal.

"Yeah, that's a little weird."

We finished and walked back to the car. Once there, I pulled out the brochure for the human trafficking conference in Dublin I'd found in Cait's room. I called the main information line and had to do some wrangling that involved the desire of the operator to not share information about attendees over the phone and my desire to find out, along with my express intent to come there and raise holy hell if she didn't help me. She finally put me in touch with one of the conference organizers who confirmed that Cait hadn't registered for the conference and as far as she knew wasn't there. I hung up.

Having heard half of the discussion, Sam asked, "She's not there?"

"They don't think so. She's not registered."

"Professor Jarlath did say she had changed her focus. So it's not a surprise."

"No. But so far we've got nothing." I looked at my watch. "We might as well head over to the club to talk to Caoimhe."

I started the car and headed out of the parking lot. "At least we know Liam is the real deal. He clearly had some influence on the security guard."

"Yeah, but I wish I knew who he was."

SEVEN

Caoimhe's club, Good Night, was on the eastern side of town in what looked like an old factory building in a large parking lot, across the street from a residential area consisting of rows of attached houses. Many of the houses looked uninhabited. The area was definitely not the tony section of town, and I suspected it would look pretty scary once the sun went down.

It was early and there was no line to get in, but two very large men in black suit jackets over T-shirts stood at the entrance. They didn't move aside as we walked up, forcing me to brush against them as I went through the doorway.

Even though it was early, the inside was dimly lit. A long bar ran the length of one side of the windowless room, separated from a seating area with tables and booths by a large dance floor. Across from us was a roped-off area with a few small tables and more booths. A set of stairs started on the back wall, leading up to a second-floor balcony that ringed the floor with offices overlooking the entire space. Staff were cleaning floors, booths, and tables, and the bartender was serving a few people seated at the bar. Standing in various places around the room and on the balcony were more of the large goon-like guys who had greeted us at the front entrance.

We were early, so while we were waiting for Caoimhe, I took the picture of Cait out of my pocket and showed it around. At the sight of the picture and my inquiry, everyone turned abruptly away. After the fifth person declined to even look at the picture, I walked back over to Sam, who was waiting by the bar.

"Wow, what the hell do you think that's about?" I asked, putting the picture away.

"Maybe they're busy?"

"I don't know. They seemed more...afraid." I was getting a strange sensation and looked around, to see every one of the goons in the place staring at Sam and me.

"Jesse?"

I turned around to see a young woman standing behind us.

"Caoimhe?" I said with relief. I was starting to get a really bad feeling about this place.

"Yeah." She put down the rack of glasses she was carrying. "I'm on break," she called over her shoulder to the bartender.

We followed her to the back of the room and through a small hallway to a door that led outside to an alley. She leaned against the wall and lit up a cigarette.

"So you're here about Cait?" she asked, taking a long pull.

"Yes. Can you tell us the last time you saw her?" I looked at the cigarette enviously. I'd tried it back in college to see what all the fuss was about. Five years and three thousand dollars in nicotine gum later, I'd given it up, but still felt the pull.

"Yeah, the night after we took our finals. I was working a shift, and she was here." She took another drag. "She was leaving the next day for break."

"She never made it home."

Caoimhe's eyes grew wide, and she stubbed out her cigarette. "What?"

If I hadn't been sure before that Cait didn't go off on a lark, I was then. This was her best friend—she'd have known if Cait had decided to take off. And she looked worried.

"She was heading home for Christmas. Are you sure she didn't go home? Did you talk to her parents?"

I nodded. "I'm sure she didn't make it back. It was her parents who called me. Have you heard from her? Do you have any idea where she might be?"

"No, no. She was definitely going home. And we haven't talked since she left the club."

She pulled out another cigarette and lit it. "Have you talked to her boyfriend?"

"Yes, he was supposed to pick her up at the Sligo bus station. She never showed up."

Caoimhe looked confused. "What? Leo went to Sligo?"

"Who's Leo?"

"Cait's boyfriend."

Now it was my turn to be confused. "Her boyfriend is Paddy Feeney."

"Who? No. Leo. Leo Doherty. Have ye spoken to him?"

Sam and I looked at each other.

"Not yet. Is he still around?" I asked.

"He's from Belfast, but I don't think he went home. I'm not sure where he is, though. The last I saw him was the day before finals. I think he might have a place in town, but I've never been there."

"Do you have his number?"

Caoimhe took out her phone and scrolled through, found the number, and gave it to me. "Is Cait going to be all right?"

There was no way to answer that question, so I ignored it. "Was she big into the club scene?" I was already wondering about drugs and other things that went along with these kinds of clubs. And this place was definitely sketchy. There was no reason they'd need so much muscle for a completely legitimate business.

"Nah, nah, nothing like that. She'd hang out at the bar with one drink all night, and we'd talk during my breaks." She looked around, then ducked her head close to me and whispered, "Are the gardaí looking for her?"

I wasn't sure how to answer that either. The short answer was not really, but that wouldn't help things. "A lot of people are." I looked at the door. "I can't get anyone here to even look at Cait's picture. What are they afraid of?"

Caoimhe looked around, then lowered her voice even more. "The owners are very strict about staff talking to gardaí. If it wasn't about Cait, I wouldn't be talking to you either. I could lose my job." She took another drag on her cigarette. "Can I do anything?"

"No, not right now. We'll let you know. If you see her, would you please call me?"

"Of course, sure. Uh, would you wait a minute before coming back in?"

I nodded.

She ground out her cigarette, turned, and went back into the club.

Turning to Sam, I said, "Not wanting staff to talk to authorities. No one even dares to look at a picture, and Caoimhe looked scared. Not to mention the place is packed with enough muscle to start their own wrestling league. What do you think is going on here?"

"I have no idea. Do you think it could be related to Cait?"

I shook my head and shrugged. We knew nothing about this place, other than that Cait visited occasionally and there was definitely something illegal going on. "I hope not."

We walked back into the club and toward the front door. We were close to the exit when one of the bouncers blocked our way. We tried to walk around him, but he stepped sideways to block us.

I craned my neck to look up at him. "Hey, Hulk, this is fun, but we've got places to be."

"You're wanted upstairs." He herded us up the back stairs and down a dim hallway, to a door with Employees Only inked on the front. He knocked and then opened it, ushering us in.

The room was paneled in dark wood, red velvet couches lining three of the walls. A bald man was sitting behind a large metal desk looking at a set of papers.

The only thing missing was a playbill on the wall of his latest porn flick.

As we walked in, he put the papers down and took his glasses off. He waved a hand dismissively at our escort. "Leave us."

Hulk left the room and closed the door.

"Jesse O'Hara and Sam Hernandez from America," he said flatly.

How the hell does he know our names?

"Who are you?" I looked around. "Are you the owner?"

He laughed a rough, mirthless sound. "I run this club. What are you doing here?"

"We're looking for a missing girl. Cait Gallagher."

"She is not here. Whoever told you she was is misinformed."

"No one told us she was here. We just came to talk to her friend. And you still haven't told us your name."

"You can call me Slobodan. But it doesn't matter what our names are. You are not welcome in this club. Do not come back."

"What the hell is this about? We're just looking for a girl who went missing. Why all the back-room, scary, ominous shit?"

He said something loud in a language I didn't know and then Hulk opened the door and ushered us down the stairs and toward the exit.

"Don't come back. You've been warned," Hulk said, giving me a small push in the back to emphasize his point as I walked through the doorway.

I didn't argue and kept walking, resisting the urge to run. I turned around a few times as we made our way to the car. He watched us the whole way.

We got in, and I started up the car and left the parking lot. A few blocks away, I pulled over. "What the hell do you think that was all about?" I said, taking a deep breath, my first since we'd left the place.

"I don't know." Sam's voice was shaky.

"There's something going on in that club. I hope it's not related to Cait. Those guys aren't messing around."

She nodded. "Are you up for a drink?" That was usually my question. She was really scared.

"When am I not?"

I drove another mile into town to put more distance between us and Good Night, then parked in front of the first pub we saw. O'Malley's. We walked in and sat at the bar and ordered drinks. Sam's cider came up right away. I watched the excruciatingly slow speed of my Guinness pour while she drank.

While I waited for my beer, I tried Leo Doherty on the number Caoimhe had given me. It went to voicemail, so I hung up. I didn't want to leave a message just yet. If he had something to do with her disappearance, I wanted to confront him face-to-face so I could tell if he was lying. I called the campus security office next, and Kelly was more than happy to help us with Leo's information, giving us both his campus and home address in Northern Ireland. I wasn't up for a trip to Belfast and hoped he was still around. I also wondered why campus security hadn't talked to him. So far, they appeared to be following the Mullarkey Method for investigating missing persons. And there was an even bigger question.

"Sam, don't you think it's strange that Cait's parents don't know about Leo?"

"Not necessarily. Lots of girls have secret boyfriends."

"Yeah. And how many of them are missing?"

She nodded, conceding the point.

"If he's really her boyfriend, he's the one we need to talk to." I looked over at my beer, which was only half full. If it even *was* my beer. I sighed. "Let's go."

Sam finished the rest of her drink, and we left. I'd already been here two days and still hadn't tried my first Guinness in Ireland. But it didn't feel like we had time to waste.

EIGHT

Leo's place was decidedly lower rent than Cait's shiny apartment, one of two flats above a chipper. The apartment was accessed via a small stairway in the back of the restaurant, which led to a hallway with four doors. I knocked on Leo's door and got no answer, then knocked more loudly.

"Jaysus, what's the racket?!" The door next to Leo's opened, and a young man stuck his head out. He was wearing baggy pajama bottoms, and his thick hair was sticking straight up around his head. "D'ye mind? I'm trying to get some sleep."

At five in the evening? "We're looking for Leo. Is he around?"

"I'm not his blasted mother. How should I know?"

"Well, Sideshow Bob, we can stand here for the next hour and knock on his door or you can try to help us." I gave him one of my sweetest smiles. "Where does he go during the day?"

"Fuck's sake. How should I—?"

"Can I help ye?" We turned around to see another young man coming down the hallway.

"Ah, Jaysus, Leo, can ye talk to these women?" Sideshow closed his door with a bang.

"Leo Doherty?"

"Yes?" His hands were full of grocery bags, and he was digging in his pocket for a key.

I reached out to take one of the bags, and he handed it to me, then put the key in the lock and opened the door. We entered to a one-room studio that was fairly neat for a college guy, other than, like Cait's rooms, the books everywhere.

Leo put his groceries on the table. "Who are ye?"

He was another in what appeared to be an unlimited supply of attractive men in Ireland. Just a hair under six feet and built, with straight blonde hair that was long enough for him to be able to push it behind his ears. He had a few days' growth of similarly tinted beard, a la *Miami Vice*. He was definitely more in Cait's ballpark than Paddy.

"I'm Jesse O'Hara, and this is Sam Hernandez. We're helping the Gallaghers look for Cait. Have you seen her?"

He frowned. "Cait? Are ye from her family?"

"No, we're just helping them. Do you know where she is?"

"What are ye on about? She's at home, in Sligo," he said, pulling groceries out of the bag.

I walked over to him and took a can of beans out of his hand. "Have you seen her recently?"

"Not since finals. Like I said, she went home for holiday."

"She's not at her home. She never made it home for the break."

"Wha'? No...that couldn't be."

"How would you know?"

"Because I put her on the bus meself. Saturday morning, the day after finals." He looked from me to Sam, then back to me. "Wait...you're saying the family hasn't seen her since?"

"No. As far as we know, you were the last person to see her."

He frowned and sat down heavily in the lone kitchen chair.

"Caoimhe tells us you're Cait's boyfriend."

"Aye."

"What about her boyfriend in Sligo?"

"Her boyfriend in Sligo?"

"Paddy."

Leo snorted. "That little wanker is nah her boyfriend. He wishes."

Sam and I looked at each other. Another piece that didn't fit. But this made more sense. Cait was smart and beautiful. Leo was much closer to her on the attractiveness scale than Paddy. And while Mik had called Paddy Cait's "one," it wouldn't be a great surprise that the dad didn't know his daughter's romantic leanings. It would be something to confirm, or not, with Rose. But I had the strong feeling that Leo was the real deal.

"Look, I told you, I put her on the bus meself. That's the last I saw of her. You're sure she didn't get there?"

I shook my head. "Weren't you concerned when she didn't call you? And why doesn't her family know anything about you?"

He sighed, looking down at the floor. "She didn't want her family ta know, not yet. She was ta tell them over the holiday. She was going ta call me after she talked ta them. I assumed she was waiting for the right time. Or maybe they told her ta fuck me off. There are...it's...complicated.

No shit to that. "Try me."

He shook his head and stood up, turning back to his groceries.

I looked at Sam, signaling it was time to put her superpower to work.

She walked over to stand in front of him, putting her hands gently on his shoulders. "Leo, Cait is really missing, and Jesse and I are looking for her. Anything you can tell us might help."

He stared at her, then nodded.

Sitting back down in the chair, he said, "I'm from Belfast."

I recalled Mik's comment about not serving protestant shite like Bushmills in his house. Was Leo protestant?

"Maybe you've heard of me dah. James Doherty."

I looked at him blankly.

"He was in the IRA. The *real* IRA, the ones that carried weapons and bombed buildings," he said with barely hidden disgust. Not a fan of Dad, it seemed.

"What are you saying? That Cait's parents wouldn't take kindly to her dating the son of an IRA guy? Seems kind of extreme. What's he doing now?" I didn't understand what the big deal was. Leo was Catholic, which seemed like the most important thing in terms of a suitable match for their daughter. And he was clearly not sympathetic with the IRA's activities.

Leo laughed grimly. "Now he's feeding the worms. He was killed just before the agreement was signed."

"Oh. Sorry..."

He waved it off with his hand. "But it's not just that. Me da was close wit Danny Ryan."

"Should I know who that is?"

Leo looked at me like I was an idiot. "He's the biggest gang boss in Ireland."

Still not getting it, I asked, "What does that have to do with you? Why would Cait's parents care about a friend of your late father?"

"Danny Ryan is me godfather. Wit me da dead, he's taken me on as his responsibility. I'm not his son, but for all intents and purposes, he treats me like one."

"Oh..." I raised my eyebrows at him. Was Leo involved in gang activities?

He put his hand up to me. "I'm not involved wit any of his business. Not at all. He's just paying for me college. I don't work wit him. But his name, that's enough ta make folks back away."

Now it was making sense. The whole violent gang-boss-as-a-godfather thing explained why Cait didn't want to tell her family about Leo.

"Have ye checked with her roommates? Caoimhe and Fiona? They're all tight," he said.

"Yes. Are there any other friends we should talk to?"

He shook his head. "Nah...meself, Caoimhe, and Fiona... we're her close friends. Cait's into her studies. Spends a lot of time wit her books. And her professor."

"Jarlath?"

"Yeah. She's been takin' more time wit him in the last few weeks. Have ye talked wit him?"

"Yes, we just came from there."

Leo went quiet, staring at the floor again. I was pretty good at reading people, and he looked genuinely surprised, and concerned.

"Okay. Thanks, Leo."

"Is there anything I can do? What do ya tink happened to her?"

"We don't know."

"Will ye let me know when ye find her?"

"Of course."

He surprised us both by walking over to Sam and giving her a long hug. She hugged him back, and we walked out of his apartment, leaving him staring blankly at his groceries.

When we were out of earshot, Sam said, "That was quick. Should we have asked him more questions?"

"He says he put her on the bus and hasn't heard from her, and that she didn't have a lot more friends here. That's in line with what we've heard from other people."

"So do you believe him? That he saw Cait get on the bus?"

"Yeah...I do. The question is, where did she get off? If Paddy didn't see her get off at the station, that means she got off somewhere between Galway and Sligo."

Sam cocked her head. "Do we believe Paddy?"

"That Cait's his girlfriend? No. That she didn't make it to the station? I don't know."

"Didn't Mik call Paddy her 'one'?"

"Yeah, but after meeting Leo and Paddy, which one do you think she's with? I mean, maybe her and Paddy were together when she was in Sligo. But now she's at the university and probably realized pretty quickly there are higher lifeforms than him."

Sam nodded. "That leaves two choices. Either Cait got off the bus before reaching Sligo, or Paddy was lying."

"My money's on Paddy." I tossed her the keys. "You can drive." I wanted to get there quickly. We had a lying Paddy to confront.

NINE

On the way back to Sligo, I called Gideon to see if he could find anything interesting on Paddy Feeney.

He got back to me immediately. "Paddy's full name is Patrick Feeney. He's currently unemployed, he took a few online courses last year, and has held a few odd jobs. His parents are deceased, and he lives in their house."

"What courses?"

"Interior design, life coaching, and something called color therapy. He didn't complete any of them."

Wow. There was way too much there to unpack. He was looking less and less like someone Cait, or anyone with a functioning cerebral cortex, would actually date. "Anything else?"

"He's been picked up a couple of times for possession."

"Drugs? What kind?"

"Coke."

That explained his behavior at dinner. Not eating, lots of trips to the bathroom, jumpy. Yep. All the signs of a coke habit.

"Thanks. Can you look up a couple of other guys for me? Leo Doherty, from Belfast, currently a student at NUI Galway." I believed that Leo was Cait's boyfriend, but I wanted more information on him. "And Daniel Ryan. He's some kind of gang boss."

"A gang boss? What are you getting yourself into?"

"Nothing, it's not like that."

"It's always like that with you. But okay. Just be careful." We hung up.

Sam looked over at me while we were waiting at a stop light. "Paddy's into drugs? Is he a dealer?"

"No, I don't think so. He doesn't seem organized enough for that. But he's apparently got a coke habit."

She nodded, not looking surprised. She'd observed the same things about him that I had.

As we approached the Gallaghers', we saw a white car with yellow and blue garda markings in the driveway. Sam parked next to it, and we went into the house.

Mullarkey was in the living room, sitting on the couch with his back to us, talking to Rose. Her brow was furrowed. It looked an awful lot like the kind of face she made just before she yelled at Brian.

"You see, Mrs. Gallagher, we're doing everything we can. I'm confident that Cait will turn—"

Rose stood up mid-sentence and took a step toward us. "Any news?" she asked, her hands clasped tightly around her rosary.

I didn't want to get her hopes up. "We might have a lead. And it looks like Cait did get on the bus in Galway." I wasn't going to mention Paddy in front of Mullarkey. He might decide to actually do some work and try to talk to him himself, and I wanted a crack at Paddy first.

He looked at us sourly. "How do you know she's not still in Galway?"

"The same way I know the chances of you solving any actual crime are the same as my chances of joining a convent and devoting my life to clean living and pure thoughts."

I glanced at Rose. "Uh, no offense Rose."

"None taken, dear."

I looked around the room. "Rose, is Paddy here by any chance?"

"No. But he lives just down the street, five doors away, in the green house."

Sam was taking her coat off. "I think I'll stay here."

I nodded to Sam, thinking that was good idea just in case Mullarkey actually said something useful. I walked back outside and down the street to the green house. It was similar to the Gallaghers', but unlike their tidy, well-kept home, it was shabby. The grass hadn't been mowed in a while, and one of the windows in the front had a piece of cardboard taped over it. The stoop was empty other than a ratty-looking rubber welcome mat and a broken vase leaning up against one of the posts. It was by far the worst looking house on the street. A rusty car was parked at an angle in the driveway, one of the flat tires resting on the lawn. I walked around it to the stoop and pushed the doorbell.

No answer.

I knocked, waited, then knocked again, harder. This time I could hear shuffling footsteps from inside. Then the door opened.

Paddy looked terrible. He was bleary eyed, his red hair standing up on one side and hanging down over his face in greasy strands on the other. He was barefoot, wearing dirty sweatpants and a torn, sleeveless white T-shirt covered in an impressive variety of stains.

He stared at me bleakly. "Yeah?" His demeanor was the polar opposite from the outgoing, helpful guy I'd met the first night in the pub.

"We need to talk. It's about Cait."

He didn't look excited at the prospect, but left the door open as he turned around. I went in after him, closing the door behind me. My hand came away sticky, and I wiped it on my pants.

The inside of the house was way worse than the outside. Mail was heaped on the floor by the door, next to which was a small pile of old boots and shoes, some caked with mud. Clothes were strewn down the narrow hallway, leading up the stairs and into one of the side rooms.

The worst part was the smell. Like something had died in the walls and been left to decompose. I tried to breathe through my mouth while I followed Paddy, stepping over clothes, shoes, and papers as he ambled through the living room into the kitchen.

Jesus Christ, somehow it got worse. Empty bottles of beer and various other alcohols were strewn across the kitchen table and covered every inch of counter space. The garbage can was overflowing with the same. Paddy, apparently, was an equal opportunity drinker. Among the empty bottles were vodka, whiskey, gin, and something called Buckfast Tonic Wine. Ireland's version of Mad Dag? I didn't want to know. There were few signs of food other than some empty takeout cartons stacked on one of the chairs.

He opened the refrigerator and took out a beer. Galahad, the Pabst of Ireland. He didn't offer me one, but I was okay with that. He popped the top and sat down heavily in the only kitchen chair not covered in garbage. I was okay with that too. I didn't want to make contact with any surface in this place.

"Let's start with an easy one. Why did you lie to me?" I'd never conducted an interrogation before, but I felt confident, as I'd seen many on television. The police usually adopted one of two approaches: either the yelling-intimidation method or the patient, "I'm your friend, let's just talk until we get there" technique.

"I didn't—"

"Stop. I know you're not her boyfriend." I could feel myself slipping into the yelling-intimidation approach. Probably a more natural fit for me.

"I *am*," he whined. He took a long drink of his shitty beer and looked down, pushing a lock of filthy hair out of his eyes.

"No, you're not. You know how I know? I mean, other than the fact that she's way out of your league?"

He looked at me stonily.

"Because I met her *real* boyfriend. Who, no offense, is also way out of your league. And because that little promise ring you're wearing"—I nodded to the ring finger on his left hand— "has a match, which is currently in Cait's jewelry box and not on her finger."

My reconnaissance of the jewelry box in Cait's room included a ring that was a perfect match to the insipid ring he was wearing, alongside a number of things she didn't care about enough to take with her to school.

"I also know she got on the bus to Sligo. The bus you were supposed to meet." I let the silence hang in the air. TV police always changed it up a bit: start with some yelling, then give the perp time to think, then come at them again.

After a moment, I said, more gently, "What happened, Paddy?"

He mumbled something unintelligible.

"What? Speak up."

"Go away. I want to be alone."

"So do I. But you don't hear me complaining."

He dropped his head to his chest and in a tiny voice said, "She said she didn't think about me that way...that I wasn't her boyfriend. I was mad."

And, bam, there it is. That wasn't so hard. Maybe I should switch to law enforcement. Clearly, I had a knack for this. Zero to confession in two minutes flat.

He continued, "I didn't know they were going to take her."

"Who?" He was beaten, all I had to do now was get the details.

"It wasn't my fault...they kept giving it to me, even if I couldn't pay them..."

"*Who*, Paddy? Who took her?"

"They just wanted to know when she was coming in."

This was taking too long. I took a couple of quick steps so I could stand over him and roughly grabbed the beer out of his hand. "*Paddy.* Look at me."

His chin was still resting on his chest, but his eyes looked up. "I need you to tell me *everything*. Start at the beginning."

He reached for his beer, and when he couldn't get it out of my hand, let out a whimper.

Fucking hell. I hated crying in any form, from any person.

"Don't start crying, you stupid little bastard. Tell me what happened before I beat you to death with a half-empty can of bad beer."

This caused him to move to full-on blubbering.

Note to self, threats may not be the best solution to crying. I should have brought Sam with me. She had the patience for this sort of thing. Maybe a career in law enforcement wasn't my destiny.

I walked out of the room to get away from the crying and stood in the living room, trying not to touch anything. When it got quiet, I returned to the kitchen. Paddy was out of his chair, with one foot on the kitchen counter and one bouncing on the floor, trying to pop himself up and squeeze through the small, now open window above the sink. He wasn't getting anywhere, but his sweatpants had slipped down in the effort, and I was getting a really primo view of loser plumber's butt.

Fuck's sake.

I grabbed him around the waist and pulled him off the counter, dumping him on the floor. He curled up in a fetal position and wept, wiping at his eyes with the bottom of his filthy T-shirt.

I desperately wished I was anywhere but there. It took every ounce of willpower I had to not kick the living shit out of him. *God, I wish Sam was here.*

"Pull up your pants, or I swear to God I'm going to drown you in your own toilet." I had no intention of really doing that, primarily because I suspected the bathroom might be even more disgusting than the rest of the house. No chance was I going in there voluntarily.

He tried to pull his pants up, but it was impossible while he was sitting down. He stood up to fumble with them. Once they were all the way up, I shoved him into his chair. He slumped down, exhausted after his physical exertion. His sobbing dwindled down to childish sniffles.

"Can we try this again? You know, without the crying and the pathetic escape attempt?"

He gave a long sigh and slid farther down into the chair. "I was doing drugs."

"*Were* doing drugs? You mean, you're over it?" I looked around the room. "I don't think so. Dude, you're not exactly the poster boy for successful rehab."

"Am...I am...I do drugs..."

"What drugs?"

"Coke, okay? I ran out of money, but he didn't seem to mind."

"*Who*?" If I'd had a knife in my I hand, I would have used it to carve the information out of his brain.

"Larkin, the dealer. He kept giving it to me even though I was behind in payments. I thought he was giving me a break."

"Yeah, because that's what drug dealers are known for, their compassion and empathy." *What a moron.* "Jesus, Paddy, how *stupid* are you?"

He started simpering. I could feel the desire to live leaving my body.

I took a deep breath and dropped the anger from my voice. "Never mind, keep going."

"Then one day a couple of hard men came. They took my wallet. There was a picture of Cait in it. They asked if she was my girlfriend." He sniffled and wiped at his eyes, this time with a dirty paper napkin from the table. I was now spending considerable effort to resist throwing up in my mouth. "I said yes." His shoulders started to heave again.

No way, buddy. I grabbed at the top of each of his arms, holding him tightly in an effort to prevent the waterworks.

Pinning his arms didn't work, and he whined himself into another full-on, sniveling jag.

Fuck's sake, what did therapists do to stop people from doing this?

"I know she's not my girlfriend," he wailed, snot and tears running down his face.

Maybe shaking him would work. I moved him back and forth

in the chair, whipping his head around. Somehow, he managed to keep bawling.

Therapists probably had some secret for dealing with crying, probably involving some kind of hypnosis.

I let him go and leaned heavily against the wall. I clearly didn't have the skills for this. I looked desperately around the kitchen for something other than shitty beer to drink.

We stayed that way for what seemed like hours. Then he said softly, "They asked where she was, and I told them she was coming in on the bus."

Maybe letting him cry it out and not threatening him was the right approach. Who knew.

"They told me to stay home...they would meet her at the station." He looked up at me for approval.

"Then what?"

"They left."

"They left?"

"Yes."

"That's it?"

"That's it." He gave me a small smile, as if he'd just finished all the peas on his plate like a good boy and was ready to be released to go out and play.

"*Jesus fuck*, Paddy!" I yelled.

He jumped in his chair and started sobbing again.

I didn't care. "Some goons come to your house, tell you they're going to pick up Cait, and you don't tell *anyone? What the hell is the matter with you?!*"

All I could think about was Rose looking out the window, waiting for the daughter that might not come home. I wanted to kill this little fucker right then.

The tears and snot on his face were now dripping down to his T-shirt, merging smoothly with the rest of the stains. "I know, I know. It's just that...if you don't pay, they come for you. They hurt you, or your family. I...I thought if they thought she was my girlfriend, they would take her instead."

I looked at him in disbelief. "You're telling me you sold out

Cait to pay off a *fucking drug debt*?" The only thing that kept me from strangling him was that it would take a little while and he was too gross to be near for that long. "Tell me who these guys were, Paddy. What did they look like?"

"I don't know, I swear. I didn't see their faces. They were wearing masks."

"Did it occur to you to tell the *fucking police*?" I looked away. I knew if I kept looking at him, I'd completely lose it.

"They said if I went to the police, they'd kill me. You have to believe me. I didn't think they'd hurt Cait. I heard...I heard that sometimes...they take people, hold family members hostage, you know? Until you can pay up. I thought once I paid them off, they'd send her back. I was going to pay them."

"Yeah, I can see you're hard at work getting that to happen."

I couldn't stand to be here any longer. I kicked over a chair, sending garbage flying, and walked out, leaving him in his filthy kitchen, sobbing into his shitty beer. I escaped into the fresh air and slammed the door behind me.

I took a deep breath of fresh, non-decomposing-body-smelling air and wondered how long it would take to get the stench of his house out of my hair. If I needed to talk to the pathetic little puke again it would definitely have to be somewhere other than his house. But I realized, despite the crying and the filthy, disgusting environment, I'd found out something action-able. Paddy had basically confirmed that Cait had been kidnapped, and we had a good idea who was behind it. I needed to share what I knew with the police. And take a shower.

I called the station and asked for Mullarkey, but it was after ten and he'd gone home for the day. I left a message, letting him know I'd gotten some key info from Paddy that might help find Cait. Maybe that would get his butt in gear.

Given the way I'd been escorted out the last time, I was pretty sure there wouldn't be anyone else at the station who'd be eager to act on my information in any kind of urgent way. But I wanted to do something. I could feel time running out for Cait, if it hadn't already. I could only hope she would be of more use as a live hostage than a dead one.

I fished around in my pocket for the slip of paper I'd gotten from Liam. He'd come through with the university security in Galway, and who knew how else he was connected. It was a small town, so maybe he could do something with what I'd learned from Paddy. I called his number and left a voicemail, telling him I'd found something out about Cait and wanted to talk. Then I started walking back to the Gallaghers'.

Less than a minute later my phone rang. It was Liam. He gave me an address and hung up. I hoped it was a bar. I really needed a drink.

Mullarkey's car was gone, and the lights were out in the Gallaghers' house. I didn't want to wake anyone, so I got in the car and drove across town.

TEN

I
t was less than a five-minute drive to the address Liam had given
me, a ramshackle house at the end of a dead-end road abutting a
number of empty lots. The driveway was full, and there were
numerous cars parked on the street. I took a spot next to the curb by
the overgrown front lawn. The house was dark, other than slivers of
light peeking from around the corners of the curtain that hung over
the large bay window. As I was getting out of the car, I could see it
being pulled back from one corner. A face peered out at me.

I walked up to the door. There was music and laughter
coming from inside the house. I rang the bell and the music
quieted. From the other side of the door, there were footsteps.

From behind the closed door, I heard, "Yes?"

"Hi...uh...I'm looking for Liam Gilmartin." Muffled voices,
more footsteps, then the door opened.

"Hiya, Jesse," said Liam.

He gestured me in to a large, smoky, dimly lit living room that
had been furnished to look like a pub. Along one side of the room
was a full bar, complete with two taps of Guinness and shelves of
bottles and glasses, a sink, and some bar stools. An assortment of
unmatched tables and chairs were sprinkled around the room,

almost all of them occupied. The walls held posters, mirrors, and a couple of large Irish flags, along with several Celtic crosses in a variety of sizes.

"What is this place?"

"It's a shebeen."

"Shebeen?"

"Basically an unlicensed pub. They pop up here and there. It's a nice way to have a drink in a friendly place." His voice was low and gravelly, but not unpleasant. Almost mesmerizing. "They're a little bit illegal, so please don't mention this to anyone. The gardaí love to close them down." He smiled at me.

I nodded. I was never in favor of closing down pubs.

"Can I get you a drink?"

I couldn't think of anything I wanted more. "Guinness, please, and a whiskey."

His smiled widened, revealing perfect white teeth. "A woman after my own heart." He walked to the bar and spoke to the man behind it, who got busy with our shots and Guinness pours. I knew enough by now to not expect it any time soon.

Now that there was more light and he wasn't wearing a hooded sweatshirt, I got a better look at Liam. He was tall, well over six feet. And he was fucking smoking hot. His longish, slightly curly dark hair reached just above his shoulders, framing dancing, intelligent blue eyes that were perfectly set off by dimples that deepened when he smiled.

When our drinks were ready, Liam grabbed them and turned to the room. "My table's in the back." His walk was straight-backed and confident, his long, easy strides moving him smoothly around the tables and chairs.

Everyone seemed to know him based on the "hiyas" between him and everyone we passed. In contrast, there were a lot of open-mouth stares directed at me. Did Liam not usually have a woman with him? Or did I stand out as not from there? I wondered how they could tell.

We reached a small table in the back corner and sat down.

Picking up my pint, I realized this would be my first Guinness in Ireland. And in a shebeen, of all places! I took a long drink.

It didn't disappoint. I'd had a lot of Guinness in my life, some on tap, most in cans with nitro charges to preserve the signature creaminess. But this...this was a whole other level of beery goodness. I closed my eyes and let the precious liquid fill my mouth.

As always, the familiar roasted flavor was accompanied by lingering notes of chocolate and coffee and just enough sweetness to counteract the bitterness often present in stout beers. It managed to be both robust and light, and the unmatched velvety mouthfeel was even more profound than any Guinness I'd had previously. I wasn't sure if it really was smoother or if drinking it in Ireland was making it seem that way. But it didn't matter. I could die right then and my life would have been complete.

"I don't think I've ever seen anyone enjoy a Guinness that much in my life," Liam said, looking at my face.

I finished my pint and put down the shot in one sip. The interaction with Paddy had left me feeling grossed out and a little shaky, and I wanted to eradicate it from my mind as quickly as possible.

I didn't feel like talking right away, and Liam didn't seem to mind the silence. He was staring at me, but not in a creepy way. More...easily familiar. He glanced at my empty glass and raised his eyebrow.

"Yes, please. Just the Guinness."

He walked back up to the counter and came back with another pint.

He picked up his shot. "Sláinte."

"Cheers."

We drank.

He continued to grin at me, studying my face. "Rough night?"

"You could say that." I smiled back.

"Maybe not your first?" he said, gesturing at the scar on my forehead.

I touched it. "No."

Unless I was looking in a mirror, I forgot I had it. The scar was largely hidden by my hair, and I didn't really mind it. It felt like less of an imperfection and more of a reminder of my friendship with Sam. I didn't expound, and he didn't push, comfortable to sit quietly. I realized I still didn't know anything about him. But at the moment, I didn't care. I felt oddly at ease. Partly because I was in a bar, no doubt, and now a few drinks in. But also because Liam was one of the most instantly compelling men I'd ever met. It wasn't just his physical appearance, although that didn't hurt. It was some combination of the intense look he was giving me, the flirty dimpled smile, and his swaggering confidence. This guy oozed charisma, and it was causing a reaction that I hadn't experienced with a guy since Ander.

I was having trouble looking away from his eyes. They seemed to reach out and grab me by the private parts.

We stared at each other for a while, and when we started talking, Liam seemed in no hurry to find out what I'd learned about Cait. He asked about my family, and what I thought about Ireland. I talked about it being the home of my grandparents and my Ireland bucket list. He was very interested in the family angle, asking where my grandparents had lived and what other family I had in the Sligo area. In addition to the Gallaghers, there were some aunts and uncles on my dad's side of the family, along with a number of cousins I'd lost track of over time.

"So you've never been here before?" he asked.

"No. My parents came back a couple of times when I was little."

"Really? When?"

"I don't know, I was pretty little. Maybe twenty-five years ago or so. Why, do you think you might know them?"

I couldn't figure out why he was so interested in my parents, and I wasn't used to sharing things about myself. When forced to attend events that required me to interact with other people, I generally adopted the Dale Carnegie approach and would be the one to ask questions. People were always happy to talk about themselves, leaving me free to daydream about more interesting things. As a result, most people I met knew next to nothing about me and I knew way more than I wanted to know about them.

"Just curious." He took a sip of his beer. "How about your da, what's he like?"

Gosh, it was hard to know where to start. Absent alcoholic? World-class level philanderer? Inveterate liar? Mother-killer? Best to summarize.

"He's in prison."

"Dad's in prison" was usually a great conversation stopper. But Liam didn't seem fazed by it. All he did was raise his eyebrows, the flirty smile never leaving his face.

Enough about me. "What about you? What do you do?"

His smile got wider, and he leaned forward. "What would you like me to do?"

Well, that escalated quickly. I could think of about a thousand things I'd have liked him to do. But happy fun time would have to wait. My main priority right then was finding Cait. And since he didn't seem eager to talk about himself, we had to get on with it.

"Thanks for the security connection in Galway," I said.

"Was it useful?"

I nodded. "We found her real boyfriend."

His smile disappeared. "Her *real* boyfriend?"

"Yeah. And we confirmed that Cait left Galway. I think she's in Sligo."

"Sligo? Why do you think that?"

"I talked to Paddy Feeney."

"Her boyfriend."

Did he know Paddy? He'd said it was a small town. "No, he's not. He used to be, at least in his own mind. But someone thought he was, and he set her up to pay off a drug debt." I described the discussion I'd had with Paddy, leaving out the parts about the yelling and the shaking and the threat of death by swirly. "Do you know anything about who runs the drugs in Sligo? If we could find the men who shook down Paddy, we'd likely be able to track them to Cait."

Liam shook his head. He was all business now, fixing me with an intense stare. "Was Paddy able to describe the men who came to his house?"

"No, he said their faces were covered. But he was in bad shape when I talked to him. I'll catch him tomorrow, after he's cleaned up." I expected that after a shower and a couple of lines of coke, Paddy would be a lot more helpful. And more importantly, less inclined to cry. "We'll get him over to the garda station to look at some photographs. As you say, Sligo's not a big place. I'll bet they can narrow down possible suspects pretty quickly." I finished my beer.

Liam raised his eyebrow again at my empty glass.

It was tempting, but it was getting late and I had to go to the station first thing in the morning. "No, thanks. I need to get going. Rain check?"

Did they do rain checks in Ireland? Probably not since it rained all the time. But he got my drift, the flirty smile returning to his face as we got up to leave.

The reaction of the people in the shebeen as we made our way out was similar to when we'd walked in. They looked at me like I had two heads.

Whatever. I liked this place. It had a laid back, comfortable feel to it, and the people seemed relaxed and happy. I wondered if I could turn my own house into a shebeen? It might make it more homey. The only potential challenge was that I wasn't sure I could find enough people to let in that I liked.

Liam escorted me out of the building and surprised me by walking me all the way to my car. When we got to the door, he put his hand on the hood next to my head and moved close, his low, gravelly voice whispering in my ear, "Fancy a ride?"

I leaned away. He was really good looking. But, wow...Irish guys moved fast. And I had things to do.

"Uh...no, thanks." Looking up into his face, I almost regretted it as the words were coming out of my mouth. "Besides, it looks like you have a lot of friends in there."

"What do you mean?"

"Well, everyone seemed to know you, and at least four of the women in there are ready to jump your bones."

"Why do you think that?" He smiled, condescending.

Shit. "I, uh, notice things." I didn't usually let on about my photographic memory when I first met someone. It tended to freak people out. "It doesn't matter. Never mind."

His look changed from flirty to skeptical. "C'mon, at least you can tell me which four are supposedly ready to jump my bones."

I didn't really want to do this, but he was challenging me. "The redhead in the back at the table with the two older guys, the only one drinking red wine in the place."

"Nora, yeah...we've, uh, dated." His brow furrowed. "Who else?"

"Two women with shoulder length black hair sitting together against the wall opposite the bar. They're sisters. Both in brown sweaters. Both drinking Guinness. And both married, although they're trying to hide it. They were seriously checking you out."

"Fiona and Molly."

"Are they married?"

"Aye. But that could have been a guess."

I sighed. "To the right of the big window in the front is a woman with her boyfriend. She's nursing a gin and tonic with two limes, and when we walked out, he was on at least his second beer and third shot. That one is sad. He's working up the courage to ask her to marry him, and she's trying to figure out how to dump him. She's ready any time you are."

He was unconvinced. "Anna and Finn. I know them. And you can't possibly know that."

As if on cue, the front door to the shebeen opened and Anna came out. Finn was behind her, imploring her to stop and talk, but she was walking resolutely to her car. We watched her get in without speaking to him and drive away. Finn looked crestfallen and slowly walked back into the shebeen.

"You must have heard them talking."

"Seriously? Okay. There were twenty-five people in there, eighteen of them men, not including the bartender. All of the men but one had beers in front of them, and twelve were also drinking shots. There are nine bottles of whiskey at the bar, three of them are unopened. The table directly in front of the window has one leg two inches shorter than the rest, and it's being propped up with a small—"

He put his hands up in surrender. "Okay, okay, you win."

I'd used my natural talent to instantly capture thousands of little details when I'd worked in forensic accounting. It was one of the things that had put me in high demand.

Unfortunately, I couldn't turn it off, and was constantly bombarded with excruciating facts of everyone around me, providing more than enough information to tell what was going on in their lives within seconds. Mostly things I really didn't want to know. I still remembered the looks and whispers around me as a child. I was different, which for a kid was a straight path to ostracization. I'd learned to keep it to myself as much as possible. People I'd worked with called it a great asset. Just about everyone else thought I was a freak.

Liam's face told me all I needed to know about which camp he was in. He took a small step back. "Jesus. I guess I'll not be playing cards with ye." He leaned over awkwardly, like he didn't want to get too close, and kissed me quickly on the cheek, then turned and walked back into the house. Maybe to the horny sisters.

Oh well. I got in my car and drove back to the Gallaghers'. This had been a complete bust. Not only had Liam not been any help, but any hopes I had of picking up a date with him after I found Cait were out the window.

That was really too bad. Booty calls to Ireland would have been way easier than going to Spain.

ELEVEN

It was still dark and quiet when I got back to the Gallagher house. As I was stepping onto the front stoop I heard, "Psst..."

I turned around to see Brian leaning around the corner of the house. He motioned for me to follow him, and we took the gravel pathway around the house to the barn in the back yard. He slid open the large wooden door and motioned me in. I walked with him to the back of the barn. It was dimly lit and largely empty, but I could see two horses in stalls, as well as various kinds of harnesses and leads hanging on the walls. Against the wall on one side was a bench on which sat some towels, buckets, and plastic bottles, some filled with yellow liquid. In the center of the barn was a lopsided pommel horse like gymnasts use.

"What's that?"

"That's a dummy mount for stallion semen collection."

I was rarely speechless, but this left me at a complete loss for words. Ideas were flooding my brain. I was already overloaded with horse jerker questions, and this was too much. I needed to ignore it for now, and I made an effort to look away from the hump dummy.

Nope, can't do it. "How does it work?"

He looked pleased to explain the details of the family business. "The handlers lead the horse to the dummy and encourage it to mount, like it would a mare."

"Why would the horse do that?"

"Stallions are trained to use these. It starts by having an estrus mare nearby—a mare that is in heat—and the horse is guided to mount and ejaculate into the dummy." He patted the hump dummy, and said proudly, "At this point, our stallions don't need a mare. We can just apply estrus urine to get them excited. We use a Missouri-style artificial vagina, AV for short."

Missouri style? That put a whole different spin on the Show Me State.

"The goal is to get them into the AV and then settle into committed, organized thrusting that leads to a one-mount ejaculation."

A one-mount ejaculation sounded like the worst date in history. "So, you, uh, don't actually jerk off the horses?" I asked, trying not to sound disappointed.

He smiled, and for the first time I noticed the slight dimples on his cheeks. "No. But it's definitely a hands-on process, and the handlers have to build up a rapport with the horses in order for it to work. And there is sometimes a need for some, em, additional manual stimulation. John and Colin are great with them. They can usually collect three or four times a day with each horse."

We walked past the dummy, toward a corner in the back of the barn, while I wondered how they built up rapport with horses, whether or not it involved long walks on the beach and candlelit dinners.

Colin, John, and Sam were sitting around on a soft pile of hay surrounded by bound bales. In front of them was an overturned crate, on top of which were a set of small glasses and several bottles of whiskey. Bushmills, something called Knappogue Castle, and three different bottles of Redbreast.

Sam had been there for a while—I could tell by the "several

shots in" smile on her face. She could definitely hold her liquor, but wasn't anywhere near my level. She was leaning casually back on the hay in between John and Colin.

John reached for the Bushmills. "Ready to try some protestant shite?"

"Definitely." I sat down on the hay as he poured a small amount into a glass.

The Bushmills was similar to Jameson in that it was light and promised more burn when you smelled it than you actually experienced when you drank it. It was a fine, serviceable whiskey but gave me no reason to think I'd ever choose it over Jameson.

After the Bushmills, we tried the Knappogue Castle and then worked our way through the three makes of Redbreast: a twelve-year-old, something called Lustau, and a Pedro Ximénez edition. Like the Bushmills, the Knappogue Castel was good, but nothing that would make me forego my allegiance to Jameson. The Redbreast was a different story. I'd always thought of myself as a committed Jameson girl, but this whiskey was making me rethink that. The twelve-year-old Redbreast had more of a burn than Jameson, which wasn't a surprise as it was higher proof. But the flavor was out of this world: caramel sweetness, accentuated by a rich mouthfeel, and a complex array of other fruit and spices.

Brian was watching my face while I tasted it. "Grand, yeah?"

"It's my new favorite." It was still lingering on my tongue. "It's...almost syrupy. I love the mouthfeel. It's like it's more viscous. And so much more complex."

"Then you can say you like triple distilled, single pot still Irish whiskey. This style is done in batches and uses only malted and unmalted barley."

"What's Jameson, then?"

"That's what we call a blend. It's a mix of one of the three Irish whiskey styles: single pot still, like the Redbreast; single malt, like the Knappogue; and single grain, which includes whiskeys with corn along with the barley and that are processed in columns rather than pots." He poured me a small amount of the Redbreast

Lustau. "This one was aged in sherry casks, along with the standard bourbon barrels that most whiskeys here are aged in. The Redbreast distillers have relationships with cask makers in Spain that make sherries and ports."

I could definitely taste the sherry. Like the twelve-year-old, this one was also syrupy and with far more flavors than Jameson.

"Usually, when distillers use special casks for aging, they only do it for a month or so. These Redbreast whiskeys, they're aged in bourbon casks and then in those sherry casks for a minimum of twelve months. It really gives the flavor." He opened up the last bottle, the Redbreast Pedro Ximénez edition, and poured it into my glass.

I sipped. "Oh my god." This was unbelievable. It took the Lustau to a whole other level. Fruit, spices, toasted nuts, and the sweetness of sherry and caramel. And like the two other Redbreast whiskeys, it was chewy, with a lingering, sweet finish. "This has to be expensive."

"Aye, it's nah something we can afford. It was a gift from a client."

"Why haven't I heard of this?" I said, taking another sip.

"The Irish whiskey industry is getting back up on its feet now. For years we've only had the three distilleries—Middleton, Bushmills, and Cooley—and all anyone outside of the country hears about is Jameson and Bushmills. Now there are over thirty distilleries and counting, but they're just getting going. It will take some time for them to produce and age great whiskeys. You know there's one in Sligo now too. Athru Distillery."

"Really? Why don't you have any of that?"

"It's very new. But maybe before you leave, we can take a tour of the site. It's on the peninsula at Lough Gill, just southeast of here." He looked into his glass, wistful. "Everyone knows about Scottish whisky. They've over a hundred distilleries in the country."

"Do you think Irish whiskey is better than Scottish?"

He laughed. "Aye, of course. They can't get the flavors we can generate. The biggest difference is the use of barley. In Ireland, we tend to use a fair amount of unmalted barley for the mash. In Scotland, they use almost entirely malted."

"Why the difference?" Scotland was a short hop across the water, so it seemed strange that they'd have such a fundamental difference in whiskey making.

He leaned forward, excited. "The reason goes back to the English Malt Tax of 1785. The English were trying to come up with money to pay for their wars against France, so they enacted a tax on malted barley. At the time, all whiskey was made with malted barley. Once the English instituted the tax, the Irish distillers innovated their process to use unmalted. Which, as it turns out, adds complex flavors to whiskey and a different mouth-feel. That's what you're noticing in the Redbreast—the creami-ness—that's from the unmalted barley. Scotland was initially immune to the tax, so they had no reason to change." Brian's eyes were dancing, and not just from the alcohol. He was loving sharing what he knew about their whiskey.

He was smart, and attractive, and I'd already seen how wonderful he was with his mom. Kind of the total package. I found myself wondering if he had a girlfriend.

"That's the main difference. The other is that most Scottish whiskies are only double distilled. Almost all of ours are triple distilled. This makes them higher proof, leaves the lighter flavors intact, and gets rid of more of the impurities."

Higher proof. I was glad we were only doing small tastes. I relaxed back against a hay bale and listened to Brian regale us with his knowledge of Irish history as it related to whiskey and other important things. When he could get a word in edgewise, John shared a few ribald stories about the family business, including particularly noteworthy interactions with their stallions.

We'd all been talking quietly for a while, enjoying each other's company and the whiskey, when Colin asked softly, "Do ya think you'll be able ta find her, Jesse?" He'd not spoken a complete sentence since we'd arrived.

Everyone stopped talking, and all eyes were on me, waiting.

They were a strong lot, this bunch, and clearly Cait meant the world to them. She seemed to be at the center of their family. It would be devastating to them to lose her. And not knowing what had happened, possibly ever, would be a horrible fate.

"I'll do everything I can." I desperately wanted to be assuring, but I didn't want to mislead them. We had some small leads, but precious little to go on at this point.

"We trust ya, Jesse. You'll bring her back," said John.

All three boys nodded, looking convinced that I would bring back their sister.

It was an awesome display of confidence that I wished I felt myself. But whatever happened, I was committed now, to Cait and her family, and I knew I would do everything I could to find her. I wouldn't stop until I did. I was filled with resolve.

An hour later I was filled with whiskey. It had been a long day, and I was tired. And while I was dreading having to deal with Paddy again tomorrow, it was time to call it a night.

I stood up. "Thanks, guys, this has been great." I raised my eyebrows at Sam.

She was comfortably laid out on a bale. "I'm not tired yet."

I knew what that meant. Someone was going to get busy tonight. And the horse semen mounting collector-thingy would make a great mood setter. Not that she needed one. Part of me envied her easy sexuality. But unless I was really wasted, it took a lot for me to hop into bed with someone. Sam described me as a cerebrosexual, and she was probably right. I usually didn't hook up unless I met someone that got my brain going.

Brian was done too. We both said our goodnights, and he walked me back to the house.

We said goodnight again, and as I started to head up the stairs, he said, "Want to try something else?"

When I didn't immediately decline, he said, "Hang on." He disappeared into the kitchen and came back with an unlabeled bottle filled with clear liquid and a couple of small glasses.

We sat down on the couch, and he poured us each a small amount.

"Sláinte."

We clinked glasses, and I put it away.

Holy mother of fuck. I was coughing and gasping. "What the *fuck* is this?" Once as a kid, I'd swallowed some gasoline on a dare. That had been way smoother than this stuff.

"Poteen. Ma makes it. She doesn't know that I know." He smiled conspiratorially.

I was still sputtering and coughing. This stuff was unbelievably vile.

"Here, try another one. The second one is always better."

I took the second shot and reluctantly drank it. He was right, it was smoother the second time. Maybe because the first one had destroyed the nerve endings in my mouth.

Brian put his second shot away smoothly, no doubt having already burned through all his mucous membranes years ago.

"So, Sam..." Of course, he wanted to know about Sam. What else was new. "You two are best mates, yeah?" He uncorked the bottle and poured another shot into my empty glass.

I drank it quickly. At this point it didn't matter. I couldn't feel or taste anything in my mouth. But this would definitely have to be the last one. I had a lot to do tomorrow. And while I was used to working hung over and not bad at it, it was starting to become a daily thing here. It was way too easy to drink in this country.

"Are you...eh...*with* each other?"

"Yes. Wait, what? No." People often made that mistake. Sam was like a sister to me. "She's probably down there getting hay in her hair with your brothers."

He laughed.

What a great smile.

"Do you have a one?" he asked.

"You mean a boyfriend?" I thought about Ander, my transatlantic booty call. "No."

"D'ya want one?"

Damn, these Irish guys were direct. I liked that. And I was

starting to like him. But I had work to do. "I'm a little busy at the moment."

"I didn't mean right now." He grinned. "Are all American women this fast?"

I smiled back at him and shook my head.

We said goodnight, and I went upstairs to bed.

TWELVE

I woke up to a headache so bad I heard banging. No doubt from the poteen. I'd drunk lots of whiskey in my life, but that homemade shit was dangerous.

It took me a few minutes to realize that the banging wasn't only coming from my head. There was something going on downstairs. I got out of bed and walked into the hallway.

Sam's door opened, and she poked her head out. I walked over to her and pulled a piece of hay out of her hair. She smiled blearily.

"Did you get any sleep at all?" I asked.

"Enough."

I guessed that meant none. Among Sam's amazing array of talents was an unbelievable ability to function at a high level and remain personable with little sleep. I could go without sleep too, but not without completely sacrificing my limited likability.

We walked down the stairs together to check out the commotion. Rose was at the door, facing two uniformed gardaí on the stoop.

One of the officers said, "Is one of you Jesse O'Hara?"

"That's me."

"Would you come with us, please, Miss O'Hara?"

"Why? What is this about?" Sam asked.

"You're wanted for questioning at the station."

Wanted for questioning? Maybe this was related to my call to Mullarkey. If so, it would be some welcome urgency to Cait's disappearance. But their manner didn't seem all that solicitous. And since when did the police provide taxi service? "Can I meet you there? I'd like to clean up."

The two garda looked at each other, and the one who'd spoken nodded stiffly. "We'll wait for you."

I went to my room and pulled on a clean T-shirt, then went to the bathroom to wash up. My head was hammering, and all I wanted at the moment was some coffee and a little food to quiet my stomach. But I needed to go to the station anyway, to see Mullarkey and tell him what Paddy had told me. Might as well get it over with.

Sam and I made it downstairs in a few minutes and convinced them to let us follow them in our car. I'd been so wasted the night before I'd left my case of Jameson in the car. I hoped it was OK.

I drove. There was no way was I going to take the chance that they'd arrest Sam for reckless driving. On the way, I filled her in on my discussion with Paddy.

"So you think Cait was taken by drug dealers to insure Paddy's debt?" Sam asked.

"That's what it sounds like. Hopefully, we can get them to bring Paddy into the station and he can make an ID on the men. Their faces were covered, but I'll bet there's not too many of those guys in a town this size and they'll be able to narrow it down pretty quickly. I just hope they haven't done anything to her."

"It's unlikely, isn't it? If she's insurance for a drug debt?"

"I hope so. What about Mullarkey? Did he share anything useful yesterday at the house?"

"Just that he's genuinely concerned." She turned to me. "I think maybe you were too hard on him, Jesse. He seems like a good man."

"Great, he's concerned. If his skillset is limited to being concerned, he should be an undertaker." Sam was always seeing the good in people, even when it wasn't there. One of the many differences between us.

When we got to the station, a garda told Sam to wait in the reception area. Officer O'Fenton eyed me disparagingly from behind the counter. After sneaking past him and then getting thrown out, I no longer qualified for his officious politeness.

A garda led me toward the back of the main office space, down a narrow hallway with several doors on each side. He opened one of the doors and gestured me into a small, windowless room. There was a table and three chairs, and a recording machine sat on the table. Two men were already sitting down, Mullarkey and someone I didn't recognize next to him. As I sat down across from them, they opened up small, identical black notebooks and took pens out of their jackets. The one I didn't recognize flipped a switch on the recorder.

"Detective Sergeant Sean Murphy with Inspector Calbach Mullarkey, speaking with Jesse O'Hara, interview commencing at ten forty-five. Miss O'Hara—"

"It's *Doctor* O'Hara."

"*Doctor* O'Hara, I need to state to you that you are not obliged to say anything unless you wish to do so, but anything you say will be taken down in writing and may be given in evidence."

"Wait...what is this?"

"Can you tell us what you know about Paddy Feeney?"

"He's a loser and a drug addict. And he might know the guys who kidnapped Cait Gallagher."

Mullarkey jumped in. "There's no evidence to say that she's been kidnapped. You don't do anyone any favors by throwing around wild speculation."

"It's *not* wild speculation. Paddy Feeney told me that the guys who shook him down met her at the bus station. It doesn't take Einstein to figure out they're the guys who kidnapped her." Hell, it didn't even take Elmer Fudd, but Mullarkey was well below him on the investigative competence scale.

Murphy continued, "What else do you know about Paddy Feeney?"

"I know he's the guy who set up Cait for the guys who kidnapped her." They didn't seem impressed with that for some reason. "Why aren't you writing that in your little books?" I said, jabbing my finger at the pages.

"When did you last see Mr. Feeney?"

"Last night. When I learned that he'd set Cait up to be taken by the. Guys. Who. Kidnapped. Her." I said the last few words slowly and with emphasis, as they'd seemed to miss that little tidbit the first two times around.

They wrote this down in their little notebooks. Finally.

"Why did you visit him?"

Fucking hell. "I found out he wasn't her boyfriend and wanted to ask him about it."

"Did you have an argument?"

"Who cares? Jesus, you need to bring him in and ask him about *the guys who kidnapped her*." Was everyone here this slow?

They just stared at me.

I recognized this as the "silent treatment" interrogation technique. "I wouldn't call it an argument, exactly." Somehow the silent treatment compelled me to keep talking. "We discussed what happened to Cait."

Best to leave out the parts about the yelling, the intimidation, and the threats.

They both scribbled into their little books.

"What would you call it?" Murphy asked.

I rolled my eyes up the ceiling. "*Seriously*? Who cares what I'd call it?"

They continued to stare at me, waiting.

I was really uncomfortable. Apparently, the silent interrogation technique was wildly successful on me. "I don't know. He cried a lot."

They raised their eyebrows.

"But, I mean, I think he's a crier, you know?"

This, apparently, was worth scribbling into their little notebooks too.

"What does any of this have to do with Cait?"

"When did you leave him?"

Jesus, it was like these guys didn't give a shit about what Paddy had said about Cait. "I don't know, it was after nine. I left a message with you last night," I said, looking at Mullarkey. "Whatever time that was." I looked around. "Look, can I get some coffee or something?"

This wasn't going the way I expected, and my irritation was turning into unease. I realized I was sweating. Jesus, I was acting exactly like someone who had something to hide.

"And where did you go next?"

I wasn't sure if I should share the meeting with Liam at the shebeen. He'd said the gardaí closed them down. I might need him again; he seemed to be pretty well connected. I didn't want to get on his bad side. "I came home. Uh, to the Gallaghers. We've been staying with them while we're looking for Cait."

"Can anyone confirm that?"

Why would they need to confirm that? "What the fuck is going on?"

They both just stared, having identified the effectiveness of the silent interrogation technique on me.

"Yes, I was with Sam and the Gallagher boys until late. It was after midnight, I think."

There was a time gap there of about an hour when I was at the shebeen. They'd turn that up if they questioned the boys and Sam. I'd need to get to them to make sure everyone's story was straight.

"Miss O'Hara—"

"It's *Doctor* O'Hara."

"*Doctor* O'Hara. Do you do drugs?"

What? "No. But you're making me want to start."

"What about cocaine?"

"I just said I didn't do drugs."

It was true. I was very comfortable with alcohol but found other substances not to my liking. I knew this based on intensive research conducted during college, when I'd experimented with just about everything. Pot, coke, LSD one time, speed, ecstasy, something that might have been a quaalude. Also mushrooms that I tried at a Grateful Dead tribute band concert, purchased in the parking lot from a woman in braids who was ostensibly selling turquoise jewelry, but once within earshot was softly calling out, "Doses, doses..." No injection drugs, though. Needles creeped me out.

Sam liked to drop the occasional hit of acid, mostly when she wanted to bring some new energy to her painting. I would stick around when she did that, just to make sure nothing weird happened and that the dogs got fed. Sometimes she created some great stuff when she tripped. Other times she'd just stare at the canvas for hours and laugh.

They continued to write notes in their little notebooks. When they were done, they closed them and looked at each other, then at me.

Murphy cleared his throat. "Miss O'Hara—"

"*Doctor* O'Hara."

"Doctor O'Hara, Paddy Feeney was found dead this morning."

"What?!"

They were both staring at me intently.

On police shows, they did this because perps revealed a lot by their faces when told of other people's deaths. The police were experts at reading guilty faces. And shit, I definitely had guilt. I'd made the poor little bastard cry and threatened to murder him with the toilet. And my DNA would be all over him. Along with undoubtedly lots of other DNA, given his aversion to basic hygiene.

I tried to make my face into a mask of non-guilt. Hmmm... what did that look like? Innocent, I guessed. Damn. That look wasn't really in my repertoire. "He was alive when I left him. What happened to him?" It couldn't have been natural causes, or they wouldn't have been questioning me. What else could it be? Death by poor hygiene? Toxic T-shirt syndrome? Lethal grossness?

"We're not at liberty to say."

Paddy could have identified the guys who likely took Cait. It struck me that with him dead, I didn't have any way to find them. I didn't have to fake the look of despair that took over my face. This apparently was enough to convince Murphy that I probably didn't murder Paddy, as much as I'd wanted to at the time.

"Dr. O'Hara, you are free to go, but please don't leave the area for the time being. We may have more questions." He reached over and clicked off the recorder.

Paddy was dead, and any information he had that could have moved the investigation along was dead with him. Probably nice for Mullarkey. It would mean he wouldn't have to do any more work.

I stood up to go, then sat back down. I did have something. "Hang on a second."

Murphy was halfway out of the room, but turned in the doorway to listen.

"Paddy mentioned the drug dealer, somebody named Larkin."

"Was he one of the men who came to his house?"

"No, I don't think so."

Murphy looked at Mullarkey, who said, "Larkin is a low-level drug dealer. He supplies many of the addicts in this town. I doubt he's involved in anything like this."

Murphy said, "We'll bring him in for a chat." He stared at Mullarkey until he nodded his head.

By Murphy's tone, I didn't think that would go anywhere. But I appreciated the fact that he wasn't ignoring the lead.

Murphy left me to Mullarkey, who walked me to the reception area. Sam was waiting for me on the little bench. She stood up and started to talk, but I shook my head. We'd talk outside.

By the time we made it out of the station, it was almost noon and pouring down rain.

"Did you tell them about Paddy and the drugs?"

"Paddy's dead. They think I had something to do with it."

"Oh no…"

"Yeah. They're not concerned about Cait. They didn't even

ask me about that." I looked at my watch. "What a fucking waste of time."

It *was* a waste of time, but I realized it didn't matter. I didn't have any other leads or anything else to do at this point. It wasn't often that I was stuck while I was investigating. Even as one line of inquiry closed down, others would open. Usually, I had too much to do and too little time.

I called Liam and left a message, though I doubted he'd have anything new for me since the night before. But I couldn't stand not doing anything, and I had no idea what to do next. I followed Sam numbly back to our car, and we drove back to the Gallaghers' house in silence.

THIRTEEN

Rose was holding the front door open for us when we got back. "Any news?"

I was starting to dread crushing the look of hopefulness on her face every time I gave her an update. "Paddy Feeney was killed last night."

Her look of shock was replaced immediately by one of fear. "D'ya believe it has something to do with Cait?"

"I don't know." I sat down heavily in the Nice Chair. "I'm sorry, Rose. I'm not sure what to do at this point." I hated admitting this to her. But it was the truth, and she deserved at least that.

Rose looked like she was going to say something, but instead walked into the kitchen. A few minutes later, she came out with a tray, on which sat a teapot, three cups, and a small basket of scones. "Jesse, you're a smart one, and I'll not be giving up on ye. Ye just need to recharge yourself." She poured a cup for each of us and sat down on the couch next to Sam.

I reached for a scone. I admired her optimism, but didn't share it. Cait had been gone for over a week. If she were a TV victim, this would have turned from a rescue into a recovery operation by now.

We drank. I'd never been much of a tea fan, and I'd always

wondered about the penchant for British and Irish folks to turn to tea in times of trouble. I watched a lot of war movies, and it was curious how British soldiers would sit around a kettle of tea and be calmed. Mortars could be dropping down around them, Germans storming the barricades, the walls of whatever shelter they were in crumbling on top of them, but they'd be sitting there drinking their tea and chatting. The only tea I'd ever had that calmed me down was the Long Island variety. Nevertheless, this was kind of soothing. I felt marginally better.

"Ye know, Jesse, when my Cait would be stuck on a problem, she'd get out and go to her favorite place to sort things out."

My favorite place was a pub, so that was an idea.

"What is her favorite place, Rose?" Sam asked.

"Knocknarea." Rose looked wistfully at the picture of Cait on the top of the mountain we'd discussed the previous night. "She'd climb to the top, to the queen's tomb. Sometimes she'd be gone for hours." She sipped her tea. "She always came home with her spirits lifted."

She always came home hung in the air, and Rose looked down into her tea. She was doing her best to keep her grief contained, but I didn't know how long she could hold out. There were few things worse than a missing child.

I felt a strong pull to do something to help her, maybe because she reminded me of my own mom. I'd lost her at eighteen and still missed her every day.

Going for a hike wasn't a bad idea. Oftentimes when I got stuck during an investigation, I'd take a shower or do something completely unrelated and let my subconscious brain work on things. It was surprisingly effective. And maybe some exercise would get things moving. I usually worked out every day, but since I'd been in Ireland, the only thing I'd really worked out was my liver. And it wasn't like we had any other options at the moment.

"I think I'll do that." The magical tea was having an effect. "Want to come with me?"

Sam looked out the window at the rain, frowning slightly. "No, thanks."

"I'll only be gone a little while." Unlike Sam, I loved this kind of weather. It usually meant I would be alone, which was better for thinking. And, overall, just better. "Do you mind?"

"No, I'll stay here and help Rose with dinner."

Rose looked gratefully at Sam, and it occurred to me how lonely she would be right now. Her husband was, for all intents and purposes, AWOL, and the boys were busy keeping the business going.

Rose got up and went into one of the back rooms, coming back with a rain jacket. "This is Cait's. Maybe it will bring ye luck."

I took it from her and started for the door.

"Jesse, please take care. It will be dark before too long, and the weather here can change in a heartbeat, very severely at the top of the queen's mountain. There'll likely be mist and fog, and this season it gets very high winds. The trail's wooden bog bridges can get slippery in this rain. We'll not be wanting to call out the Mountain Rescue folks.

"The wind has bundled up the clouds high over Knocknarea and thrown the thunder on the stones for all that Maebh can say."

I looked at her blankly.

"That's Mr. Yeats. You know he's from Sligo. This is from his *Red Hanrahan's Song About Ireland*."

"Yes, thanks, Rose. Don't worry. I'll be careful." I studiously avoided Sam, who I knew was rolling her eyes. She'd heard that lie hundreds of times.

I left the house and took the car to Knocknarea, which was only five miles or so away. There was no traffic to speak of, and I got there in ten minutes. I pulled into the empty main parking lot and took one of the spots.

Cold rain came down now in sheets, and, as I'd hoped, there was no one else there. It wasn't tourist season, and the locals had better things to do than walk around a mountain they saw every day.

From the map mounted in the parking lot, I could see there were three trailheads: the main one I was at, one on the Strandhill side of the mountain near the water, and a third at Caillte Rochcarrick, some kind of forest. There was a six-kilometer loop that went up the mountain and then through the forest and back to the parking lot. Six kilometers was close to three and a half miles, with an elevation gain of only three hundred meters. It would take me about two hours, short enough that I'd make it back before dark. I was feeling invigorated by the cold rain and decided to do the loop. I left Cait's jacket in the car and headed up.

My trailhead was the closest to the top of the three, and I made it up the gently sloped mountain in fifteen minutes. At the top, I saw Queen Maeve's cairn. The cairn itself looked like a large gravel cone with its top cut off. Placards noted that it was close to sixty meters across and ten meters high and built around 3,400 BC. It was one of the largest monuments ever built in prehistoric Ireland. Signs posted nearby implored people not to climb on the cairn. I could see where it had been eroded from people who apparently couldn't read.

The most striking thing to me was that, unlike the Carrowmore tombs, Queen Maeve's cairn had never been excavated. In the age of exploring and tearing everything down, this was extremely cool. At least people had been able to leave one mystery on earth.

Supposedly there were six more neolithic monuments nearby, five on the summit, but all I could see was low grass and a number of narrow dirt trails leading away from the cairn. But the view from the top was stunning, even as it was limited by the rain. To the west and south was the ocean, and to the north a band of thick forest ran alongside the mountain. East of me were bright green fields and softly rolling hills.

The path to continue down and around the loop was marked with red arrows painted on narrow wooden posts. I left the tomb and headed north. The trail up to now had been simple gravel or dirt, surrounded by low grass and brush. It led gradually downward to a signpost that gave me a choice to continue north to the Strandhill trailhead or west to follow the path around the loop. I'd been going down, but now the loop path was starting to slope upward again, the gravel replaced by steep wooden stairs that led toward the forest. I stopped a little ways up at one of the viewing platforms.

The platform looked out over the grassy slopes and farther out the tide flats of Ballysadare Bay and the ocean beyond. It was a spectacular view. I could see why Cait loved this place.

After the platform were a series of switchbacks, and the trail continued to weave in and around the edge of the forest. Eventually, the steep wooden steps gave way to a less steep dirt path with wooden planks. The planks continued for a little while and then I was back walking on dirt, and all of a sudden, completely in the forest. The sun hadn't set yet, but it was cloudy and dark. I turned on my phone light.

Somehow this made things eerier. I couldn't see anything other than a few feet of the path in front of me. The available light showed just enough to outline the tall trees, but not all of the way to the top. The effect was that of being surrounded by trees of infinite height and who knows what looking down at me from above.

It was getting late and would soon be even darker when the sun set, which I estimated to be about a half hour away. It was time to get back to the car, so I sped up. There now seemed to be little signage, and I hoped I was going the right way. Nothing to do but keep walking.

The rain had finally stopped and among the trees the wind had died down to a gentle wave. The path was taking me to the edge of the forest, which was now thinning and letting in more light. I was relieved when I saw signs for the Caillte Rochcarrick trailhead. To my left I could see through the trees, into green fields. I estimated I was halfway around the loop when I heard an engine.

I stepped behind a tree and looked toward the sound. Not far from where I was, an old pickup truck was moving toward me on a narrow gravel road that came almost up to the edge of the forest. The truck stopped at the end of the road, and two men got out. They went to the open back and levered out two large, square plastic containers from the bed. They dumped them on the ground and got back in the truck.

The road they'd come up originated from a small farm. I watched them drive slowly back down, where they stopped about a hundred feet away. They parked next to a warehouse-like structure and a few more trucks. Farther on I could see a shed, some cars, and something that looked like a small oil tanker. All of the vehicles and the structure were hidden from the main road by a row of trees.

I left the forest path and walked toward the containers they'd dumped at the end of the road. They were covered with some kind of sludge and smelled strongly of gasoline.

The sun had set but the clouds were gone and the moon was out. I could see the two men get out of the truck and walk into the warehouse through a small door next to the parking area.

Part of my mad skillset included what Sam referred to as terminal curiosity. And while I knew I should get back to my car, it looked like something interesting was going on here. It wouldn't hurt to take just a quick peek, so I walked down the road to the warehouse.

As I got closer, the smell of gasoline got stronger and I could hear voices and banging from inside the warehouse.

Maybe there was a window in this place. I walked to the far side of the warehouse and turned the corner. No windows on that side. I continued to walk around the perimeter. I was almost all the way around, picking my way through the dense trees up against the back of the building, but they eventually became impenetrable and I turned to go back. I was getting uneasy.

It was time to get out of there. I didn't know what I'd been thinking. I was out in the middle of nowhere, after dark, butting into someone's business.

I retraced my steps along the side of the building. Added now to the smell of gasoline was cigarette smoke. I was about to turn to the front and back to the gravel road when I heard the warehouse door open. I crouched down and peered around the side. One man was standing in front of the warehouse lighting a cigarette. I'd need to wait him out before going back to the forest.

Wait...if he was just lighting up now, why did I already—?

"Who's this?" A heavy hand gripped my shoulder.

FOURTEEN

An extremely large man lifted me up and pushed me forward around the corner to the front of the warehouse, easily holding me in place with one beefy hand wrapped around my upper arm.

"Who the hell is that, Lynch?" Just Now Smoking Guy walked toward me, dropping his cigarette to the ground and putting it out with the toe of a worn work boot.

He was short, under five foot five, and thin, with buggy green eyes barely visible under strands of brown hair that fell over his forehead. He was wearing jeans and a flannel plaid shirt over a long-sleeved T-shirt.

"Dunno. Found her 'round the side."

Lynch, AKA Lurch, was not the brains of this operation.

"What are you doin' here, little lady?" Small Guy brushed my hair back from my face and gently touched my cheek.

Ew.

"We better take her to Quinn." Small Guy wasn't the brains either. Probably good for them.

"C'mon, guys. I was out for a walk and just got a little lost. I was checking out the queen's tomb. Which was very inspiring, by the way. Makes you want to go grab a spear yourself, amiright?" I gave them my most winning smile.

"It's not the weather for hikin'," said Lurch, Master of the Obvious.

Small Guy grabbed my other arm, and the two of them frog-marched me into the warehouse.

The smell of gasoline hit me like a wave when we walked in the door. No wonder they went outside to smoke.

The warehouse looked bigger on the inside than it had on the outside. Bare bulbs hung down from the ceiling at intervals, lighting up the space in an overlapping series of weak spotlights. The room was dominated by a large, horizontal white tank along one side of the building. Laying around it on the floor were a variety of tubes and funnels and shelves stacked with sacks of... kitty litter? I counted over sixty of them. There were no cats in sight. Gas cans were strewn about the floor between makeshift shelves overflowing with plastic bottles, some of them with skull and crossbones poisonous materials labels. Along the other walls were generators, pumps, and something that looked like an air compressor. A man was tying plastic around another one of the large sludgy containers I'd seen them dump earlier. A fourth man was flipping through a clipboard near the door. He was older but looked fit, a muscular fifty-something, with a craggy, pock-marked face. His gray hair was shaved close to the scalp.

Small Guy pulled me over to the older man. "Quinn! Look what I found nosing around outside."

Lurch let me go, apparently fine with letting Small Guy take the credit for me.

Quinn looked up from his clipboard, saw me, and threw his head back in exasperation. "What the fuck, Firbis? What were ye doing outside?"

Firbis looked down at his feet. "Having a fag."

Quinn smacked him across the side of the head. Maybe Lurch wasn't as dumb as he looked. "Put her over there and tie her up." He nodded to the back corner of the warehouse.

Firbis pushed me to the rear of the building and shoved me to the floor. It was wet from gasoline in rivulets making their way from the various gas cans and tubes to pool in small puddles on the floor. I tried to sit in a space between the wet spots. He picked up a piece of twine from the floor and tied my hands with it. Quinn put his clipboard down on a barrel he was using as a table and walked over to me. Lurch and the other one joined us in a semi-circle around me.

Quinn loomed over me. "Who the hell are ye? What are ye doing here?"

"Just out for a stroll."

No way was I giving them my name. I'd seen a lot of war and spy movies and knew what was coming next. They would ask me questions, threaten me with torture, but I would be strong and brave and refuse to answer, gaining their grudging respect, and eventually bring them over to the side of good. I was confident I could resist pressure to—

Quinn leaned down and slapped me hard across the face.

Ouch. And damnit. My eyes welled with tears. I don't know why getting slapped hurt so much. It did way less damage than breaking a nose or getting hit with a bottle, as I knew from experience. But why did it hurt so much fucking more? The side of my face was on fire. I lifted my tied hands to rub it.

"Don't play with me, ye poxy cunt. How'd ye find us?"

One of the strategies that spies often used successfully was humor. Everyone loved to laugh. "Irish yellow pages. I was looking for my Lucky Charms. Because, you know, they're magically deli—"

The words were barely out of my mouth when, in an economy of motion, one of Quinn's fists flew forward into my face. It hit me right above the left eye, rocking my head to the side and knocking me over to the ground.

I was wrong. This hurt way more than getting slapped.

Quinn nudged the fourth man and said, "See what she's got on her."

The fourth guy pulled me back up and roughly went through my jacket and jeans pockets, taking out my keys, phone, and wallet. He handed them all to Quinn, accompanied by a stream of energetic, slightly high-pitched chatter that might have been, "Here is her stuff." His accent was so thick I was having trouble recognizing any English. It also could have been, "She's pretty, in a Debra Winger sort of way." Or, "I'll bet her best friend is smoking hot." Or, "Where are our cats?"

Quinn didn't seem to have any trouble understanding Irish Kenny and nodded. "Good idea." He turned back to me. "Where's your car?"

When I didn't answer right away, he reached a hand behind his back and pulled out a handgun from his waistband. He pushed the gun's muzzle into my kneecap. "Don't take a piss, or I'll be happy to change your stride for ye."

The gun to the kneecap technique was even more effective than the silent interrogation method. I wasn't interested in permanently joining the Ministry of Silly Walks and gave out information faster than a Jehovah's Witness at a block party. "Knocknarea parking lot. The main one near the Glen Road. It's the blue rental, third spot from the entrance."

"Go get the bitch's car and bring it here." He tossed my keys to Lurch, who caught them and hurried out the door.

Quinn opened my wallet, pulling out my driver's license. "*Fucking hell*. American. Just what we fuckin' need." He tossed the wallet to the floor and stood glaring at me, thinking.

Irish Kenny said something else that I didn't catch.

Quinn nodded. "Yeah, I'd rather Firbis'd not brought her here in the first place either. Fucking eejit." So that was the hierarchy, then—Quinn at the top, then Irish Kenny, then Lurch, and way down on the pecking order was Firbis, the fucking eejit.

Quinn turned his back to me and pulled out his phone, punching in a number. "Boss, hi, yeah, sorry to bother ye. We've got another trespasser."

Another trespasser? I looked around the room.

He pulled the phone away from his ear. I could hear the yelling from the other end.

"An American. O'Hara."

He listened for a moment, then said, "Yeah. Okay. Will do."
He hung up.

"Does he want us to do the same thing we did with the other
hoor?" Firbis said, leering at me.

The other hoor? I presumed he meant *whore*, so another
woman, in Irish thug-speak. Could it have been Cait?

"No. He'll take care of her. He's coming over later. We're to
keep her until then."

Firbis looked disappointed. I wondered what they had done
to the other hoor to make him so excited.

All three men were still standing around me.

"*Get off yer duffs and finish up the run.* We need to be out of
here by tomorrow. We've got bigger things to do shortly," Quinn
yelled.

Firbis and Irish Kenny hustled away.

They left me alone after that, and got back to whatever it was
they were doing. Firbis and Irish Kenny were at the big tank,
siphoning liquid out of it into a large plastic bin. Quinn went
back to poring over his clipboard.

I wasn't all that familiar with drug operations, but this didn't
have the feel of drugs to me. For one thing, I didn't see anything
that resembled drugs or drug packaging. In *Scarface*, they'd used
kerosene to process cocaine. All of the liquid in this place was
gasoline, although maybe that didn't matter. But there was no
white powder in sight, and none of those kilo-sized packages that
you always saw drug buyers cut into with impressive-looking
knives and then put their little finger in to taste.

Also, thankfully, no chain saws. But it definitely had an illegal
feel to it.

In a little while, Lurch came back and reported to Quinn,
returning my keys.

"Like we don't have enough fuckin' things to worry about,"
Quinn swore. He threw the keys on the ground and returned to
studying his clipboard.

He'd said the Big Boss was going to take care of me, and I was
very interested to know what "take care of" meant in this

context. I hoped the options might be, "give heartfelt regrets and let me go," or, "escort me to my car," or, "make Quinn apologize for calling me a poxy cunt." But I didn't want to wait around to find out. It was time to get out of there. These guys might have taken Cait, and I needed to get the gardaí to check them out. And I was pretty sure I didn't need to be taken care of, whatever that meant.

The main problem was that the only door in the place other than the garage door was the small one at the front, and I was sitting on the other side of the building. No way could I get across the warehouse without them seeing me.

One problem at a time. I leaned over nonchalantly and felt around my boot for the Datu. Waiting until all of their backs were turned, I slowly pulled the knife out, stuck it between my feet, and rubbed the twine around my wrists across the blade, cutting through the ratty rope easily. I left it in place to make it look like I was still tied up.

The other two things I had on me were my lockpicks, always hidden in my boot, and a lighter that they apparently didn't think was important enough to take. The lighter was an artifact of my collegiate smoking days. Those days were over, but I felt naked without it and it occasionally came in handy.

I looked around. There was shit everywhere, plastic containers, garbage, cardboard. No cigarette butts, for obvious reasons. Close to me was a messy pile of the heavy paper kitty litter sacks, empty ones, lying next to some gas cans and plastic bottles with poisonous material labels.

Quinn had walked out of the warehouse, maybe for a smoke, and the other three were busy siphoning liquid from the tank. They were sloppy, sloshing liquid over the side of the bins and onto the floor. All of them were fully concentrating on the tank.

I slid over to the kitty litter sack pile and cut off a piece of one of the sacks. Sliding back to my spot, I lit the edge of the heavy paper with my lighter, watched it catch, and then tossed it toward the pile.

I waited.

A tiny wisp of smoke rose from the edge of the pile and then nothing.

I tried again, sliding over and cutting off a larger piece of the heavy paper. I lit it and waited a little longer this time, until it was well over halfway burned and almost singing my fingers, before I tossed it into the pile.

This time I was rewarded with a small visible flame. It moved quickly to the center of the pile, which started to smoke. I watched licks of flames emerge and waited for one of the hoods to notice.

No one turned around. They were completely absorbed in their tasks.

The fire was growing, flames now visible in various places and smoke making its way up to the rafters.

I wondered if their sense of smell had been burned out from inhaling gas fumes all day.

The fire continued to spread. Several of the sacks had completely caught, and the entire pile was on fire now, sending billows of smoke up and across the top of the warehouse.

How could they not notice this?

There was a small *pop* and then *whoosh*, and a large flame shot up from the edge of the pile, then another, and another. I watched it move low across the floor, following the rivulets of gasoline.

My primary concern had been that the men would see the fire and put it out too easily before I had a chance to get out. I needn't have worried about that. The dumb sons of bitches still hadn't turned around.

Stacks of plastic bottles propped up a set of makeshift wooden shelves, on top of which were some of the fuel barrels that I could see weren't empty. The fire was quickly moving toward them, making me worry. In addition to the fuel containers, there were puddles of gas all over the place and the bales of sludge scattered around the warehouse looked like they would go up in a heartbeat. Once the fire really started going, I'd be stuck in the middle of it.

What the hell was the matter with these guys? We could all burn to death before they noticed their building was on fire.

"Hey!"

All three men turned around at my shout.

"*Fire! Fire!*" Firbis yelled, dropping the siphon tubes and running toward the exit. He grabbed the handle and flew through the door, smacking into Quinn, who was walking in at the same time.

Quinn looked around quickly and pulled his gun out. He waved it at Firbis and the others, who were also more interested in getting out than putting out a fire. "We're not leaving all this. Put it out."

The men ran to the back of the warehouse, toward the burning piles. No surprise that the illegal operation wasn't equipped with sprinklers and extinguishers. They frantically beat at it with their jackets, and Firbis threw buckets of water on it. At least, I hoped it was water.

Now that they were all otherwise engaged, I slipped across the warehouse floor, grabbing my keys and wallet on the way. I could hear one of the men coughing as I opened the door and ran outside.

My car was next to the tanker, and I jumped in and started it up, reversing my way out of the parking lot and then racing down the gravel road between the trees. At the main road, I turned left to go back to town. I heard a loud *boom* behind me, accompanied by a flare of light that flashed in my rearview mirror.

I hoped they'd made it out of there. Less for humanitarian reasons and more because I needed them to tell the gardaí that they were the ones who had kidnapped Cait and where they were keeping her. And maybe the gardaí could raid the place when the Big Boss was there later that night. That is, if the warehouse was still standing. Catching the Big Boss would be a bonus. But even if that didn't happen, at the very least the gardaí could find out what those guys had done with Cait and shut down whatever it was they were doing in the warehouse.

Nailing a crime boss and shutting down an illegal operation, whatever it was, would be a big-time feat in this town. Maybe they'd give me a medal or a key to the city. That would be cool. I was taking a liking to this place, and the idea of becoming a local celebrity was appealing. I'd probably never have to buy my own drink in Sligo again.

No time to think about that now. I hit the gas and the car lurched forward.

It was dark, but the clouds were gone and the street was lit by the full moon. I was able to take the curves at speed, and I'd be back to town in a few minutes. I turned the heater up to its maximum setting to offset the chill from my wet clothes.

Best to let the gardaí know right away. I reached for my phone to call the station, then remembered Quinn had taken it.

Sometimes Sam left her phone in the car. It was a long shot, but I leaned over to run my hands over the passenger's seat and then leaned over to open the glove compartment.

It was awkward, driving on this side of the car. Usually, I was on the left side, reaching with my right hand. But it was—

BANG.

The air went out of my lungs in a *whoosh* as the car came to an immediate stop, throwing me forward toward the windshield. Everything went white.

FIFTEEN

I woke to the hissing of a deflating airbag. I'd missed a turn and run into one of the low stone walls that were all over this fucking country.

Fortunately, I'd taken the entire impact of the crash on my face. I brought my hand up to my nose and touched it gingerly. It was broken, not for the first time. I was dizzy and a little nauseous. Probably a small concussion, also not for the first time. But this was a much better outcome than going through the windshield.

I took a panicked look in the back seat. *Whew.* The case of whiskey was safe, still secured snugly by the seatbelt.

The front of the car had accordioned, the way it was supposed to. I was fairly intact, as was the wall I'd run into.

I turned the key. The engine ground weakly, then stopped. I tried it a few more times and heard clicking. I wouldn't be driving out of here.

The car's headlights were on, and my car was jutting out into the road. I made an unsuccessful attempt to turn off the lights, but apparently the switch had been broken in the crash.

There was no one behind me, yet. I wasn't sure if they were following me, but if so, they wouldn't be able to miss me.

I was on a quiet, deserted stretch of road, with thick, impenetrable woods on one side and open fields on the other. If I'd gotten lucky, Quinn and the gang had either not followed me or had gone the other way. But if not, they'd spot me too easily if I tried to go through the fields. I wasn't optimistic about my chances of outrunning men with guns, and that didn't leave a lot of options. I had to wait for daylight, or until someone else drove by. But I didn't want to stay in the car and be an easy target.

The seatbelt buckle wouldn't open, so I cut myself out and reached for the door. No luck there either. The impact had bent the frame, and the door was stuck. I used the butt of my knife to smash the window, then wriggled out, trying, and mostly succeeding, to not cut myself on the glass.

I was able to open the undamaged back door and undid the seatbelt around the case of whiskey, then grabbed it and pulled it out of the car. I climbed over the wall and sat down on the wet grass, setting the case next to me. I opened the case and took out a bottle. If they were going to get me, I'd at least have a few drinks to soften the blow. I screwed off the top of a bottle of Jameson and took a sip.

Maybe they'd given up or turned around. Or maybe they hadn't even followed me. There was that boom...it could have been that everyone was lost in the fire.

A minute passed. Then another. I took another drink, hopeful.

The sound of car engines approaching broke the silence. They were moving fast, then more slowly, then they stopped. Car doors opened and closed.

"Firbis, see if she's in the car. Maybe she saved us the trouble. You others get the torches out of the boot." Quinn's voice.

So much for the luck of the Irish. Although, now that I thought about it, he was more Irish than me, so I guess the saying held true.

It was quiet again, other than Firbis's footsteps slowly approaching my car.

"Save them the trouble" sounded like they were no longer

interested in holding me until the Big Boss came around. And there were four of them with at least one gun. My chances of getting out of there alive were looking bleak.

I looked up at the moon. It was a beautiful night. I was in Ireland, the land of my ancestors, drinking my favorite whiskey. Or what used to be my favorite whiskey before trying the Redbreast. Still, it wasn't bad.

If this was how it would end for me, fine. There were worse ways to go. I took another drink.

It was kind of a shame, though. There was so much more I wanted to see in Ireland. From the minute I'd stepped off the plane, I'd felt an immediate affinity for this country. These were my people, as much as any people could be. Millennia of rich history, and a culture forged by eras of suffering, struggle, and revival. The builders of the Irish megaliths; Queen Maeve the warrior; the Famine, whose effect was still evident in the Irish diaspora; Irish independence, and the great Michael Collins; the tragedy of the Troubles in Northern Ireland, and the start of a solution through the Good Friday Agreement; the Celtic Tiger economic resurgence in the late '90s.

Too bad I'd never finish my Ireland bucket—

The Troubles...

Leaning the bottle against the case, I hurriedly removed my jacket and stripped off my T-shirt, which unlike my jacket had stayed relatively dry. I put my jacket back on and then used my knife to start a tear in the shirt. I ripped a strip off the bottom and then wadded it up and stuffed it halfway into the mouth of the open bottle, turning it over once to wet the fabric. Then I waited.

Firbis was close. "Nah, don't see 'er." I imagined him peering into the car.

I lit the end of the whiskey-soaked T-shirt strip with my lighter and tossed the bottle over the wall, in the direction of my car.

Glass tinkled on the pavement, and there was a flash of light. I felt a small wave of heat.

"Holy fuck!" *Bitch!*" I heard running steps, then car doors opening and slamming and cars backing up.

I peeked over the wall. Maybe they'd decided I wasn't worth the trouble.

Nope. They weren't leaving, they'd just moved their cars back about fifty feet. The doors were opening again.

"There she is!"

My head was perfectly framed above the wall by my car's headlights. I heard a gunshot and a *chink* and felt a sharp pain in my neck. I dropped down quickly and touched my throat. My hand came away sticky. A piece of the wall had splintered off from the bullet and nicked me. I pressed my hand against my neck to slow the bleeding, staying low behind the wall as a flurry of gunshots flew over my head.

They definitely had more than one gun. I counted at least three sets of shots coming from different weapons. Some were hitting the wall with sharp metallic pings and others were buzzing over the top of the wall just above me. They seemed to have a lot of bullets.

I waited, but there was no letup in the barrage. I reached into the case for another bottle. I unscrewed the top and took a drink, then tore off another piece of T-shirt, lit it, and heaved it farther over the wall, in the direction of their cars.

There was another tinkle of breaking glass, and the gunshots stopped.

"*Fuck!*"

I waited again, the only sound muffled voices from the direction of the cars. Too low to hear what they were saying. Or maybe it was Irish Kenny, unintelligible at any volume.

A few minutes later the gunshots started up again, chinking into the wall and flying inches over my head.

I slid lower down behind the wall and grabbed another bottle from the case. In a rush to cut the next T-shirt strip, I sliced myself with the knife. Blood dripped from the palm of my hand onto the cloth as I stuffed it into the bottle. I lit it and sent it over the wall, again stopping the shooting and keeping them back and down behind their cars.

The first two bottles had sent up flashes of light and small waves of heat when they broke, until the whiskey burned itself out on the pavement. After the third bottle, the light continued to shine unevenly. Something bigger had caught fire. Probably my rental car.

When cars caught on fire in movies, they'd blow up. But I'd heard that was a myth and that in real life they'd just burn themselves out. I hoped that was the case. The car was right up against the wall, and if it exploded, I would spend eternity as little bits in the Irish countryside. But there was nothing I could do about it. And I'd rather blow up than let those bastards shoot me.

We went on like this for almost an hour. They'd shoot at me, I'd send over a bottle, they'd wait, then start firing again when the flames died down. They knew enough about Molotov Cocktails to know that you didn't want to be on the receiving end of a flammable liquid and a flame. In some ways they were scarier than bullets. Bullets could miss; flame searched for a target.

My bottles were consistently landing between their cars and my wall, and I mentally thanked my dad. He hadn't done much I was thankful for, but the time he'd spent with me as a kid developing my hand-eye coordination by tossing baseballs around had definitely paid off.

Bullets were chipping off pieces of the wall at a regular clip, causing them to fly off in different directions, some of which ricocheted into my head. Warm blood was now flowing slowly down my neck from a dozen tiny impacts. I ignored them. They weren't causing any major damage, and by now I'd had enough to drink that I barely noticed them.

I'd made a point to send over the bottles of regular Jameson, as it seemed a shame to waste the higher end stuff. But I'd used all six of them and all I had left were five bottles of the Jameson 18 and the single bottle of Rarest Vintage Reserve. I pulled one of the Jameson 18 bottles out of the case. It was in a stouter, slightly shorter bottle than regular Jameson and with a cork instead of a screw top. I pulled out the cork and took a sip.

Damn...this was really good. Very smooth, with a long finish that managed to taste fruity and caramelly at the same time. I took one more long drink, then ripped off another strip of T-shirt and stuffed it into the bottle, sighing.

What a fucking shame.

I lit the cloth, in the process also lighting my pants on fire. Not really surprising, as by now I was starting to get loaded. I'd learned the hard way years ago that inebriation, flammable liquids, and an open flame was not a recipe for success. I smacked my thigh to put the flame out, burning my hand a little bit in the process. The flame had put a quarter-sized hole in my jeans. Not too bad, though. It could be kind of—

Oh shit.

I was still holding the whiskey bomb. I quickly sent it over the wall and waited for the satisfying crash of glass on the pavement.

Instead, I heard a thud. The bottle had landed on the hood of one of the cars.

"*Ha!* Nice try, bitch. Firbis, grab that bottle and put it out."

I heard scuffling.

"Hey, she's using fuckin' eighteen-year-old whiskey!"

Irish Kenny said something I didn't catch, although I did comprehend his righteous indignation.

"Damn. *Hey*," Quinn yelled. "How about ye stop wasting good whiskey and just come with us? We'll not be hurting ye."

"I've got a better idea. I'll trade you the rest of my whiskey for your guns. Here's a free one to show my good faith." I adjusted my aim and sent another bottle over the wall. I was rewarded with a satisfying shatter. It was gratifying that eight shots of Jameson hadn't affected my aim. I might light myself on fire, but I wasn't going to miss a throw. All those years of drunken softball games were paying off.

"*Ahhhh!*" I heard Firbis scream.

Direct hit. I stood up unsteadily to see the damage. He was in front of the first car, rolling on the ground. The others were beating him with their jackets.

"*Ha!* Take that, kitty litter users." Not one of my better insults, but I was well past the point of being clever.

"*Poxy cunt!*" I heard doors opening and closing and engines starting. Were they leaving now?

No, just backing up a little more. The engines stopped and the doors opened again.

"How much fucking whiskey does she have back there?"

Not much more, unfortunately, and my T-shirt was used up. I took off one of my boots and stripped off my sock, then pulled another bottle from the case. The fires illuminated the label, and I studied it. Beneath the crest on the front were the words *Sine Metu*. Without Fear. The Jameson family motto. I pulled out the cork and took a long swallow.

Sine Metu was spot on. I was definitely feeling fearless at this point.

Not just fearless but also pain-free despite the fact that I'd been nicked in the head a dozen times by flying stone chips, lit myself on fire, and my hand was still bleeding steadily. I wasn't really feeling the cold either, even though I was shirtless, soaking wet, and missing one shoe and sock. Between the adrenaline and the thought that this might be my last night on earth, I was immune to cold, or pain, or poxy cunt insults. Or maybe it was the ten-plus shots of whiskey I'd put away.

Probably the whiskey. At this point in my life, I was very familiar with my own stages of intoxication. There were three of them. The initial stage was what I referred to as Whoville, a period of singing and friendly interactions with other humans, where I would be a reasonable facsimile of a normal person. The second was Animal House, which involved bad dancing, the occasional hookup, and lighthearted fun that only rarely resulted in minor jail time. Most of the time I'd stop drinking in the Animal House phase. Because the next one was dangerous territory. I thought of it as Thunderdome. A little like Mad Max meets Jackass but more extreme, usually resulting in major property damage, a trip to the

ICU, and/or waking up in bed next to a spectacularly poor decision (hello, coworkers and felons).

The few times in my life that I'd seen therapists, usually by court order, had involved lengthy discussions related to the "wellspring of rage" that lurked inside of me. For the archetype ACOA poster child, this wasn't all that unusual; like other kids with alcoholic fathers, growing up in that environment resulted in a variety of behavioral characteristics that served to mitigate the accompanying sense of childhood abandonment. For many people, this lingered into adulthood, manifesting in depression or sadness. I wasn't fond of those emotions. Anger was a far more comfortable place for me. But left unchecked, it could be damaging. I generally kept it under control by employing a variety of safeguards. These included a fair amount of drinking, a sophomoric sense of humor, and mild misanthropy that helped me keep my distance from most people. Those safeguards went away with Thunderdome. It was a "release the Kraken" situation, where the only thing between the inner me and the world was my imagination. And Sam, if she were around.

As bad as it was, the most negative aspects of Thunderdome came the day after, when I'd be dealing with the repercussions of the night before. The following morning, I'd have a fierce hangover and spend the day slowly remembering my cringeworthy behavior, or having it remembered to me, sometimes by very angry and occasionally litigious people, and often by law enforcement.

At this point in the evening, I was many shots in and solidly in Thunderdome territory. But as I was struggling with the lighter, now slick with blood, I realized that some of its aspects were actually working for me. I wasn't feeling any pain or cold, and my aim was still on point. And, in this case, there would be no repercussions. There wasn't going to be a day after. For the first and only time in my life, I could sit back and enjoy Thunderdome with no fear of consequences.

It was liberating. I took another bottle out of the case and cut my sock in two pieces. I stuffed the two cloth pieces into the tops of the bottles. Finally getting the lighter to light, I set it to both wicks, this time also lighting my hair on fire in the process.

Ooops. I laughed. Who cared? I could burn all of it off and it wouldn't matter. I patted the burning hair with my bloody hand, putting it out, and in the process getting a fair amount of my hair stuck to the blood. A small patch of it pulled out of my head as I threw the two bottles. That didn't hurt either.

The bottles went flying over the wall, and I heard again the pleasing shatters of whiskey on pavement, one after the other.

"Take that, leprechaun fuckers," I taunted.

"That's the best you can do? Leprechaun fuckers?" Quinn yelled.

Irish Kenny said something, and they all laughed.

"Yeah, you're right. What's wrong with being a leprechaun fucker?"

Damn, Irish Kenny sounded kind of smart and funny. I wished I could understand what the hell he was saying.

I took out my last bottle of Jameson 18 and took several long drinks. I stripped off my other boot and sock, and after one more long sip, sent it flaming over the wall. I heard it break on the pavement.

"That's eleven." Quinn had been counting too. "If there's just the case, she's only got one more."

Bastard. He was right. I was down to my last bottle. The Jameson Rarest Vintage Reserve. I wished I had another case. This was kind of fun and I could die of alcohol poisoning, which seemed like it might be way less painful than being shot to death.

With a heavy sigh, I pulled the bottle out of the case and looked at the label. My fingers weren't working quite as well, and with some difficulty, I stripped away the seal around the cork and pulled it out. I took a sip.

Holy mother of God.

I'd only had this stuff a few times in my life and it was always a revelation, how sublimely gifted humans were at creating wonderful things when they put their minds to it. This was a pinnacle of human achievement. Rich and luscious, with an unbelievable complexity of flavors, including fruit, pepper, cinnamon, fudge, and wood. I vaguely wondered how much more amazing this would taste if it had been the first sip of the evening instead of after a whole bunch of other ones.

Oh well.

I put away another long drink, then took off my jacket. The only cloth I had left was my bra. I reached behind me to take it off.

Fucking hooks.

Usually, when I was this wasted, I'd just leave it on and sleep in it. I struggled with it, twisting the band around and pulling as hard as I could in various directions.

Fucking hell.

Kevlar had nothing on bra hooks. No force on earth could pull these apart. I gave up and pulled it over my head, struggling and eventually succeeding to get my arms through the straps. When I finally got it off, I was panting. *Jesus.*

In the effort to remove my bra, I'd dropped my knife. I felt around on the ground for it.

Ouch. There it is.

I'd cut myself again, not that it mattered. I brought the knife up to the bra and started the cut for the last wick, for the last Molotov Cocktail.

Sine metu.

My hand froze, and I stopped, watching the blood from my hand drip onto the bra.

I couldn't do it.

This bottle was a gift from Sam. The last gift. My best friend in the world. My personal link to the rest of humanity and possibly the most compassionate, wonderful being on the planet. There was no way I could send it to die on a backroad in Sligo. I'd held them off as long as I could. If no one had seen us by now, it wasn't going to happen. Quinn and his team of boneheads would come over the wall and shoot me. It was over.

So be it. I put my jacket back on and leaned back against the wall. I tipped the bottle toward my face, mostly missing my mouth, and thinking about the places I'd never get to see. The whiskey dribbled down my chin and onto my chest.

The Guinness plant and the Midleton distillery, Dublin, the megaliths, the Wild Atlantic Way. My relatives, I guess. And poor Rose, she might never find her daughter. I would never see Sam again either. God, I would miss her. Or maybe not, since I'd be dead. Maybe she'd miss me.

I took another drink, working a little harder to make sure it ended up in my mouth.

So, so good, this stuff.

I'd never get to hug Gideon again, or politely ignore his rambling technology explanations. Tatiana would have to find someone else to argue Russian cultural superiority with. Gram, Shannon and Seamus, and the little nieces or nephews likely coming soon. I'd always wanted to be an aunt. And Chaz...well, that was one bright spot. I wouldn't miss his ugly ass one bit. But the rest of the dogs...I desperately wished I had one of their furry selves with me. Dogs made everything better. I started feeling a little weepy.

Shit.

I wiped my eyes with my bra. I needed to suck it up. I was not going out crying.

I leaned back against the wall, rubbing away the tears that had fallen onto the bottle I was holding tightly against my chest.

Nope. Not throwing this one. They could fucking pry it out of my cold, dead hands.

The rain had started up again, clearing the air of the smell of whiskey, smoke, burning hair, and my own blood. I gripped the knife tightly. If they got close enough, at least one of them was going to pay for killing me.

I closed my eyes and waited for them to come over the wall and the last bullet. I had a vague awareness of colorful lights and voices nearby before my head dropped to my chest and I passed out.

Sixteen

"Jesse.

"Jesse, can you wake up?"

I was laying down on something warm and soft, curled around something cold and hard. I reached down and pulled the half-empty bottle of Rarest Vintage Reserve from under the sheets.

"We couldn't get it out of your hands last night," said Sam from a chair next to the bed. "How are you feeling?"

"Ugh." I moved each of my arms and legs and felt my face. Everything seemed to be at least connected and functional. I winced when I touched my broken nose. "Like I went ten rounds with Apollo Creed in hell." I was surprised I didn't feel more hungover. I looked around. I was in a hospital room. "What happened?"

"When it got late and you weren't back, I got worried. I called the gardaí, but they weren't going to help until you'd been gone for at least forty-eight hours. You didn't exactly make any friends over there."

What else is new.

"Brian and I drove to Knocknarea. The fire got our attention, and I called the gardaí. That got them to come out."

"Thanks for saving my life."

"I owed you one."

"No, you didn't. I'll get you a fruit basket." It was the same thing she'd said to me when I'd rescued her from the attack in college. That was five years ago, and we'd been best friends ever since. I wasn't sure why; Sam was a fully functional, happy adult, and I was pretty much the total opposite. Maybe it was surviving a near-death experience together that brought us close. Or maybe I just amused her. In any case, I trusted her more than anyone I'd ever met, and she knew I always had her back.

She laughed; it sounded like relief. "The little wall we found you behind was filled with bullet holes. I can't believe there's none in you."

"For the record, I'm not one hundred percent sure there aren't." I tried to sit up and lean forward, but fell back onto the bed, too woozy to complete the move.

Ah...that explains it. I wasn't hungover because I was still loaded. "Did the gardaí get them?"

"Who?"

"The guys who were trying to kill me."

"There was no one else around when we got there."

"Damn."

"We heard shots as we drove up. They must have left when they heard us coming. The gardaí are up there right now looking for evidence."

"There should be plenty of shell casings lying around. And I need to tell them about the warehouse. They were running some kind of illegal operation." I tried to sit up again, this time with a little more success. "We need to get to the garda station. I think these guys might be the ones who took Cait."

"They want you back there anyway. I convinced them you needed to see a doctor first."

"I don't need a doctor. Let's get over there." I swung my legs over the edge of the bed and looked around for my clothes, until I realized I was still wearing them. What was left of them, anyway. I was shirtless and barefoot but still in my jacket and pants. Everything was damp, and there were red smears of blood on my bra that was stuffed into the front pocket of my jeans, which were covered in grass stains and mud and smelled like whiskey.

"They tried to put you in a hospital gown, but you fought them off. They'll do tests once you've sobered up. That is, if you don't die of a cerebral hemorrhage in the meantime."

That was one of things I really appreciated about Sam. Her utter lack of drama. And the fact that she didn't freak out when I got myself into trouble.

"Did you happen to grab my boots?"

Sam pointed to the floor at the end of the bed.

They were both there. Good thing. I'd only brought the one pair with me.

She was looking at me and wincing. "Uh, Jesse, maybe you should wash up. I brought your bag."

I grabbed the bag and stumbled into the bathroom. Turning on the faucet, I ran warm water gingerly over the cuts in my hand. Thankfully the bleeding had stopped. I looked up at myself in the mirror, then jerked back. *Holy shit.* This was bad, even for me.

My hair was laying down in matted strands, framing dark bruises that had formed under both of my eyes. On one side, the bruise merged into a larger contusion where Quinn had punched me. Dried tracks of blood ran down my face and neck, in some places capturing pieces of hair that were stuck to my face in wild patterns. Black sooty smudges filled in the spaces between the blood trails. On one side of my head, some of the hair was singed short and there was a small bare patch where it had been pulled completely out. I would give *Evil Dead*'s Mia a run for her money.

I washed the blood and soot off of my face and attempted to run a comb through my hair. It stuck in the blood, so I soaked a washcloth in warm water and ran it over my head. *Ouch.* The stone chips had nicked me in a dozen places that were still tender.

Now that I was sobering up, the physical toll of the night before was coming on in full force. Based on how I looked, it would get worse before it got better.

I rummaged through my bag for a clean T-shirt, bra, and socks. The jeans I had on would have to do. I only had a couple of pairs and wasn't going to waste one on a trip to the garda station.

Sam had followed me to the bathroom and was leaning against the door. "Are you sure you don't need to see a doctor?"

"No, I'm fine."

"You're definitely *not* fine. You look like you had a burning building collapse on your head. Are you dizzy?"

"No." *Not much, anyway.* "Can you give me your phone? I need to call Gideon."

She handed me her phone. Gideon answered on the seventh ring. He was irritated and short. "What do you need?"

"What's wrong?"

He sighed heavily. "I'm sorry, I'm tracking down a ring of pedos and the trail keeps going cold in Athens. I could use a distraction. Whaddya need?"

Gideon usually found helping me very satisfying, primarily because it either involved research and tracking down information, which he loved to do, or technical problems with solutions like, "Turn it off and turn it back on," or, "Plug it in."

"I've got something that will cheer you up." I cut to the chase, explaining the warehouse set up, the equipment and supplies I'd seen. "Any idea what they might have been doing?"

I heard his fingers dancing on his keyboard. Gideon could pull information from the internet faster than anyone I knew. "Can you give me a little more?"

"I smelled gasoline, and there was a tanker parked outside."

More typing. Then, "It sounds like they were running a fuel laundering operation."

"Fuel *laundering*?" There was nothing clean about that place.

"Yeah." More keyboard clicking. "So here's the deal. In Ireland and the UK, fuel is heavily taxed. They basically pay for a liter what we pay for a gallon. But they sell a lower-taxed version to farmers they call agricultural diesel. It's quite a bit less expensive, and they don't want the farmers reselling it at a profit to people for car fuel. So, to prevent farmers from reselling their cheap fuel at a profit, they put dye into it to mark it. In Ireland, the marker's green."

"Makes sense."

"Yeah, but the thing is, it's not that hard to remove the dye."

"Are you telling me these guys were removing dye from fuel?"

"Yeah. One of the ways to do it is to use a bleaching agent."

"Bleaching agent?"

"Yeah, like silicon dioxide. Something with a small particle size that can absorb dye."

I thought for a moment. "Would kitty litter work?"

"Yeah, the less sophisticated operations use that. In any case, they either use a bleaching agent or acid to clear out the dye. They put it in a big container, like a tank—here, I'll text you some pictures."

"Never mind, they took my phone. Send them to Sam."

"Okay. So, they put the dyed fuel in a container, like a big tank, throw in the bleaching agent, pump in some air, and in a couple of hours, the particles sink to the bottom, taking the dye with them. And voila, you now have bleached fuel. They siphon it out of the tank, and it's ready to go."

This was consistent with what I'd seen in the warehouse. But the operation didn't look that big, and it seemed like a lot of trouble to go through for a few bucks.

"It's hard to believe there's enough money in something low tech like that to be worth the effort."

"There's *tons* of money in it. Some of the operations are huge. Last year, the gardaí busted one that was turning over five million gallons of fuel a year. That's"—I could hear him typing—"over ten million dollars of profit a year from that one plant alone."

"Holy shit."

"Yeah. Then they sell it at a discount to gas stations who aren't too picky about where they get their gas."

"And that's all money that would have gone to the tax revenue base."

"Exactly." His fingers were flying over the keyboard. "Ireland's been losing millions in tax revenue every year to fuel laundering.

But recently they've stepped up their efforts on stopping it and have been largely successful. A few years ago, they came up with a way to mark the fuel by using a tracer."

"Tracer?"

"A chemical they add to the fuel. It's inert—it doesn't interact with the fuel—and it's generally undetectable unless you have special equipment. Most importantly, it's virtually impossible to remove."

"So why would they still try to launder it? If it's traceable?"

"The laundering sites are set up in remote areas, so they're hard to find. And they sell the fuel to small, out of the way stations, or set up their own temporary ones. The authorities don't have the resources to find and test every station. There aren't enough people, and the detector units themselves aren't cheap. They usually find the laundering operations when something bad happens, like if there's a spill or some kind of environmental crisis. As you can imagine, the guys doing this aren't that concerned about the environment. The bleaching process creates large quantities of solid waste, and they either leave it at the site or dump it. Here, I'll send you a picture."

He texted a couple of images of waste in the form of large square bundles. They looked exactly like what I saw Firbis and Lurch dumping near the forest.

"Who organizes this kind of thing?" Quinn and his gang of assclowns didn't look like they could operate a lemonade stand, much less set up and operate a fuel laundering operation on their own. Someone else had to be involved. Someone higher up, like the Big Boss on the other end of Quinn's phone.

"Historically, it's been the within purview of the paramilitaries—the IRA, UDF, those guys. Typically, they set up their operations near the border, usually on the northern side. A lot of illegal stuff happens near the border, which makes it easy to transport things back and forth."

Uh-oh. I lowered my voice. "Are you saying the guys that tried to kill me were IRA?"

"Someone tried to kill you?"

"Uh, yeah. But they didn't. You were saying, you think they're IRA?"

"Maybe. But not necessarily. These days, some of the gangs are getting into it too. It doesn't take much to set up, and they can make a pretty good buck with smaller operations like the one you found. They even have mobile units, where they can operate the whole thing out of an open-sided truck or trailer. You really only need a big container to throw the fuel and bleaching agent in and some way to get it in and out."

So Quinn and the gang weren't necessarily IRA. That was marginally comforting.

"It's also really, really bad from an environmental standpoint. The sludge from the bleaching agents is nasty. Using acid to remove the dye is in some ways worse than the bleaching agent. The waste is in liquid form and runs off from the process, getting into streams or lakes. It's really toxic and kills everything: plants, animals, microbes, whatever. And it's really hard to clean up once it gets into the soil."

I thought about the puddles of gasoline on the floor and the sloppy way they were siphoning liquid out of the containers. And how bloody stupid they all were. It wasn't surprising that they were causing a huge mess. "Anything else?"

"Yeah. If you see really, really cheap gas, I'd be wary. It's likely been laundered. And the laundering process leaves a lot of residue in the gas that reacts to heat. If it's in your car, when it gets going and heats up, it can freeze up your engine."

Whew. Maybe more than I wanted to know. Especially the bit about the IRA. "Okay, thanks, Gideon."

"Then there's the link between these operations and the massive amount of money laundering that has to happen to be able to use the cash." He was on a roll now. "There are some pretty sophisticated—"

"Gotta go! Thanks!"

"Any time!" He sounded way happier than when I'd called.

Sam reached for her phone. "Fuel laundering?"

"Yeah, I'll explain on the way."

I tried to fast walk out of the room and got hit by a wave of vertigo. I wasn't sure if it was the concussion or the fact that I would still fail a breathalyzer. I stopped and put my hand against the wall to keep from falling.

Sam didn't bother saying anything, just looked at me with one of those "I know you're not fine and you're making a mistake not to see a doctor" looks. It got a lot of use when we were together.

"I'm fine. Really. Let's just get out of here." I started to leave the room, but saw Rose sitting in the hallway on a bench and ducked back inside.

"Can you run interference with Rose? I don't want her to see me like this."

Sam nodded and left the room. Cracking the door open a smidge, I watched her talk to Rose and then escort her to the elevator.

Even cleaned up I still looked like hell, and it would terrify Rose even more about what had happened to Cait. And I still didn't have any answers for her.

SEVENTEEN

Since our rental car was now a burned-out wreck, the Gallaghers had let Sam borrow their car, and we left the hospital. On the way to the garda station, I filled Sam in on fuel laundering.

Once we were at the station, I checked in with O'Fenton, who was apparently the only person in the place who qualified for reception duty. His chilly tone signaled that I was still on his shit list.

This time it wasn't long before a uniformed garda opened the door to the back and gestured me in. "Dr. O'Hara? Could you come with me, please?" The state of my face didn't seem to faze him.

I left Sam to wait and followed the officer. As he led me toward the back, I passed him. "I know where I'm going."

I walked into to the same small room I'd been in before. This time there was just one man sitting at the small table, and he motioned me toward the seat across from him. The officer who had escorted me left the room and closed the door. The guy at the table was older than the other detectives I'd seen and looked tired. He didn't have a notebook in front of him, just a thin manila folder.

"Dr. O'Hara, I'm Chief Superintendent Murphy."

"Murphy? What's your first name?"

He frowned slightly. "Sean. Now, can you tell me—?"

"Isn't the other guy here Sean Murphy too?"

"Uh, yes, Detective Sergeant Sean Murphy."

"Doesn't that get confusing?"

"Em, no, not really."

Maybe they went by Older Sean Murphy and Younger Sean Murphy. But more importantly, how many Murphys were there in this fucking country? But this one was a chief superintendent, which was good. I was working my way up the garda food chain. Maybe this guy would actually do something. Friendly Nice Jesse would need to make an appearance.

Smiling regularly wasn't in my nature and never had been. When I was a kid, my mom had adopted a shorthand to tell me when I needed to smile, even when I didn't feel like it, usually during family picture taking sessions. She called it Good Attitude. Good Attitude meant I needed to plaster a smile on my face regardless of how I was feeling. This resulted more often than not in a toothy grimace that was unflattering at best but apparently good enough for family photos.

I nodded politely to Chief Superintendent Murphy and added in some Good Attitude. He winced at the effort. Or maybe at my face, which even without the Good Attitude was pretty frightening at the moment.

"How long have you been in Ireland, Dr. O'Hara? Three, four days?"

"Four."

"Four. Yes, well, it's been a busy four days for you."

I started to respond, but he held up his hand to stop me. He pulled on a pair of reading glasses and opened the folder, then lifted out a piece of paper and held it in front of him by the edges. Reading from it, he said, "In four days you've managed to get thrown out of my station, be the last person to talk to a murdered man, involved yourself in an illegal fuel laundering operation—"

"*Involved* myself? You mean, got kidnapped and threatened

by the guys doing it?" *What the fuck?* I could feel Good Attitude slipping away "Look, Chief Murphy—"

"Chief Superintendent."

"Whatever. I'm here to share what I know about Cait's disappearance. The guys who kidnapped me might be the ones who took her."

It was like I hadn't spoken. He continued to read from his little paper. "Rammed into a pasture wall, participated in a shootout on a public road—"

"*Participated?!*" I stood up quickly. I was beaten up, concussed, injured, and still fairly drunk. Whatever niceness I'd intended to display evaporated. "You mean, got shot at and almost got killed?" *Whoa.* The room spun and I sat back down, grabbing the edge of the table for support.

"Destroyed a rental car and apparently did your best to light our countryside on fire."

So much for getting the key to the city. "It's not my fault there's all kinds of sketchy shit going on in your town." I folded my arms and leaned back into my chair.

Mr. High and Mighty wasn't going to make me the bad guy. And I wasn't going to let up until I got some fucking answers, or at least a commitment to look into Quinn and the gang. "The guys who were laundering fuel, I think they're the ones who kidnapped Cait. You need to find them."

"I've got men looking into it."

"They better look into it soon if you don't want the whole town to go up in flames."

He looked up from his little paper and peered at me over his glasses. "Did you have something to do with the warehouse fire?"

"I was kidnapped and held there. I had to, uh..." It probably wasn't a good idea to admit I was the one who had started the fire that had blown the place up, so I went on the offensive. "What do you think? A bunch of morons around thousands of gallons of fuel. Yeah, no chance of anything going wrong there. But, sure, blame me for it. Fuck's sake." I shook my head in feigned disgust.

My yelling and swearing at him had no effect. He continued

to speak matter of factly and didn't raise his voice. This guy wasn't going to get into a shouting match, which was too bad. I usually won those. "Fortunately, we were able to save the warehouse. The fire department managed to put out the fire with some help from the rain. We're investigating the scene." He put the paper back into the file and closed it, then leaned back in his chair, taking off his reading glasses and putting them back in his pocket. "So...em...Dr. O'Hara, how long will you be staying in Sligo?"

The previous guys had told me not to leave the area. Now this guy was hinting that I should get out of his town as soon as possible. *Make up your fucking minds.* "Until I find Cait, you wanky fuck."

I wondered what it would take to get him to raise his voice or get angry. Apparently, *wanky fuck* was not all that offensive. His expression remained stubbornly neutral.

"Speaking of which, have any of you looked into the guys who came for Paddy? You know, the ones who met her at the bus station and probably kidnapped her? Have you looked for *them*? They might be the same guys who were operating the fuel laundering operation. And what about all of this CCTV that's supposedly all over this fucking country? Just show it to me. I can probably ID them."

"I doubt that. It was dark, and by the looks of things, you experienced significant trauma."

Oh yeah, buddy? "Really? Let's see. I'm still well over the legal limit, likely concussed, and running on two hours of sleep over two days. But let me see what I can do."

Murphy leaned back in his chair.

"You know I've only been at this station three times, including this one, yeah? And one of those was extremely brief."

"Yes, I'm aware."

I closed my eyes for dramatic effect. "The recording device at the table is missing the cap on the rewind key. The serial number on the side is 87009876. There's a scratch mark above the volume button, just under a centimeter long. The station is old but was renovated seven years ago. You currently have fifteen open cases being handled by eight inspectors, seven if you don't count Mullarkey: ten burglary, two missing persons, and three murders. You're fifty-nine years old and recently divorced. You're missing one of the back molars on the right side of your mouth, and you have a mole approximately two millimeters wide on the left side of your neck just above your collar. You had eggs for breakfast, and you prefer tea to coffee. You take it black." I opened my eyes and leaned back, crossing my arms.

Cracks had formed in the look of bland affability that had been on Murphy's face. I was winning.

"So, Chief Superintendent Sean Murphy, let's try this again. Show me the camera footage, and maybe I can ID the guys who took Cait."

"Yes, em, we have no record of her getting off the bus in Sligo."

"No record? What do you mean, *no record*? Don't you have that camera shit at the bus station?"

"Yes, em, there are cameras there. But the recording is, em, unavailable..." He expression changed again. He looked embarrassed.

Someone had screwed up. He wasn't trying to keep me from looking at the tapes because I wouldn't be able to ID anyone. He wasn't showing them to me because he didn't have them and didn't want to tell me why.

"What? *Unavailable*? How?"

"It was lost." Older Sean Murphy was now looking longingly at the door to the hallway.

"*Lost*? Are you fucking kidding me?" I was starting to hyperventilate and took a deep breath. "Wait, let me guess...that idiot Mullarkey, right?"

He sighed. "It's being dealt with." He stood up. "I'm sorry." He turned to leave.

"Hey! What about the fuel laundering guys? Don't you want to know about that?"

He was almost out the door to safety but turned around.

"Oh, yes." He exhaled loudly. "Stay here a moment. Someone will be with you shortly." He left, looking relieved to be able to hand me off to someone else.

Probably someone else who was more interested in getting me out of their hair than in looking for Cait. But I wasn't going to leave until I got some goddamn answers. I settled into my chair to wait it out. I'd been a hostage, and if the IRA guys couldn't break me, the garda certainly wouldn't be able to.

Although, now that I thought about it, the IRA guys had broken me fairly easily. Once Quinn had pulled out his gun, I caved faster than Anna Nicole Smith's underwire. But hopefully the garda wouldn't be pulling any guns on me.

I was startled when the door opened only a few minutes later.

A middle-aged man in a black suit, white shirt, and tie walked over to me. He started to extend his hand and stopped, looking startled. Probably at my face. He quickly composed himself. "Hello, Dr. O'Hara, I'm Chief Inspector Dick. PSNI."

Chief Inspector Dick? I wondered what his first name was. God, I hoped it was Harry. *Please, please let it be Harry.* I stifled a laugh.

"PSNI? Am I supposed to know what that is?"

"Police Service of Northern Ireland. I understand you came across a fuel laundering operation."

Damnit, Harry wasn't looking for Cait either. I couldn't imagine a cop from Northern Ireland was going to be any help in tracking down a missing woman in Sligo. Fuck him, despite his name. I got up to leave.

"Please, Dr. O'Hara, I'm here to help identify the men who kidnapped you."

Fucking finally. I sat back down. He'd obviously been listening in on my discussion with Older Chief Sean Murphy.

"Let me give you some background. Most of the fuel laundering operations have historically either operated in Northern Ireland or near the border. We've been fairly successful at shutting them down. But now we're starting to see them pop up farther away in the Republic, in remote areas, away from gardaí observa-

tion. I'm here on special assignment to help track down operations in this area and put a stop to them. Many of the people
involved are the same players with whom we're very familiar in
Northern Ireland. It's a long and tedious process to find these
operations and capture the fuel launderers. It requires
surveillance, often in remote areas, that has to be extremely covert.
If they get a whiff of law enforcement anywhere around them,
they simply walk away and leave everything behind. This costs the
governments—on both sides of the border—a lot of money, not
just from the expense of surveillance, but in lost tax revenue and
the clean up of what are fairly devastating environmental
impacts."

Tracking these guys and their operations down sounded like
incredibly difficult, dirty work, not to mention mind-numbingly
boring. I guess someone had to do it. *Good for you, Inspector Dick.*
"That sounds really great for you. But I'm looking for a young
woman who's been missing for over a week. It doesn't sound like
this has anything to do with finding her."

He put his hand up in a placating gesture. I'd seen that hand a
lot in my life. It normally irritated the hell out of me. Harry
Dick's version was slightly less annoying. "I've read the file on
Cait Gallagher—"

I snorted. "You mean the single piece of paper that documents
the gardaí doing fuck all to find her?"

"And your interview with detectives Mullarkey and Superintendent Murphy. It sounds to me like the men you encountered
participated in something like a tiger kidnapping."

"Tiger kidnapping?"

"Yes. It's common among the paras. They choose a member
from a prominent family and take him or her hostage, holding
them for ransom, and usually release them once it's been paid."

"Usually release them" sounded promising. But there hadn't
been any ransom demand, and while the Gallaghers were living
comfortably, they weren't exactly rolling in dough. "The
Gallaghers haven't received any ransom demands."

"Yes, I didn't say it was a tiger kidnapping, but that the MO resembles more of a para operation than a criminal gang. And since the fuel laundering operation is also typically within the purview of the paras, there might be a connection. Can you describe the men who kidnapped you?"

Now we were getting somewhere. I walked him through detailed descriptions of Quinn, Lurch, Firbis, and Irish Kenny—how they looked, what they were wearing, what they said to each other, and how they sounded. He wrote everything down in his own little black notebook, apparently standard issue for law enforcement on both sides of the border.

"Do any of these guys ring a bell to you?" I asked.

He nodded. "We know James Quinn. He's from Belfast, a mid-level IRA lout. He's been operating up there for years. He's loosely affiliated with one of the IRA splinter groups, but he's basically a mercenary and has worked for a number of them. Like many of his ilk, he's not got a true political affiliation. I don't know the others, but from the sound of it, at least one of them is from Northern Ireland too. The Belfast accent is very distinctive and can be unintelligible if you're not used to hearing it. Could you pick up any words?"

"When we were in the warehouse, I heard him say something like *naff* and *wick*."

"He was likely referring to someone he thinks is stupid." That made sense. Firbis was an idiot.

"And when they were shooting at me, I heard *peelers*, *kex*, and *melter*."

"Hmmm...well, *peelers* is the police. *Melter* is Northern slang for someone who is annoying. Might he have, em, been talking about you?"

That sounded about right. I nodded.

"Are you sure he said *kex*? It sounds like he was talking about underwear. Why would he say that?"

"No idea." I wasn't interested in putting on record the fact that I'd used my underwear to make Molotov cocktails.

He wrote more notes into his book. "Is there anything else you can think of?"

"Only that none of them seemed smart enough to put something like this together without a lot of help." I described Quinn's phone call with his boss.

"Did you hear anything else about this boss?"

"No. But after the call, Quinn told his guys that they had to get everything cleaned up to move out the next day. They were getting ready to leave, they had something else, something big, to start working on. He sounded kind of...excited. I'm thinking it might have something to do with drugs."

Harry looked up. "Did they mention any specifics? Did they actually use the word *drugs*?" He was trying to sound nonchalant, but there was an edge to his voice.

"No. But if they were the same guys who came for Paddy, it makes sense, right? That they're involved in drugs too?"

Harry closed his notebook and tucked it into his pocket.

I'd hit on something important. "What? What do you know?"

He stood up and turned to go. "Dr. O'Hara, I need to ask you to please stay with the Gallaghers for the next few days or so. Or better yet, take some time away from here, see some sites. This is not a good time to be prying around Sligo." He looked at my face. "And you, uh, you look like you could use some time to recuperate."

Normally, I would have torn his head off for keeping something from me. And stayed in the little room until they had to physically throw me out. But he'd given me something that would help with my next move.

"Okay."

He turned to me sharply. "Okay?"

"Sure, I'm pretty beat, anyway. I could use a few days off. And it sounds like you have some leads. I'll leave you to it." I smiled pleasantly.

He looked suspicious and waited for me to say something else, but I stayed silent. He opened the door and escorted me out of the room and into the reception area where Sam was waiting. We shook hands, and he walked away.

As he was stepping through the door to the back rooms, he turned to face me. "Dr. O'Hara, I truly implore you to stay away from all of this. Just for a few days, please."

EIGHTEEN

We left the station and walked to our car. Sam didn't speak until we were on the road back to the Gallaghers. She drove; I was still probably over the legal limit.

"They didn't throw you out this time. You're moving up in the world."

"Ireland's having a calming effect on my personality."

"Who was that, and what is it that you're supposed to stay away from that we both know you won't?"

"Chief Inspector Harry Dick, from Northern Ireland. He didn't say it, but there might be some kind of connection between Cait's disappearance and drugs. And, uh, maybe the IRA."

I said the last part quietly, but Sam turned from the road to look at me with wide eyes. "Oh my God. Jesse..."

"I know...but you know I can't let this go."

She turned back to the road and nodded slightly.

We'd both bonded with the Gallaghers, Sam in the biblical way. At this point, there was no turning back. We were in it for the duration. Not to mention that once I started things, I liked to finish them.

"If this is about drugs, then we need to find out who's running them in Sligo, who the main players are, and where they hang out. Whoever it is probably killed Paddy and is connected with Quinn and the gang." With Paddy dead and Quinn in the wind, I wasn't sure where to go. Harry had given me this clue, but it wasn't taking me anywhere. Paddy had mentioned Larkin, but I had no idea where to find him or guys like him.

We drove in silence the rest of the way back to the house. Sam turned off the engine and leaned back in her seat. "Wouldn't that be something that a gang boss would know about?"

"What?"

"Whoever is distributing drugs in Sligo. Or anywhere else for that matter. Gangs bring most of the drugs into the country, right?"

"Right..." I wasn't sure where she was going with this.

"Leo's godfather is Daniel Ryan. If he's that big of a gang boss, he's bringing in more drugs than anyone else. So he'll know the major players, won't he? Maybe he'd give us a lead on who it was that might have taken Cait. Or even where we could find men like that."

"I don't know. Do you really think a gang boss is going to want to talk to the two of us?"

"More likely than he would talk to the gardaí. And Leo said he treated him like a son. Leo loves Cait, and if Ryan really does think of him as a son, he'll do what he can to help him find his girl."

Sam was right, as usual, when it came to people and their motivations and emotions. It was worth a try. "Leo took a liking to you. Can you call him, see if he can set up a meeting?"

She nodded and pulled out her phone. The call was a quick one. "He's going to call Ryan and see if he'll meet with us. He'll let me know if Ryan will do it, and when and where. What now?"

"Let's assume we can get a meeting. Limerick is two hours away. Let's get going."

"Are you sure? You don't need a nap? Or, uh, a shower?" She didn't bother asking me if I would go see a doctor.

"Okay. But let's get in and out quick."

We went into the house, and I managed to avoid Rose while I went upstairs for a quick shower. I knew seeing me right now would scare the shit out of her.

In fifteen minutes, we were back in the car and on our way to Limerick.

While Sam drove, I pulled out her phone and looked at my email. I'd asked Gideon to put together some information on Daniel Ryan, and he'd sent me a summary.

Daniel "Danny" Ryan was the head of the largest criminal gang in the Republic of Ireland. He had his hands in all kinds of illegal activities, the biggest of which, in terms of volume and money, was drugs. He moved cannabis and ecstasy, but his primary product was coke. Recent reports listed him as controlling half of the total cocaine business in Ireland, an astounding achievement at his relatively young age of fifty-two. He was smart and well organized. His business, at its center, was a family-run operation, with sons acting as lieutenants in the major areas of the island. Gideon's report included that Ryan's operation was divided into regions and identified which specific family member was responsible for operations in each area. Ryan also had one daughter, Teagan. She was relatively young, but had recently been put in charge of the Sligo area. Ryan was ruthless. In an industry not characterized by compassion, as a young man he was known as an exceptionally brutal enforcer. His rise to the top of the drug kingpin pile was linked to numerous assassinations of rival drug barons, some in particularly cruel ways that often involved their families. He was also untouchable. Some of his many millions of dollars went to lawyers, judges, and, rumor had it, gardaí. So, despite all of the drug running, murders, and associated money laundering, he hadn't spent a single night in jail in his life.

I finished reading the report and stared blankly out the window. "Holy shit, this guy is big time. And bad news."

A text message beeped from Leo, confirming a meeting with Ryan, an address, and a time.

"We're confirmed. Limerick it is," I said.

The mother of all hangovers was starting to kick in, and I was tired and sore. But we had a plan. We were going to meet with Danny Ryan, the biggest crime boss in Ireland.

NINETEEN

The Limerick address for the meet Leo gave us was a restaurant, Fómhar, which Sam informed me meant *harvest* in Gaelic. It was the most expensive restaurant in Limerick and one of the most highly rated in the country, one of only a few receiving two Michelin stars. The head chef and owner, Noah Boyle, had won numerous Irish Food and other international culinary awards. He was known for farm to table cooking, working with local purveyors, and highlighting Ireland's natural abundance of fresh ingredients.

Sam parked a few blocks away from the restaurant, and we walked over and went inside. We'd gotten there a couple of hours before our meeting to take advantage of the chance to try the best of modern Irish cuisine.

A smiling hostess greeted us as the door. "Can I help you?"

The restaurant was small, with seats for thirty at tables and six more at the counter in front of the kitchen area. The décor was modern and minimal, brick walls adorned with a few pictures of the Irish countryside and coast, the entire space tastefully lit by pendant lights.

"Hernandez for two, please."

The restaurant was near full. I had no idea how Sam had

managed to get us a table on such short notice, but by now I was accustomed to her ability to navigate all things related to travel and dining.

"Yes, hello and welcome." The hostess led us to a small table next to the front window. We sat down and she handed us menus. "Your waiter will be with you shortly."

We looked over the menus, but it was a foregone conclusion that we were going to do the chef's tasting menu. There really was no better way to try the best a chef had to offer than to go through a multicourse meal chosen by him or her.

Our waiter, Jamie, took our order, and we were visited by the sommelier. As usual, Sam handled the wine selections, and he came back shortly with a bottle of something white. We were barely into our first glass of wine when the food started arriving. Almost all of the ingredients were locally sourced and included things I'd never heard of. The first course was a red mullet tartare with a caviar cream topping, a shrimp and scallop emulsion, and acacia flower and water pepper vinegar. The fish was briny and oddly addictive. And the water pepper vinegar was far spicier than anything I'd expected to eat in Ireland. After that, two more small plates arrived in rapid succession: a roasted scallop and blue lobster ravioli and a seared pork belly with black garlic mushroom sauce. The ravioli had no sauce to speak of, just melted butter, but it reminded me how deeply serious and expert the Irish were about their dairy products. These dishes were followed by a duck breast croquette with caramelized cauliflower risotto and pickled turnip.

By now the white wine was gone, and Sam ordered another bottle of something red. The sommelier seemed impressed by her choices, which I knew reflected an expert's eye for the best value on the wine list. As we waited for the bottle, we were presented with a cucumber and gin sorbet, a palate cleanser that signaled we were now moving into the heavier dishes.

We started on the bottle of red, then were treated to wild halibut with smoked eel and peas, razor clam, and green apple sauce. The last savory dish was Guinness braised beef cheeks with colcannon, one of Ireland's many versions of mashed potatoes.

We were stuffed, and fortunately the dessert was fairly light: an apple soufflé with cardoon ice cream and tonka bean sauce.

"What's a tonka bean, and how come I've never heard of them?" I asked through a mouthful of ice cream. The sauce was like nothing I'd ever tasted...an ethereal mix of vanilla, cherry, and cinnamon.

"They're illegal in the US."

"Illegal?" I liked the idea of eating something illegal.

"Yes. Tonka beans contain coumarin, a chemical that the FDA has deemed unsafe in high quantities."

"How high?" I said, stopping the spoon just before it entered my mouth.

"Consuming thirty beans in one sitting could affect your liver."

"Yikes." I put the spoon down.

She laughed. "One bean provides enough flavor for about eighty servings. You're safe."

We finished the dessert and the wine, turned down the cheese board, and Jamie brought our bill.

I looked at my watch while Sam was signing. "We're here to see Daniel Ryan. Is he here?" I asked Jamie. I hadn't seen anyone who might be Ryan come in since we'd arrived, and it was close to our meeting time.

His smile disappeared, and he turned away.

A minute later, the hostess came to our table, her lips pressed tightly together. "Follow me, please."

We stood and followed her through the dining room and down a short hallway that led to a closed door, out of sight of the dining room. She knocked once and walked away.

After a short pause, the door was opened slightly and a large man looked down at us.

"Hi. We're here to see Daniel Ryan."

He stared at us.

"Uh...Jesse O'Hara and Sam Hernandez?"

He closed the door.

We waited another thirty seconds until he opened it again, stepped aside, and gestured us in. We'd barely gotten in the door when he blocked our way and proceeded to give us a thorough pat-down. Then another guy came over and used one of those wand things they use at the airport, the ones they wave around you to see if you had any metal on you. He found my knife but didn't seem bothered by it. Satisfied that we weren't packing heat, they stepped aside and gestured us in.

The windowless room was almost as big as the dining room, but with just a single, small table in the center. A full bar with a copper counter and plush leather bar stools ran along one side of the room, behind which a bartender was idly wiping bottles down with a towel. Standing against the other three walls were four more of the same guy who had opened the door—tall and big, wearing suit jackets that looked two sizes too small, and all sporting noses that had been broken numerous times.

A single man, presumably Danny Ryan, was sitting at the table in the middle, waiting as a nervous-looking waiter opened a bottle of wine. He took out the cork and poured, then watched as Ryan took a sip. He grunted and nodded his head, and the waiter filled the glass and left the bottle on the table. He disappeared through a side door next to the bar.

We were escorted by the wand guy over to the table. Ryan was cutting a piece of steak, and without looking up motioned to us with his knife to sit down. There was one other table setting next to him that I assumed wasn't for either of us, so I took the seat across from him. Sam sat down in the other seat next to him. I would owe her for that.

Up close, Ryan didn't look all that scary. He wasn't a large man and had wispy brown hair, a ruddy complexion, and a small nose. His dominant feature was a large mouth slightly turned up at the corners, like it was always just about ready to smile.

He looked up from his food at Sam, and I could see a familiar look of appreciation on his face. His eyes turned to me, and he stopped and stared. He started to cough. One of the goons standing by the wall moved quickly over to help, but he waved him away with an impatient shake of his hand.

"Mr. Ryan? I'm Jesse O'Hara. This is Sam Hernandez."

He stared at me, slowly chewing his meat.

My thoughts about him not being scary changed instantly as I looked into the coldest eyes I'd ever seen, like two things that had been dead a long time.

"Uh...thank you for seeing us. Leo thought you might be able to help us find the whereabouts of a young woman who went missing in Sligo."

He continued to stare at me.

I didn't know what else to do, so I stared back.

Finally, the corners of his mouth turned up, and he chuckled. "Dr. O'Hara and Miss Hernandez. Yes, I know who you are. Can I offer you something to drink? Some wine? This is a malbec from Irish Family Vineyards. I also have whiskey. I understand that's your drink of choice." His voice was low and rasping, like he'd smoked a pack a day for his entire life.

I wasn't sure how I felt about drinking with a murderer, but I didn't want to be rude. And we needed his help. And, well, whiskey. "Whiskey, neat, please."

"I'll try the malbec," said Sam.

Out of nowhere the waiter appeared with another wine glass, two shot glasses, and a bottle of whiskey. He filled all three glasses and set the bottle on the table, then disappeared.

Ryan raised his glass to us. "Sláinte."

"Sláinte," Sam and I said at the same time.

Wow. It was like drinking happiness. Even after the whiskey tasting in the barn with the boys and my new love affair with all things Redbreast, this was the smoothest, most flavorful whiskey I'd ever had in my life.

Ryan nodded appreciatively at my reaction. "Grand, yeah?"

"What is this?" I said, not recognizing the label.

"It's my own batch. The kind distillers at Dooley's make twenty bottles only each year for me. It's a special blend." He leaned his head toward the bottle and raised his eyebrows.

I nodded.

He poured me another shot, and I drank it.

Wow, again. I wasn't completely over the drinkfest from the night before, and it seemed as if this country was determined to keep me in a permanent state of inebriation. I'd need to be careful today. We had work to do.

"So," he said, leaning back in his chair, "Jesse O'Hara? Of the Sligo O'Haras?"

"Yes, I think so."

Ryan nodded but didn't say anything, still looking at me strangely.

Damn. I wished I wasn't so susceptible to the silent treatment. It was really uncomfortable.

After what seemed like hours, he said, "Dr. O'Hara, before we start, I want to make clear to you that whatever is said here is between us. I'm not in the habit of sharing information with anyone, at least not without receiving something in return. And definitely not with people I don't know. I'm doing this as a favor to Leo." He took a sip of his wine, wiped his mouth, and set the glass back down. He picked up his knife and fork and cut off another piece of meat. He chewed slowly, then swallowed. "But if I find out that you've shared anything about our discussions, or what you learn here, with the gardaí, things will go very badly for you." He pointed to me with his knife. "Very badly."

I stared at the knife, unable to take my eyes away from the little bits of meat and blood stuck to it.

"Do we understand each other?"

"Yes." I tried, and was mostly successful, in keeping the waver out of my voice. "I'm only interested in finding Cait. Everything else is none of my business."

"I'm glad we understand each other." He went back to his steak.

I heard the door open and then looked at the empty setting. "Are we expecting someone else?"

"Yes, my daughter. She works in the west part of the island and might know more about your missing girl."

I heard the door close, then a woman's voice. "Get your hands off of me, ya feckin' eejit."

Sam glanced over to the door and her jaw dropped. She turned her head to me and then back to the door.

I leaned around in my chair and looked. At myself.

TWENTY

"Who the *feck* are you?" The woman who was me grabbed the empty chair, pulled it out, and sat down heavily. She turned to Sam. "And what the feck are *you* staring at?"

Ryan cleared his throat. "Dr. O'Hara, Miss Hernandez, please meet my daughter, Teagan."

I looked at her, and she glared back.

We were dead ringers for each other. Like me, she was five ten and about a hundred and thirty pounds. She had straight dark hair that went just past her shoulders, blue eyes, pale skin, the same curve to her mouth, and the same unremarkable nose. Also like me, an oldish-looking silver locket hung around her neck. I wondered if, like mine, it had been a gift from her mother. We were even dressed similarly. She was wearing jeans and a T-shirt and a black leather jacket. The only major difference between us was her expression. Her brow was furrowed and her lips were pressed tightly together in what looked like a state of permanent rage. It was like looking in an angry mirror.

Teagan didn't seem to notice the similarity; maybe because I was sporting two black eyes and lots of purple bruises, or maybe she did, but didn't care. She waved at the bartender, who returned shortly with a pint of Guinness and a shot glass. She took a long sip of the Guinness, then poured herself a shot from Ryan's bottle, putting it away immediately.

Ryan looked at her with irritation, then at me. "So, what is it you think I can help you with?"

"As you know, Leo's girlfriend, Cait, has disappeared. She left the university to go home for Christmas break and never made it back to Sligo. We think she's been abducted."

He smiled. "And you think I had something to do with that?"

"No, no," I said hurriedly. "But you know, uh, you know a lot of people."

"Teagan, you live in Sligo. Do you know anything about this?"

"Why would I care about some fancy university cunt?" She looked at me. "Did you lose a fight, you bruised-up bitch?"

Bitch? "Really?" I started to get up, but felt Sam's hand on my leg, exhorting restraint. I settled back down, though not before seeing the glint of satisfaction in Teagan's eyes. She was happy to get a rise out of me. She probably got in a lot of fights. *If she keeps this up, she might get in another one tonight.*

I wondered what it would be like, fighting myself. Could I throw a punch at my own face?

"You'll have to forgive my daughter. Living beyond the pale has robbed her of her manners."

"Beyond the pale?" I asked. I'd heard the phrase but had never been exactly sure what it meant.

Sam knew, of course. "The original phrase comes from the British several centuries ago. It referred to the area outside of their authority in Ireland, which at the time included the larger Dublin area. If you were outside the pale, you were considered to be in a savage and uncivilized environment."

Ryan nodded. "Savage and uncivilized, yes. Still a fair description of Sligo."

Wow, he really hated the place.

He looked at Teagan. "Do you know anything about a missing girl?"

"No," she barked, taking another drink of Guinness.

I continued, "The guys who took her, we believe they were also involved in fuel laundering. We found an operation they were—"

Ryan interrupted me with a wave and laughed. "I don't deal in small-time shite like that."

I believed him. I couldn't imagine him being involved in something as low rent as the fuel laundering site I'd seen. Teagan, however, was looking down and away.

Ryan moved his gaze to her. "Don't tell me you're messing about with that poxy bullshit?"

She stared at him defiantly. "We're just taking a bit off the top. We can't very well go and let them operate under our noses for notin', can we?" She looked at me with hatred in her eyes. "You need to mind your own business, girly."

I hated being called *girly* for some reason. And yes, I decided, I could throw a punch at my own face. Teagan took Resting Bitch Face to a whole new level. It would be extremely satisfying to smack her in the middle of it.

Sam gave my leg a squeeze.

I took a breath and helped myself to another shot of Ryan's heavenly whiskey. "Okay. I just I wondered if you might know them. Someone named Quinn, and Firbis, and two other guys. They mentioned someone else they'd kidnapped and—"

"*What?*" Ryan hissed, turning angrily to Teagan. "What are those gobshites doing messing around with that junk?"

So he *did* know Quinn. But he apparently wasn't the boss Quinn had been talking to in the warehouse.

Teagan shrugged.

He stared at her until she looked down. "We'll talk about that later," he said, turning back to me. "I'm sure Quinn and his men had nothing to do with a kidnapping." He didn't look like he was lying, but it was hard to tell. He was probably really good at it.

I took a deep breath. "We think the reason Cait was taken may have been related to drugs."

Ryan looked at me stonily.

I waited, but apparently the silent treatment didn't work on him. "Does the name Paddy Feeney mean anything to you? He told me that some men were looking for Cait, but he was killed before he could identify them. He thought they were there because of a drug debt."

"Paddy Feeney?" Ryan looked again at his daughter.

"A customer."

"One of ours?"

She nodded. He stared at her, and she said irritably, "I had noth'n to do with him getting killed. He was behind on his payments, but we hadn't gone after him yet."

"How far behind?"

"Three months?"

"*Three months?* You know you can't let those things go," Ryan said condescendingly.

"Ya, I know, Da, but you know, I've been pretty busy with bigger fish to fry lately."

I wondered what the fish were but wanted to stay on topic. "What about a dealer named Larkin? Could he have taken Cait for some reason? Or killed Paddy?"

Teagan looked at Ryan, who nodded and said, "Larkin's one of ours. There's no way he would do anything to one of our customers without approval from us. And he didn't have fuckin' approval."

Ryan looked back at me. "It looks like we know nothing about what happened to Cait or to Paddy Feeney. Anything else?"

Ryan knew Quinn and the gang, but I believed him, that he hadn't had anything to do with Paddy's death or Cait's disappearance. And given that they had the drug business wrapped up in Sligo, it wasn't likely that some other drug lord had done it. That meant Paddy was killed for some other reason and Cait was taken for something that might not have anything to do with Ryan and his drugs. Would Quinn's boss have her kidnapped just because she found his fuel laundering site? They'd tried to kill me for the same thing. But then it would mean it wasn't related to Paddy or drugs.

This wasn't helping. My head was spinning, and I was getting increasingly uncomfortable under Ryan's steady stare. Time to get out of here, but I had to know. "Just one more thing. Do you know a Liam Gilmartin?"

Teagan gave a quick inhalation.

Ryan shot her a glance and turned back to me, his face expressionless. "You've certainly been getting around. Yes, I know him. We do a little business from time to time."

That would explain Liam's secrecy. He was involved in the drug business. But it didn't sound like he was in Ryan's gang.

"Why do you mention Liam?" Ryan asked.

"He's been helping us, to find Cait."

Teagan was staring daggers at me.

She was younger than me, but already I could see lines starting to form in her skin where she scowled. It made me think of when I was a kid and I'd get mad and scrunch up my face, and my mom would say I'd better knock it off because if I did it for too long, "your face will freeze like that." I'd spent my early years terrified of my face freezing into anything, so had made a point as a kid to change expressions on a regular basis.

Ryan was looking at Teagan. "Would you excuse us for a moment, Jesse and Sam? Reed will take care of you at the bar." He nodded to the man who'd been wiping the bar counter since we walked in. "Reed, would you share some of Mother's finest with them?"

Reed nodded and bent down below the counter.

As Sam and I walked over to the bar and took seats in the soft, leather stools, I could hear Ryan speaking in low angry tones to Teagan.

Mother's finest? I wonder what— "Oh no."

"What is it?" Sam said.

Reed had pulled out an unlabeled bottle filled with a clear liquid, and I had a sinking feeling I knew what it was. He poured two generous shots and put them in front of us.

"Uh, no, thanks. I think I've had enough for today."

"Mr. Ryan insists," Reed said.

I got the feeling that when Mr. Ryan insisted, you didn't have a choice, so I picked up my shot reluctantly.

Sam was looking at me strangely. She'd rarely seen me turn down alcohol, and I hadn't told her about Rose's poteen. She drank her shot.

Immediately, her face reddened and her eyes watered. "Oh my God."

"Yeah." I closed my eyes and put the shot away as quickly as I could, trying to keep it from touching the surfaces in my mouth. It didn't matter. It was like drinking a really bad vintage battery acid. I coughed at Reed, "We'll need some bleach chasers. Or Guinness, if you have it."

Reed turned to the Guinness tap before I remembered how long it would take to pour. We waited in pain until he brought it over. Sam and I emptied the beer into our mouths as quickly as we could.

We'd just put our glasses down on the bar when Reed said softly, "I think Mr. Ryan is ready for you."

We walked back to the table and sat down. The mood was noticeably darker. Somehow Teagan managed to look even angrier. And Ryan's face was locked into a cold, dead stare, aimed at me.

He lifted a finger at one of the goons, a signal that we were about to be escorted out. He said to me, rasping softly, "I suggest that you lay low for now. Go to the beach or take some time in Dublin. We have some business to wrap up in Sligo. In a couple of days, that will be completed and I will help find Leo's girl. But until then, I wouldn't want anything to get in our way. Do we understand each other?"

"Yes, completely. Thank you." I stood up. I couldn't wait to get out of here.

He surprised me by putting out his hand. I shook it, and he quickly pulled me toward him, squeezing so hard I thought it would break bones. When my face was next to his, he put his mouth up to my ear and hissed, "The whiskey I shared with you earlier. It was very smooth and delightful, wasn't it?"

"Yes."

"And what did you think of mother's poteen?"

I didn't trust myself to speak.

He laughed, a mirthless sound. "It was harsh, aye, I know." He squeezed again. "You have a choice working with me. Things can go smoothly, like the whiskey. Or much harsher, like the poteen. You understand what I'm saying, yeah? Do what I say, get out of town, and stay out of my way. And don't breathe a word of this discussion to anyone."

He let go of my hand, and I backed away. The big goon led us to the door, and we left the restaurant.

I was rubbing my hand as we walked back to the car. "Ryan is scary as fuck. Exactly as billed. But Teagan, Jesus, what a piece of work."

At least one mystery was solved. All of the looks I'd been getting, the staring, the double-takes, were from people who knew Teagan Ryan and initially thought I might be her. Even Liam had been looking at me strangely. Now I knew why.

"Who does she think she is? Her dad is a criminal, and she acts like she's some rock star. And where does she got off calling *me* a bitch. *She's* the bitch." She'd gotten under my skin in a way no one had in a long time. "And, hello, can anyone say daddy issues? Did you see the way she was looking at him?"

Lost in my ranting, it took me a while to realize Sam hadn't said anything since we'd left the restaurant.

I looked over at her. "What?"

"What?"

"What's with the silent treatment?"

"It's not a silent treatment."

"What, then?"

Sam looked away from me. "It's just...uh, it's just hard to fathom that there's an *angrier* version of you running around."

"Oh," I said more calmly. "Yeah. You know, it kind of reminds me of that old *Star Trek* episode where Kirk and Sulu and some of the other officers are accidentally transported to another dimension. The other dimension is almost identical to their dimension, but it's populated with evil, angry versions of themselves. Do you remember that episode? I think it was called 'The Enemy Within.'"

"I must have missed that one."

"Yeah, there was scary, evil, angry, volatile Kirk in one dimension and nice, benevolent, calm Kirk in the other."

Sam thought for a moment. "Maybe there's a third, intermediate dimension? Somewhere between the two? I envision you in that one."

"Very funny."

We'd made it to the car and were standing beside it.

"What did Ryan say to you, there at the end?"

"That we should get out of Sligo for a few days until he's done with some business there. And to stay out of his way."

"Was there an 'or else' attached to that suggestion?"

"Definitely implied." I leaned against the car and looked up. "So, let's see what we have. A fuel laundering operation in Sligo run by some IRA guys who may have kidnapped Cait without Ryan's knowledge for something that may have been related to drugs but not to Ryan's drugs. That is, if we believe Ryan."

"Do we?"

"I think so. I don't think he'd kidnap Leo's girlfriend. And he seemed genuinely surprised when he found out Quinn and the gang were involved in fuel laundering."

"Agreed."

"We have a dead drug addict, some mysterious boss of Quinn's, and a national gang boss's daughter who is Satan, if Satan looked like me, who's running his operations in Sligo. She knows Liam, who we still don't know much about. Last, Ryan's got some big thing that's happening in Sligo in a couple of days, something that involves Quinn and the gang. Something way bigger than fuel laundering."

"And didn't Harry tell you to stay out of Sligo for a few days too?" Sam asked.

I nodded. "I'll bet it's the same thing. I mean, how much big stuff could be going down in Sligo at one time?"

"That means the gardaí have some idea of what's going to happen."

"Yeah." This was a lot to process. "Let's make it simple. Quinn and his gang kidnapped some other woman. Let's assume it was Cait. So, to find her, we need to find them."

Sam nodded. "But we have no idea where they went or even if they're still in Sligo."

"They're probably still around, right? They're going to be working with Ryan on whatever it is he has coming up. If we can find out what it is, maybe it will lead us to Quinn."

"Well, I don't think Ryan is going to talk about it. And the gardaí haven't demonstrated they're interested in sharing anything with us. Or at least with you."

"What, you think you could have done better?"

"Probably not. But I wouldn't have gotten thrown out. And we'd likely have someone there who would at least be willing to talk to us."

She was right. This wasn't the first time I'd let my personality get in the way of getting what I wanted from people.

"You're right. Next time, I'll let you do the talking. But, regardless, we know they're not doing anything to find Cait."

We were silent, lost in our own thoughts. After a few moments, I said, "You know, Liam still might be able to help. Teagan obviously knows him, and Ryan said he worked with him from time to time. Liam could be in on whatever Ryan has going. And if not, maybe he could find something out from Teagan."

"Yes, but we're back to the same problem. Why would Liam tell you now if he hasn't already?"

"He might not, but it won't hurt to ask. We've learned a few things in the last couple of days. Maybe if we share what we know with him, he'll realize he knows something he didn't realize was important before. And he *was* interested in helping us find Cait. And, uh, I think he'll talk to me."

"Why do you think that?"

"I just do." I started to get in the car.

Sam grabbed my arm. "Spill it."

Damn. She always knew when I was keeping something from her. "When we met at the shebeen. He made a...uh...move on me."

She smiled. "You mean a romantic overture?" For some reason she was acutely interested in my, comparably negligible, love life.

"Something like that."

"Something like *what*?"

Argh. "His exact words were, 'Fancy a ride?'"

She laughed. "I'm not sure that qualifies as romantic. What did you say?"

"I turned him down. And then I did the memory thing." About the only time I used the memory thing outside of my job was to drive away guys who were hitting on me, because it was an extremely effective deterrent.

She rolled her eyes. "And you think he's still interested after *that*?"

"Probably not. But he still might talk to me. And he hasn't met *you* yet. We'll double team him. Can I have your phone?"

She handed it over, and I called Liam. He didn't pick up, so I left a message.

"What if he doesn't call you back?"

I didn't like the idea of sitting on my ass waiting. "Let's go find him."

"Do you know where he lives?"

"No, but I know where he hangs out. Let's get back to Sligo."

"Okay. But I'd prefer from here on we stay away from Danny Ryan, and the IRA."

TWENTY-ONE

I t was two and half hours back to Sligo, so Sam drove to let
me grab a little more sleep. We got into town at two a.m.,
and she woke me for directions to the shebeen. We soon
parked on a side street that gave us a view of the door.

Before we went in, I called Gideon. "Hey, did you find
anything out yet about Liam Gilmartin?"

"No, nothing. I mean, there are a ton of Gilmartins in Sligo
and a few Liam Gilmartins, but no one with any criminal background and none of them are the right age."

"We think he might have ties to Danny Ryan. Does that
help?"

"I checked that. Ryan has no known associates with that
name."

"Can you expand the search to the rest of Ireland?"

"Already did. Same thing. Nothing remotely interesting that
might be linked to the guy you described."

Damn. "Okay, thanks, Gideon." I hung up. "Gideon can't
find anything."

"So he's still a mystery man," said Sam.

"Not for long." I started to get out of the car, but stopped,
quickly ducking back inside. "Sam, look." I pointed to a black

SUV that had pulled up in front of the shebeen. A woman was getting out. "That's Teagan. She made it back here fast."

"What do you want to do?" Sam asked.

We watched her go up to the door and be let in before I replied, "Let's wait. She'll have to come back out sometime."

A half hour later, we saw Teagan come back outside and Liam was right behind her. They walked to her car and stood next to it, talking. It was dark, but the lone working streetlight was not far from her car, and we had a good view of them. Teagan's hands were moving restlessly, and she was whipping her head around as she talked. At various points in the conversation, she waved her hand and pointed. At one point she started to get into the driver's seat, but Liam grabbed her arm and leaned toward her.

"I wonder what they're saying," mused Sam.

I scowled and lowered my voice to match Teagan's.

"I want to leave. I have people to insult and drug addicts to intimidate."

Sam laughed and did her best to mimic Liam's gravelly tone. "Don't go yet. By the way, don't you love my manly dimples?"

"Unfortunately, yes, I'm still standing here listening because you are so good looking. But I have work to do."

"You should learn to relax."

"You relax! You know I hate it when people tell me to relax."

"You sure are angry."

"No, I'm not. And fuck you."

Whatever he said to her must have worked. They stopped talking, and Teagan closed the front door and then opened the back one. They both got in.

"I guess he won the argument," Sam said.

"Can you see what they're doing?"

"No, the windows are tinted."

After a few minutes, the car windows started to steam up. Then we saw the car begin to rock gently.

I rolled my eyes. "Oh, Jesus. They're doing it in her car."

"I hope it's got leather seats."

"This shouldn't take long. Car bangs never do."

After a few minutes, the car stopped moving. "I guess that was it." I looked down at my watch. "Four minutes." I no longer regretted turning Liam down.

"No, look. It's started up again."

The car was rocking, this time more vigorously.

We waited. Forty minutes later, we were still waiting.

"That's...uh...impressive," Sam said, her eyebrows raised.

It went on another ten minutes before it stopped. We waited to see if they were done for real this time, and Liam got out of the car. Teagan came out after him. He gave her a kiss on the cheek and went back inside the shebeen. She got in the front seat of the car and started it up.

"Well, now we know how they know each other," I said.

"What do we do now?"

"We know where we can find him. Let's stick with her."

Sam started up the car and we followed Teagan at a discrete distance to another residential neighborhood a few miles away. She pulled up into a driveway, got out, and went inside. The lights went on briefly and then they went out. The house was still and quiet.

"I guess she's tired." Sam said.

"No surprise there."

Liam hadn't called me back, but maybe it was because he'd had other things on his mind. I called him again and got his voicemail. I left another message, asking him to call me back on Sam's number. I told him it was urgent.

Sam was fidgeting; she hated waiting. "Now what? Should we go back to the shebeen?"

"I don't know. Let's give it a few minutes." I hated waiting too; it was one of the few things we had in common. But we were getting to the end of our options and I wanted to give this a chance.

Fifteen minutes later, Liam still hadn't returned my call.

I sighed heavily. "All right, let's go to the shebeen. We want to be face-to-face with him, anyway."

Sam started to turn the car on, but stopped. Turning to me,

she said, "Jesse...what if Liam is involved with Ryan more than a little? Ryan said they worked together from time to time, but what if he's deep into whatever it is Ryan is planning? I mean, he's sleeping with his daughter. And we really don't know anything about him. Well, other than that he's apparently got some stamina."

She was saying what I'd been thinking but didn't want to. Liam might be a bad guy. I nodded slowly and picked her phone back up. Time to change tactics.

I got his voicemail. "Hey, it's me again. I know you're banging Teagan Ryan, and if you don't call me back right away, I'm going to the gardaí and telling them that you're in with the fuel laundering gang, or the IRA, or the UDF, or whatever I can think of to make up about you. And that they can pick you up at the shebeen."

I hated saying that. I didn't want to be responsible for getting a pub shut down. But he wasn't leaving me any options.

Two minutes later, my phone rang.

"Hi, Liam." I nodded at Sam. "No. In person."

"Not there. Meet me at Murphy's. Four o'clock this afternoon."

The call ended, and I gave Sam her phone. "He's not happy. But he's agreed to meet."

"Why didn't you talk to him over the phone?"

"We might need your special powers. And I want to see his face when we talk."

"Four o'clock?"

"Yeah. The pub's not open yet, and I'm dead on my feet. I need some sleep."

Sam started the car and we headed back to the Gallaghers.

TWENTY-TWO

S am engaged Rose while I snuck upstairs to take a nap. At a quarter to four, we left and went to Murphy's.

I was surprised at this time of day to see that the pub was almost full. I recognized some of the regulars, including four men at the bar sitting in exactly the same places they'd been in when I'd met with Mik and Paddy the other night.

Most of the people were there to hear music. Many of them had moved their chairs to face the group of trad musicians settling in at a table in one of the corners. Three men and a woman, with pints in front of them, were taking instruments out of cases.

Liam was already there, sitting at a small table in the back. He looked distracted and wary, and even before I sat down, he said brusquely, "What is it you want, Jesse?" He looked over at Sam and did the typical Sam double take. He stuck his hand across the table and managed a smile. "I'm Liam."

She shook his hand. "Sam. Nice to meet you."

Even though I'd threatened him, I needed him on my good side. "Can I get you a pint?"

He looked around and nodded absentmindedly.

I went to the bar and came back with three pints of Guinness and three shots of whiskey.

He took the Guinness and left the shot on the table. He looked at me closely for the first time since I'd walked in and winced. He hadn't seen me since I'd crashed the car, and I still had black eyes and large purple bruises on my face.

"What happened to you?"

"I crashed a car into a wall and flame bombed some criminals."

He rolled his eyes. "Whatever. Jesse, I'm really busy. What is it you want?"

"I'm serious. I'm trying to track down some guys who tried to kill me. They might be IRA."

His eyes grew large.

"I thought you might know where I could find them." I was really curious about his relationship with Teagan, but my main focus was tracking down Quinn.

"*What?*" he hissed. "Don't be throwing that around here." He looked around and lowered his voice. "What are you on about?"

"I, uh, stumbled across what might be an IRA fuel laundering operation. They were talking about a woman they'd taken. I think it was Cait." I left out the parts about the kidnapping, and using my clothes to make Molotov cocktails.

"What makes you think I would know anything about men like that?"

Answering a question with a question...he *did* know something. But unlike earlier, he wasn't interested in helping me. We'd come a long way since "fancy a ride."

"It doesn't matter. I met with Danny Ryan and Teagan."

His eyebrows went up at the mention of Ryan.

"It was pretty clear that she knows something about Cait. Since you *know* her"—I drew out *know* to make it clear I meant in the biblical sense—"I thought maybe you could ask her about it. You know, as a favor, to me."

"Teagan doesn't know anything about Cait."

"How do you know? Did you ask her?"

"Jesse..." He took a long sip of his beer. "You need to back off.

Don't go near Danny Ryan, or Teagan. And leave me alone. I told you what I know. I can't help you anymore."

"What the fuck is going on, Liam? You were the one who approached me, remember?"

"That was a mistake."

He didn't know me very well if he thought telling me to back off was going to get me to back off. And while he'd been motivated by my call to meet with us, it wasn't enough to tell us what we needed to know. Time to change my approach. At this point it was clear that Liam wasn't going to help us and was no longer interested in finding Cait. I needed to give him more of an incentive.

I leaned forward and glared directly into his eyes. "It wasn't a mistake. And you know something."

"I didn't say that."

"You didn't have to. I can see it in your face."

"You can't possibly know that." He sat back and crossed his arms across his chest.

"You know I know a lot of things." I looked down at the table in front of me. "There are thirty-two people in the pub right now, twenty men and twelve women. Six are sitting at the bar on stools, including two men in their sixties in the center and two younger ones sitting around the side. The older ones are brothers. The younger ones at the end are sitting with pints, and neither one has taken a drink since we walked in. They're friends of the bartender, who—"

"Stop it." He tried to sound casual, but I could sense his unease. Unease was good.

"You seem to be well connected, and you said you wanted to help."

He took a long sip of his beer. "You don't know what you're asking," he said without looking up.

"I know there's a young woman who's been missing for over a week, and her family is devastated. I know you tried to help me before. And I know that she might be in big trouble and the guys who took her are involved in some big thing that's happening this week and is linked to Danny Ryan and his daughter. And I know you might be involved too."

His head snapped up and he started to say something.

I put my hand out. "But I don't know what it is, and I don't care. I just need to find them, or get the gardaí to bring them in and question them. They're the only link we have to Cait."

"Jesse, you need to stay the *fuck* away from these guys and especially from Danny Ryan's—" He suddenly looked down into his pocket, then reached into it and took out a phone.

"Yeah? Hang on." He got up from the table and walked toward the door of the pub.

"Sam, did you see that?" I asked her quietly.

"See what?"

"His phone. The one he answered. It's not his regular phone. It's a burner."

"And did you see his eyes when I mentioned the big thing with Ryan? He's definitely involved."

Liam was frowning and whispering urgently to whoever it was he was talking to. He looked over at us, then pushed open the door to the pub and walked outside to continue his call.

"I want to know who he's talking to."

"I doubt he's going to tell you."

"Probably not." I took a sip of beer. "We need that phone. Do you think you can get it?"

Among Sam's many skills was a pretty slick ability to pickpocket. She was perfect for it. It wasn't her manual dexterity or deft fingers, although she had both of those. Sam's pickpocketing expertise had more to do with how distracted other people were around her, because of how desperately they wanted to be close to her. When she moved next to people, they tended to get flustered, and when her hand slipped into their purses, pockets, or jackets, they'd only register her closeness and forget all about their possessions. The last thing anyone cared about when they were around Sam was their stuff. She didn't do it often, but she was money when she needed to.

She nodded. "Do you think you can create a distraction?"

"I was made for distractions. Are we talking spilled drink, fake choking, or nuclear?"

"Something on the order of nuclear, I would think. We don't want to take any chances. And he doesn't seem like the type to be easily distracted."

"I'm on it."

Liam walked back into the pub, slipping the phone into his coat pocket. As he came back to the table, I finished my beer and downed the shot, then I got up and went to the bar. Inserting myself roughly between the two older regulars and speaking more loudly than I needed to, I ordered another pint of beer and three more shots. I carried everything unsteadily back to our table, weaving slightly on the way. I could feel the men at the bar watching me.

I set the shots down. "Peace offering. Sláinte!" I yelled, downing my shot.

"Thanks, Jesse, but I need to go." He left his shot on the table, and I looked at Sam.

She knew the drill. "None for me either."

I pulled my face into a sulk, then picked up the other two shots and in quick succession put them down.

"*WHOOOO!*" I slammed my fist on the table, sending one of the shot glasses to the floor, where it bounced away and rolled underneath a nearby chair. I picked up my pint of Guinness and put it away in one long gulp.

I got up from the table with my glass, pushing my chair back roughly, knocking it to the floor. The people at the nearest table looked over and frowned.

No one else was even looking our way. The trad players had started up, and everyone's attention was toward the other side of the bar, listening to the music. I would need to ramp things up.

I stumbled up to the bar again and shouldered my way rudely between the two older men. I raised up my glass and waved it back and forth at the bartender, who was now studiously avoiding making eye contact with me. He turned and walked to the other end of the bar, drying glasses with a towel.

"Hey!" I yelled drunkenly at his back.

The two regulars the bartender was talking to looked over at me, frowning.

"*Hey!*" I yelled again. "Who do I have to blow to get a drink around here?"

This caused him to put down his towel. He came over and leaned across the bar. "Miss, I think you've had enough."

They were probably used to tourists overindulging in the local spirits. What they didn't know was that I was well under my limit. I'd always had an extremely high, possibly genetic, tolerance for alcohol. And in the last six months with Tatiana around, it had been honed to a world-class skill. Tatiana could drink like no one I'd ever met, and I'd worked up my capacity to keep up with her. It had been quite a challenge. Early on in her stay with Sam, she'd come home with some bottles of Baltica beer to try, and a thermos. After pouring us each a glass of beer, she'd opened the thermos, which I learned was full of vodka, and dumped it into the beer. I guess beer by itself wasn't high enough proof to bother with. I only vaguely recalled the rest of the night, the first of many like it. I never reached her level of consumption, but it would take more than a few shots and beer chasers to put me over the edge. But the people in the pub didn't know that.

"*Enough?* No fucking way." I slammed the glass down on the bar. "More Guinness, and more shots." I wondered how long his fuse would be.

Not long, as it turned out. He'd had enough, no doubt having dealt with his share of overserved assholes in his life. He looked over at the big men who'd been sitting quietly at the other end of the bar and nodded his head in a brief dip.

They both got up and came over to me. One of them grabbed my arm and tried to pull me away from the bar.

"What the *fuck*?" I reached out for the metal bar railing with one arm, gripping it tightly. I wrenched the other one loose from them and was now holding on for dear life with both hands. "Let *go* of me!" I yelled as loud as I could. I kicked a nearby stool, sending it flying.

The trad singers stopped playing, and everyone was watching as the two men tried to pull me away from the bar.

"Get your hands *off* of me! Help! Guards! I'm being assaulted!"

One of the men held my arms while the other one pried my fingers off the railing. They pulled me away, one on either side, gently but firmly escorting me out of the pub, my feet barely making contact with the floor.

I snuck a look over at Sam and Liam. They were still sitting down, albeit with looks of mortification on their faces. Time to turn things up to eleven.

"Back *off*, shamrock sniffers!" I started kicking my legs and waving my head around like a mad woman. I managed to wrench my arms away and grabbed at one of the wood support columns, wrapping both arms around it in a hug. "Fuck *you*, and *fuck* Ireland!"

The men proceeded to patiently work on pulling my arms away from the column. No one else was paying any attention. Where was their national pride?

I'd been throwing a stream of obscenities that seemed to have no visible effect on anyone. Time to get personal.

"U2 are posers! Enya sucks!" I'd locked my fingers around the beam—they were not going to get me off of it quickly. "Pierce Brosnan was the worst Bond!"

I was settling in, and the men were struggling to unlock my fingers. But so far, no reaction from the crowd.

"Maureen O'Hara was a terrible Jane!"

This last one was tough. Maureen O'Hara was one of my mom's heroes, and my full name—Jesse Maureen O'Hara—was in honor of her. But everyone in the pub was still sitting patiently in their seats, sipping their pints, and waiting for the commotion to die down so they could get on with their music.

"Michael Collins was a wanker!"

That seemed to move the needle. Angry muttering was now coming from several tables.

"Yeats is overrated!"

Sligo's famous son was not to be disparaged. The muttering got louder. I heard *slag* and *wagon*. I wasn't sure what they meant, but I knew I was getting close. Time to go full nuclear.

"Brendan Gleeson is a mediocre actor!"

Twenty-five chairs scraped against the wooden floor at once as everyone in the pub stood up. The three male trad players moved quickly over to us, grabbing my arms and easily peeling them from the column.

Now that I'd gotten the trad players to rampage, Liam was standing up, although with no apparent inclination to help me out. Sam was standing closely next to him. She gave me a small nod. Mission accomplished.

It was a good thing, as I was out of insults. I went boneless and let them pull me toward the door, my feet dragging limply on the floor.

They took me outside, dropping me more roughly than necessary onto the edge of the sidewalk, then one of them kicked me into the street. I landed in a heap up against a parked car.

Sam came out of the pub a minute later. She stood on the sidewalk, looking down at me. She didn't bother helping me up.

"Shamrock sniffers?"

"I was improvising." I stood up, brushing dirt from my pants.

"I noticed you didn't say anything about Chris O'Dowd or Amy Huberman."

"I'm not a savage, Sam."

She looked back at the pub. "I really liked that place," she said wistfully.

"You said you wanted a distraction. You said nuclear."

"Yes, I know. I think I'd forgotten how committed you can be. Humming 'God Save the Queen' the whole time was a nice touch. Too bad we can never come back here. Or, you know, visit this town again."

"Did you get it?"

"Yes." She pulled Liam's burner phone from her purse and handed it to me, then looked back to the entrance. "You should hurry, he's going to realize it's missing pretty soon. We're lucky he didn't follow us out."

"I don't think luck had anything to do with it. I'm guessing he's in there pretending like he doesn't really know us."

I turned on the phone and entered the password I'd watched him use the day before on his other phone, and hoped it was the same one.

It was, and I hastily opened his call record. Just two numbers with numerous calls in and out over the last two months. I committed them to memory and handed the phone back to Sam.

"Let me use your phone." She handed it to me and then turned and went back into the pub to retrieve whatever she'd purposely forgotten there so she could slip the phone back into Liam's jacket and make apologies for my behavior.

While she was inside, I called Gideon. It was three in the morning his time, but he was up and answered on the second ring. "Hey, Jesse." He sounded way better than he had the other day.

"Hey, you're up."

"Yeah, I'm tracking some pedo activity. It's boring, but I have to monitor it all night. What can I do for you?"

"Can you track down a couple of phone numbers for me?"

"Sure, let me have them."

I gave him the two numbers from Liam's phone. "Any chance I can get this soon?"

"Yeah. You know me, the ultimate multitasker."

"Thanks. I owe you."

"I know," he said cheerfully. We hung up.

Sam came back out of the pub. "Now what?"

"Now we get something to eat and wait for Gideon to call us back. And I need a shower."

TWENTY-THREE

We went back to the Gallaghers, and I took a shower. I realized it had been several days since my last one, not counting sponge baths. The water felt good, and the nicks and cuts I'd gotten the other night were starting to be less painful. I stayed under the warm stream for a long time. I was tired. It took a lot of energy to humiliate yourself in front of a crowd, even though I was used to it. I dried my hair and laid down for a moment on the bed.

I woke up an hour later. *Damnit.*

I hurriedly put on my only pair of clean jeans and walked down the stairs to the empty living room. The boys were working late, and Mik was nowhere to be seen. Likely at a pub. Rose was in the kitchen, and I walked in to join her. She hadn't seen me since I'd stumbled upon the fuel laundering site. And while I'd been healing, I still had two black eyes and a large bruise down the side of my face, at this point a spectacular blend of purples and emerging yellows.

"Oh, you poor dear!" She put the spoon she was using down and came over to me, putting her arms around and giving me a full body hug. "Here, let me get you something." She disappeared into the laundry room off the kitchen and came back with the bottle of poteen Brian had shared the other night. She pulled down two small glasses from the cupboard and poured a bit into each, handing one to me and picking the other up herself. She raised it to me. "Sláinte." She drank hers easily and poured herself another.

I had no desire to put this stuff into my body again. Once was enough for a lifetime. But I didn't want to insult her, and I didn't want her to know that Brian had discovered her stash. I drank it. The fact that I was prepared this time didn't make it any easier. I'd heard that dung-smoked testicle beer was all the rage in Iceland. I wondered if it would be an improvement over this stuff. I couldn't imagine it could be worse.

Through a coughing fit, I gasped out, "Thanks."

"It's poteen." She poured me another glass. "I make it meself," she said proudly. She lowered her voice conspiratorially. "I don't share it with the boys. It's just for us girls." She clinked her glass against mine and drank it down.

I followed her again, coughing fire.

I was relieved when she put the top back on the bottle. When I was able to talk again, I asked, "Have you seen Sam?"

"I think she's in the barn with the boys. Will you two be staying for dinner?"

"I'm not sure. You should probably not count on it."

She looked at me hopefully. "Does this mean you've found something about my Cait?"

I sighed. God, I hated this. "We have one lead we're following." I wanted to tell her not to get her hopes up, that Cait had been gone now for almost two weeks and it was getting more unlikely that we, or anyone else, would find her, and that it wasn't clear she was even still alive at this point. And that we might not even find her body. But looking into her eyes, I couldn't make myself say the words. Who was I to take away her hope? It could be the last thing she'd have left of Cait, and she might as well hang onto it as long as she could. I gave her a small smile and headed out to the barn.

Sam and the twins were out in the pasture, next to the stallions that I'd privately named John Holmes and Ron Jeremy. Sam was stroking Ron Jeremy's nose. As I approached them, I tried to see if the stallion had more of an affinity for Colin or John, to give a clue as to his preferred jerker, but at the moment he was wholly focused on taking an apple out of Sam's hand.

She was good with horses. No surprise there. It was a safe bet that she was good with most carbon-based life-forms.

Sam's phone was still in my pocket and it was vibrating. I pulled it out. It was Gideon.

"Hey, I tracked down your numbers."

"Go ahead."

"One is a Teagan Ryan."

That made sense, he'd be calling his girlfriend. But why didn't he call her on his regular phone?

"The other number is registered to a James Quinn."

A cold lump started to form in the pit of my stomach, and I could feel my chest tighten. "Can you see his call history?"

"Yeah."

"Was there a call made to Quinn from Liam's phone two days ago at around two p.m.?"

"Yep. Lasted about a minute."

Shit. "Okay, thanks, Gideon."

"Sure. Anything else?"

"Yeah. You said you couldn't find anything on Liam Gilmartin?"

"Yeah, nothing useful."

"Did you look at Northern Ireland? Or just in the Republic?"

"Damn...no. I should have. I'm not thinking clearly. Too much work and not enough sleep. Give me a couple of hours, and I'll get back to you." He hung up, sounding a little embarrassed.

I knew it was a mistake a lot of Americans made, thinking that the Republic of Ireland and Northern Ireland weren't truly different countries, not realizing they were completely separate governments, with completely separate systems.

Sam had stopped feeding the horse and was looking at me. She knew it wasn't good news.

"Well?"

I shook my head and walked back toward the house. Sam followed me; once we were out of earshot of the twins I said, "Liam is with the IRA."

"Oh no..."

"It gets worse. He's the boss, the one that's behind the fuel laundering operation.

"He's the one who ordered Cait's kidnapping."

Twenty-Four

The signs had been there. And I couldn't use the excuse that I didn't notice them, because I noticed everything. I just hadn't realized the significance of what I was seeing.

The shebeen was an IRA hangout. The flags, the Celtic crosses, the posters of Bobby Sands and Michael Gaughan. It was all there—I just hadn't put it together. I'd been a little too focused on the hot guy I'd been drinking with.

"Should we go to the gardaí?" Sam asked.

I exhaled loudly. "I don't know. These guys are dangerous. I mean, Quinn was going to kneecap me just to get me to tell him where my car was. Whatever it is they're working on now with Danny Ryan, they're going to be way more serious about that than the location of my car. And if Ryan finds out we're still poking around..."

"But wait...if Liam is the one who gave the order to have Cait kidnapped, why was he helping you find her?"

"I don't know." I'd gotten to the front stoop but didn't want to go in yet. Rose didn't need to hear this. "And *was* he really helping? He sent us to Galway. But now we know she definitely left to come back to Sligo."

"So you think he was putting us off the track? Trying to get us out of the way?"

"Yeah, I do. He's probably involved in this big thing Ryan's got going on too. And both he and Ryan basically told us to back the fuck off until it was over. Why else would he send us to Galway if he knew she was coming back here?"

"So you think he knows where she is?"

"I'm sure of it. And for some reason he doesn't want to tell us." I didn't want to say out loud that maybe the reason he didn't want to tell us was because she was dead.

"So why don't we go to the gardaí?"

"And tell them *what*, Sam?" I was frustrated and angry. The one guy we'd counted on had not only completely let us down, but was responsible for the whole thing.

"That we know Liam, and that he knows Quinn, who they can't find. That we think he's tied to the IRA, like Quinn. That he drinks in a shebeen. That he sometimes works with Danny Ryan."

Who the fuck was I to be searching for a missing person, in Ireland, no less? I'd been completely wrong about everything. I was way out of my depth, and a young woman might die because of it. I was scum. I sat down on the stoop and dropped my head to my chest.

"Jesse, this isn't your fault. You've done more than anyone here to find Cait, and you've gotten closer to it than the gardaí have."

I shook my head. "I think it's over, Sam. I don't know what to do at this point. We've used every card we have."

"Have we?"

I looked up.

"Liam was worried enough about your investigative abilities that he made the effort to send you to Galway."

"So? He's a prick. But he'll find out soon enough that my abilities are overrated."

"And he knows you've been at the garda station."

"Sure, yeah, they think I'm a suspect, for fuck's sake."

"Yes, but does Liam know that? For all he knows, you've been working closely with the gardaí, helping them move things along. He doesn't know you're at the end of your rope. Remember, he made a point to tell you at Murphy's to back off. Whatever he's doing, he's worried enough about you to make that threat."

"Ryan made the same comment," I said, thoughtful.

"And we know that the gardaí know something about whatever is going to happen, yes? Harry warned you off too, the last time you left the station. He told you to stay away for a few days."

"Yeah, well, fuck him." Everyone had been telling me to stay away. "Fuck *all* of them. Fuck Liam for pretending he was helping find Cait when he was the one who had her kidnapped. Fuck Mullarkey for not doing his job. Fuck Danny Ryan for his fucking drug business. Fuck Teagan for looking like me. And fuck Quinn for taking my phone."

Enough personal pity party. "When I was in the fuel laundering warehouse, they talked about another trespasser. That means Cait stumbled upon the same thing I did. And we know that the fuel laundering isn't the main thing they're working on. They probably took her because she'd found something else out... something about their upcoming operation. Why else would they go to the trouble of kidnapping her?"

Sam was nodding excitedly. "Exactly. And Liam knows we've figured a lot out already, so he might believe that we know what it is."

The next move was clear. "We can threaten Liam with outing his connections to the IRA and to Ryan and his big operation and all of these other connections to the gardaí. I'll make him think we know more about Ryan's operation than we really do. We'll tell him we know he had Cait kidnapped, but we just want to know where she is. It might be enough to get him to give her up. He knows that's all we care about."

Sam had stopped nodding.

"What? What's wrong? Do you have a better idea?"

"No. But if Liam really is with the IRA, should we be threatening him with *anything*?"

She was right. It was one thing to get him to meet with us by saying he was with the IRA when we knew it wasn't true. It moved us into a whole other realm to do it when it was the truth.

"Maybe not. But do we have a choice?"

Sam was shaking her head. "And not just Liam. Danny Ryan is linked to dozens of murders and disappearances in Ireland. If you start interfering with his business..." Her voice trailed off, but the point was made.

"I know, I know." I stood up from the stoop wearily. "But what are we supposed to do? Tell Rose, 'Sorry, we're too scared to go after your daughter. Good luck, see ya'?"

Sam was silent for a few moments, then said quietly, "You're right, of course. We don't have a choice."

"Nope. And we also have to keep this from the gardaí. If a miracle happens and Liam does believe we know enough to mess up his business, getting the gardaí involved could do more harm than good. He might just decide to take us out. And Cait too." I didn't say, if he hadn't done that already.

We turned to go into the house, when Sam's phone rang.

She answered, "Hi, Gideon."

"Did he track down Liam in Northern Ireland?" I asked.

Sam waved me off. She listened for a minute, then said goodbye and hung up. I could see by her face that it was more bad news. Just what we needed.

I reached for the phone to call Liam and leave my message bomb.

She held onto it. "Jesse, I need to tell you something."

"Let me guess. Gideon's decided he's not gay and wants to marry you."

She shook her head. "Your dad is out of prison."

"What? *Why?!* He's got two years left on his sentence."

"His last parole hearing was a few days ago. He's been a model prisoner, and they're dealing with overcrowding."

I sagged more than sat back down on the cement. The man who had killed my mother was out on the streets.

She gently put her hand on my shoulder. "Is there anything I can do?"

"Yeah, get me a drink. And when we get back, I'll need to borrow your gun." I wasn't sure if I was kidding or not.

"He's been in prison almost thirteen years...that's a long time." Sam was trying to put a positive spin on things.

"Not long enough." I put my head between my knees, fighting nausea. Rose's poteen wasn't helping. "Does Shannon know?"

"Yes, she picked him up at the prison."

He'd been out of my life for over a decade, but it seemed like just yesterday that he'd been put away. Shannon had said he'd changed, and I wondered if that were true. I doubted it. He'd been a lifelong drunk, and even if he was sober now, he would still be the same irresponsible, thoughtless asshole who had gone to prison. As far as I knew, there wasn't a rehabilitation program in the world that could fix that.

Whatever. I had a job to do. I would think about his sorry ass later. I got up and walked into the house.

Twenty-Five

We were upstairs in Cait's room, where I called Liam and left a long voicemail. This would either work or it wouldn't. But the only chance we had was if I really sold it, hard.

"Liam, this is Jesse. We know you're with the IRA, and we know you're working with Ryan on his operation. I know all about that. The good news for you is that I don't care about your shady business. I just want Cait back. We haven't talked to the gardaí. But we will if you don't get back to me." I made my voice sound angry, which wasn't hard, as I was still thinking about my now unincarcerated dad. "I also know you're responsible for her being taken, you son of a bitch. Get back to me with her whereabouts, or we're going to the gardaí with all of the details about you, Ryan, and his operation. You know me well enough to know that I see things other people miss. Like the number for your super-secret burner phone that I'm calling you on now."

As far as he knew, only a couple of people had this number. Between that and what he'd seen of my powers of observation, I was hoping he'd believe I knew more than I actually did about his business.

"You think I've been stirring things up? I haven't even started.

I can fuck your shit up like no one you've ever seen. And I'm not going to stop until Cait is returned to her family. You know what I can do. And how do you think Ryan will react when he finds out you're the reason his big operation got blown up?"

Even if Liam didn't completely believe I knew everything, he wouldn't want to be responsible for anything interfering with Ryan's business. Unless he had a death wish.

I hung up the phone and gave it back to Sam.

"Nicely done. What do we do in the meantime?"

"If he calls our bluff, we're fucked. We don't know anything about what they've got going other than it looks like it's going to happen soon, it's in or around Sligo, and Liam's in it with Ryan. The gardaí probably know more than we do at this point. If he figures that out, he'll just ignore us." *Or decide he wants us out of his hair and throw us in a bog.*

"I think there's a good chance he might believe you. He's seen you in action."

"Sure. But just in case, maybe we should prepare for the eventuality that he doesn't buy it."

Sam nodded. "Agreed. Why don't we use the time to see if we can find out what Ryan's operation actually is?"

That did sound better than sitting around waiting to be killed. "Any ideas where we should start?"

"Wasn't that Professor Jarlath's research area, the business about how paramilitaries and gangs are linked? He might be able to tell us something useful."

"Good idea." I'd skimmed through one of the papers he'd given me. It wasn't exactly electrifying reading, but his understanding of Ireland's underworld was extensive. If anyone could give us some ideas about what was going on with Danny Ryan and the IRA, it was him.

Sam started to hand me her phone, but I shook my head. "I think we should go back to Galway and meet him in person."

"What if Liam calls while we're gone and wants to meet?"

"It's only a couple of hours away. If Liam calls, we'll turn around. But it might be a good idea to get out of town anyway. In case, you know, he decides that there's another, more efficient way to deal with us."

Sam didn't argue, likely coming to the same conclusion I had. We got in the car and headed out. She drove, and I called Jarlath on the way. He was around and agreed to see us. We were thirty minutes from Galway when Gideon called again.

I picked up Sam's phone from the console between us. "Hey, Gideon. What's going on?"

"You were right. I found your Liam Gilmartin in Northern Ireland."

"Okay. Thanks." I wasn't surprised he'd found him there. I already knew Liam was IRA.

"It's funny, though," he went on. "It was like he didn't exist before two years ago. Then all of a sudden, he sprung on the scene and since then has been really active in IRA circles. He's been arrested a couple of times and spent some time in Maghaberry Prison."

"Any particular faction? NIRA? PIRA? People's Front of Judea?"

"He seems to be all over the place." That made sense. Jarlath had told us that there were people associated with various causes who weren't motivated by politics. Quinn might just be in it for the money. "But regardless of where he's been, he's been moving up rapidly. Cigarette smuggling, fuel laundering, and, more recently, drugs. Bigger deals every time. He was arrested twice in Belfast last year for cocaine distribution. But no jail time for that, as far as I can tell."

I wasn't surprised. Liam was smart, charismatic, and one of the smoothest talkers I'd ever met. He would have made sure there wasn't the kind of evidence to make any major charges stick.

"Thanks, Gideon."

"Sure. And, uh, Jesse, I'm really sorry about your dad."

"That's okay. Thanks for letting us know. How are you doing?"

"We're all fine. Chaz seems to be perfectly happy hanging out with Tanya—"

"Tanya?"

"Tatiana. She told me the other day to call her that."

I put my hand over the phone and said to Sam, "Tatiana told him to call her Tanya."

Sam's eyebrows went up.

When Sam had invited Tatiana to live with her, I wasn't overexcited at the prospect. She came across as a real bitch when I first met her. But I hadn't realized she was that way because she and her father were being blackmailed and she'd thought we were part of it. Now that she was away from that situation, she was, well, still kind of a bitch. But we were growing to trust each other. And I knew enough about her now to know that her asking Gideon to call her by the diminutive Tanya was a big deal.

"Dude, do you realize what this means?"

"Uh, no. It's a nickname, I guess."

"Sure, but in this case, it's closer to a declaration of love."

"Oh. What should I do?"

"Well, if she offers to show you her etchings, I'd politely decline."

"Thanks a lot. Listen, can you give me some—?"

I made a scratching noise into the phone. "...going through a tunnel...gotta go." I hung up. Turning to Sam, I said, "Liam is definitely IRA."

She nodded. There wasn't much to say. Neither of us were surprised at this point. But it was a bummer to have it confirmed.

I looked out the window at the countryside. "When this is done, I want to spend more time here."

"Here?"

We were on the N17 between Sligo and Galway. It had looked like a major highway on the map but for most of the trip was a scant, three-lane strip of asphalt running through low green fields.

"The Wild Atlantic Way is on my list. Fifteen hundred miles of beautiful coast and small towns." Now that we'd put ourselves squarely in the crosshairs of the IRA, I found myself thinking more about my bucket list.

"So, tell me about the things on this list."

We had some time to kill. And it would help take my mind off our imminent danger for a few minutes. So, I began telling her my list. "Drink a Guinness in Ireland, buy some whiskey from the original Jameson distillery, visit the Guinness brewery, visit the Whiskey Museum in Dublin, have a drink in Sean's bar in Athlone—"

"I'm sensing a theme here. And who's Sean, and why do you want to drink in his bar?"

"It's the oldest bar in the fucking world. And don't interrupt. Visit Carrowmore, eat fish and chips at a chipper, go to Newgrange during the winter solstice. And one I've added since I've been here. I want to visit one of these Gaeltacht places and see for myself that people are actually speaking that language on a regular basis."

"You're not interested in the Blarney Stone?"

"No. Kissing a rock is stupid. What about you? Do you have one?"

"An Ireland bucket list? Not exactly, but I do have some things I want to do before we leave. Visit the Hunt Museum, the Irish Museum of Modern Art, and the Highlanes Gallery. Visual in Carlow is supposed to be stunning. And, of course, the National Museum of Ireland."

We pulled into the university parking lot near Jarlath's building. Sam turned off the car and took a deep breath.

I knew she was feeling the same thing I was. None of this would matter if we couldn't find Cait. Ireland would forever be cemented in my mind as the land of a missing young woman and a destroyed family.

"Not too much overlap in the lists, is there?" I said.

"No, there never is. But we always seem to manage it."

It was true. We'd traveled comfortably together for years. My mood turned somber as I found myself wondering if this would be our last trip.

TWENTY-SIX

"Hello, Jesse, Sam," Jarlath greeted us with a smile. All of the academics I knew relished the chance to help out with real world problems. "What can I help you with?"

"We've found some things out while looking for Cait." I shared with him the fuel laundering and the fact that we had information indicating she'd been kidnapped by Quinn and his IRA friends.

"Yes, that makes sense. When we discussed changing her major, Cait said she'd found something like that fuel laundering facility."

"Really? Why didn't you mention that before?" I said a little harshly.

He leaned back in his chair, like he'd been slapped. "Uh, I don't know. I didn't see how it was relevant."

Not relevant? I leaned forward, getting ready to let him have it. If we'd known that earlier, it might have taken us in a completely different direction.

Sam nudged me with her leg, reminding me that we needed this guy and I shouldn't go all nasty Jesse on his ass.

I took a deep breath and leaned back. "You said your research focus was on the intersection of gangs and paras?"

He nodded, looking a little afraid to speak.

"So you know who Danny Ryan is?"

"Of course. He's the most influential crime boss in Ireland. At least when it comes to drugs. And, of course, money laundering to deal with all of the cash he brings in."

"We believe he's working with the IRA on something big. Would that be odd for him?"

"No, Danny Ryan's organization distributes all over the island." Jarlath was looking a little more comfortable now that I was speaking more gently to him.

What a wuss.

He continued, "That includes Northern Ireland. And he works with all of the paras—the IRA splinter groups, as well as the unionist groups—along with smaller dealers and distributors."

"Who are the other players in the drug game?"

"There are three families. Ryan is the biggest, he controls about half of the cocaine that comes into the island." That went along with what Gideon had told me. "The Meany and Bolan families split the other half."

"Where do they work?"

"As far as I know, Ryan is strong in Limerick, Dublin, Cork... he distributes in Northern Ireland and has recently taken over most of Sligo. Meany operates in Galway and Donegal, and he used to have the Sligo business, but Ryan has been moving in on that. Bolan is the smallest player...he works primarily in Northern Ireland and along the border. They each bring large shipments of drugs into the country, then distribute to those regions, to the lower-level tiers of distributors. The distributors sell it to the dealers to sell on the streets. Of course, it gets cut multiple times, so whatever they start with gets multiplied by eight to ten times with fillers."

"How do they get drugs into the country?"

"Historically, they bring it via boats of all kinds—trawlers, fishing boats, cruise ships, basically whatever floats—through the major harbors. But the gardaí have been cracking down on that, so they've been getting more creative. Ireland has over three thousand kilometers of coastline, and the guards can't watch all of it all of the time. They're starting to bring it ashore in more remote locations. Getting it ashore is the obviously the tough part. Once it's through the port, harbor, or wherever—"

"Wherever?"

"As I said, the ports are cracking down, so they've been bringing it in at other points on the coast. They don't need a harbor. Small boats can bring it right up to the shore. Anyway, once they get it ashore, it's just a matter of splitting it up and shipping it to each of their territories for distribution."

"How much cocaine comes in to Ireland each year?"

"No one knows for sure. Last year, the gardaí seized over fifty million euros' worth of cocaine in the Republic alone. Note that this is just what was *seized*. If we assume that ninety percent of it gets through, we're talking about hundreds of millions of euros' worth. And this is the bulk value. After it gets cut, the street value ends up being over seventy euro per gram."

Holy hell. This was hundreds of millions of dollars. "So with this much money, there must be conflict between the gangs."

He laughed grimly. "Of course. They're constantly trying to take territory from each other. And the younger lieutenants want to make a name for themselves, and they can get very aggressive. And violent. When someone inevitably dies because someone else wanted a little more of the pie, it sets off a sequence of killing, revenge for that killing, and so on. It gets bloody very quickly, and once it starts, the revenge cycle can go on for years, even decades. But the conflicts aren't just between the gangs. More and more, the paras are getting involved in the drug trade. It's too lucrative for them to leave it alone. In some cases, they work cooperatively with the gangs. In others, they try to keep the whole thing—the supply chain, as well as distribution—to themselves. As you might imagine, the gangs don't look kindly upon paras encroaching on their territory. Either way, once the paras get involved, that opens up a whole new set of opportunities for conflict. All of these groups have cultures of retaliatory and escalating violence. And that's not even considering the enmity between the two para sides—unionists and republicans. That brings in a whole other facet of built-in animosity."

"Isn't all of this violence bad for business?"

Jarlath nodded his head. "Yes. That's why the smart organizations, the bigger ones, learn to avoid it, if at all possible. Too much killing gets the gardaí involved, and none of them want that."

"What would cause one of the bigger players to kill someone?" I was thinking about the bodies they'd found in the bog.

"Like I said, it could be a lower-level person in the organization who's out of control. If so, he or, rarely, she would be dealt with harshly. It could also signal that one of the groups is making a move to take over more territory. It's hard to be sure."

Time to get to the point. "We know Danny Ryan is planning some big operation and believe it's going to happen in the next couple of days, probably in Sligo. We also think he's working with some IRA guys. Any idea what that could be about?"

Jarlath leaned back in his chair, looking up at the ceiling. "I'm not sure. He is, of course, involved in drugs, but I don't know why he'd do something like that in Sligo, of all places. His base of operations is Limerick. And he only just recently started to take over the Sligo area, and Teagan is a relatively new lieutenant." He shook his head. "No, it's not drug-related. You know, he has his hand in a lot of other things. Maybe it's related to money laundering. Or smuggling. Sligo is close to the border."

"You seem very sure of that." As was typical of academics, whenever he was asked to speculate, Jarlath had been couching his remarks with *likely* and *probably* and *might*. I'd learned to do that myself as a PhD student, and that the only appropriate answer to any question was, "It depends." But he'd said definitively that it wasn't drug related. How could he know that?

"Well, uh, it's just that Sligo is a really out-of-the-way place. It's unlikely."

"What about human trafficking?" I asked, remembering the club where we'd met Caoimhe.

"Even more unlikely. Those businesses are generally operated by immigrants, usually of Eastern European origin. And I've not heard anything that indicates Ryan is involved in that. Is there anything else I can help you with?" He seemed to be in more of a hurry now.

"Yes, what can you tell us about tiger kidnappings?"

"Well, tiger kidnappings are basically money makers for the paras. They kidnap someone of means, demand a ransom, and hold them hostage until it's paid."

"We know that part. Can you tell us anything else? Any other details of how these things work?"

"I write about that extensively." He looked around on his desk and picked up a paper and gave it to me. "Here, you can read it," he said, looking at his watch.

"Spatial Patterns in Tiger Kidnappings" was ten pages long. "Can you summarize it for us?" I didn't need to look at another one of his boring papers.

He sighed. "Among other things, the kidnappings usually only involve a few people. One or two to do the kidnapping and transport to the storage location, and one, as needed, to keep an eye on the victim until the ransom is paid. Usually, the storage location is close by, in territory that's known to the kidnappers. This is particularly true here in the Republic, where the kidnappings are more often conducted by gangs rather than by paras as in the north. The gangs are less organized and confident about the process, so rely more heavily on familiarity in choosing their abduction and hostage storage locations." He started to pack up his briefcase. "You really should just read the paper. It goes into detail about the distance-decay function." Without looking at me, he said, "Do you think this is what happened to Cait?"

"We don't know. Maybe."

"If so, it's a good thing."

"A good thing?"

He looked up at me. "Yes. As a matter of course, they don't

usually kill or even harm their hostages. It defeats the purpose. If they did that, no one would trust them, which would make it harder in the future to extort ransom money from people."

"Yeah. The only thing is, the Gallaghers don't really have much money."

"Oh. Well, then maybe not. Tiger kidnappings are purely a financial thing." He closed his briefcase and stood up. "Is there anything else I can help you with?"

"You don't happen to know a Liam Gilmartin, do you?"

I'd thrown it out as a flier, but Jarlath's face turned white. He looked like he was going to be sick. "Uh...no."

"Are you sure?" Jesus, he was a bad liar. I wondered if I should call him on it.

"Yes, definitely." He looked at his watch. "If we're done, I have some other things I need to attend to."

"Okay. Well, thanks for your time."

He didn't look up as we left his office. I closed the door behind us. Through the window on the door, I saw him pick up his phone.

TWENTY-SEVEN

"Is there anyone in this fucking country who isn't hiding something?" I said to Sam as I pulled out of the university parking lot.

"You definitely hit a sore spot."

"I don't know what his deal is, but I'm going to ask Gideon to look into him too." My mind was running in high gear now. "Can you give him a call?"

"You're thinking of something. What is it?" she said as she punched in his number.

I waved at her to wait, and when he got on the line, put my hand out for the phone.

"Hey, Gideon...a few days ago they found two bodies in a bog a little south east of Sligo. Slieveward Bog. Can you find out for me who they were?" When we'd learned that the bog bodies weren't female, I hadn't thought anymore about it. Until now, it hadn't seemed important.

"Bog bodies? You mean, those thousand-year-old guys, the ones that are really well preserved?"

"Yeah, but more recent. Like, recently killed recent."

"Oh, okay, sure. Hang on." He'd been in bed. I heard him get up and walk to his desk, and then fast typing. "According to the gardaí, one was Kevin Larkin and the other was Ciaran Beamish. Do either of those names mean anything to you?"

"Larkin is a local drug dealer, if it's the same Larkin Paddy Feeney mentioned. I haven't heard of the other guy."

"Let me check." A minute later he came back. "Ciaran Beamish has been arrested several times for drug dealing."

"Cocaine?"

"Yes."

"In Sligo?"

"No, some place called Letterkenny."

"Letterkenny? Where's that?"

"It's north of you. It looks like the largest city in Donegal County."

"Okay, thanks, Gideon."

"What's going on? You're staying away from that Gilmartin guy, right? Those IRA dudes are dangerous."

"I know, I've already run into some of them. I'm being careful. See ya."

I was feeling excited. Things were starting to click into place. I handed Sam her phone.

"Are you going to share?" she asked.

"Those bodies they pulled out of the bog when we first arrived in Sligo? They were both low-level drug dealers. One from Sligo, and one from Letterkenny."

"And you think that's related to Ryan's upcoming operation? Drug dealing is a dangerous life. It doesn't necessarily have anything to do with Ryan."

"Yes. But don't you think it's a big coincidence that shortly before his big operation in Sligo, two drug dealers in the area turn up in a *bog*? This wasn't some bar fight that got out of hand. They were murdered and disposed of by someone who was thoughtful about getting rid of them."

I was sure of it. "And I don't care what Jarlath said, I think this whole thing is all about drugs. And I think Jarlath does too. Did you see his face when he told us it's not about drugs? Dude's a terrible liar."

"I find that somewhat comforting, given what he does for a living."

We were back on the N17 that would take us to Sligo. I was starting to really enjoy the long stretches of green between towns. "Maybe Ryan, or someone who works for Ryan, killed them. Maybe Liam did it. We already know he has no problem kidnapping people. But it doesn't matter. The question is *why*."

Sam pursed her lips, something she often did while she was thinking. "Okay. Let's suppose you're right, that they were killed by someone with an agenda. But Jarlath said that Bolan runs the drugs in Donegal. So why would Ryan go to the trouble of killing a couple of low-level dealers, one of which isn't even in his sphere of influence?"

I was great at reading people, telling when they were lying or hiding something, and no one could match my gift for catching details. But when it came to people's behavior and their motivations, Sam was the master. I waited for her to answer her own question.

She was nodding as she worked it out in her head. "For the same reason he does everything. Because they're interfering in his business."

"Okay. So, how could a couple of low-level dealers interfere in Ryan's business when his business isn't even in those areas?"

She snapped her fingers. "Because he *wants* to do business in that area. Ryan is expanding."

That made sense. "We know that Ryan has about half of the drug business on the island. That means half of the drug dealers, the guys on the streets distributing it, and their suppliers are getting it from someone other than him."

Sam was energized now too. "And Ryan is the kind of man who wants it all. But why would he bother killing two low-level drug dealers? It's not like they're in charge of anything other than taking the drugs and putting them in the hands of addicts."

"Yes, but remember what Jarlath said. Any kind of killing of the families or the paras sets off a cascading wave of revenge murders. But no one cares enough to start revenge killing if a couple of low-level dealers get whacked."

"But that still leaves us with, why bother killing them?"

I could feel things slipping into place. "Suppose Ryan's got a big deal coming up, one that will give him control of most or all of the drugs on the island."

She frowned. "The whole island?"

"Sure, why not? He's already got connections in Northern Ireland. And we know he's working with Liam, who's from there. And it's not like the border is hermetically sealed. In that scenario, what do you think he'd do with any dealers who refused to get their drugs from him instead of their previous suppliers?"

"He might use them to send a message to the others. 'Buy from me, or else.' And if they didn't..."

"He'd kill them and have their bodies thrown in a bog. This way he avoids a retaliatory assassination war between the gangs."

She'd been looking out the window but turned to me. "And the dealers are caught in the middle."

"Exactly. The dealers either stay with their current supplier, and run the risk of Ryan's murder squad, or they jump ship."

This felt right. And it explained a lot.

"So where does that leave us? If we think Ryan is consolidating all of the drug business into his organization?"

I slowed down to avoid a stray sheep that had made it past one of the limestone walls and onto the road. It was a good thing I was driving; if it had been Sam, we'd be having mutton for dinner. "Well, we know this would mean he's got to be bringing in a lot of drugs. A *lot* of drugs. And both he and Liam were warning us off for a few more days. I think they're in the process of bringing a shit ton of drugs into the country. They're doing it near Sligo, and it's happening soon. Once the drugs are on land and on their way, then it's a matter of transport, and we already know that the police in Northern Ireland and the Irish gardaí aren't staffed to deal with it once it's in the communities. They have to try to control it at points of entry."

"Like Sligo Harbor?"

"Yes. But I don't think they'd try to bring it in there. Let's face it, there are thousands of miles of coastline in Ireland, and Jarlath told us most of it isn't watched. They're probably bringing it in somewhere off the coast near Sligo, then splitting it up for distribution into the territories."

"Why Sligo?"

"Because national law enforcement has gotten pretty good at stopping this shit from coming into Dublin, and they've made a lot of busts off the coast of Cork. They have tons of law enforcement there looking for that stuff. We're on the other side of the island, where there are way fewer police, fewer eyes watching." The more I talked, the more I felt sure about this. "And Teagan...did you see her when we met with her and Ryan? She's desperate for his approval." I was an expert on daddy issues, and she had them in spades. "Sligo is her territory. I'll bet she's convinced him to do this in her region. It's her way of impressing him."

She nodded. "I think you're right. But how does this help us? We don't know when, or where, this is all going to happen."

"No. But remember when I talked to Harry, he said I needed to stay away for a few days. I think that means the gardaí must have some idea what's going on and when it's going to happen. They might know where too. If that's true, we might be better off just going to them right away about this rather than waiting for Liam to call us. At this point, it doesn't look like he's going to."

She was frowning again. "Go to them with what?"

"I wonder if they even know Liam's involved? And that he's working with Ryan, and that he's the one responsible for Cait getting kidnapped? If not, it might help their investigation. And we know where he hangs out." It was too bad I'd have to give up the shebeen. But it was a sacrifice I was willing to make to get Cait back. His buddies could find another house to drink in. "Maybe something we share will help them. Liam knows where she is. If he gets arrested, he'll have to trade that info for a lesser sentence, right?"

Sam looked skeptical. "That's a lot of ifs."

"I know, but it's all we have to go on. Let's go to the station and talk to one of the Sean Murphys."

"Not Harry?"

"No. He's from the PSNI. He might know about what Ryan's doing, but it would be the Sligo gardaí who will be the ones to deal with it."

I stepped on the gas, racing the rest of the way into town.

I felt good. In my gut, I knew we were right. We were getting closer to Cait.

As we approached the station, traffic was snarled and we came to a complete stop a few blocks away. We parked on the street and got out to walk the rest of the way.

Gardaí cars with flashing lights were blocking Chapel and Abbey Streets, and officers were putting police tape across the sidewalks. Some people were moving toward the barricades, and others were running away from them.

I grabbed a man who was moving to the barricade. "What's going on?"

"There's been a bomb threat at the Abbey."

TWENTY-EIGHT

The garda station was only three blocks from the Abbey, and the area was in chaos. We pushed our way to the barricade on Abbey Street. It looked like every single uniformed garda was on the street. This was a big deal. As Sligo's oldest landmark, it would be all hands on deck to protect the Abbey. They'd also called in the Special Response Unit. One of them in a puffy Michelin man outfit and helmet got out of the back of a truck across the street from the Abbey and walked into the open courtyard near the tower.

It was like swimming upstream to get into the garda station. Uniformed officers were still rushing out the door. We wove our way through them and into the lobby.

I went to the counter and cringed when I saw O'Fenton, who apparently never went home.

"Can I help—?" His eyes narrowed. "Oh. It's you."

"We need to speak to Sean Murphy."

"Which one?"

"Either one."

"It's not my job to choose who you want to talk to."

"It doesn't matter. I just need to see either one of them."

"You have to pick one."

I sighed. "Okay. The older one."

"Chief Superintendent Murphy?"

"Yes."

"He's not here."

Argh. "Okay. Then can I please speak to Officer Murphy?"

"There is no Officer Murphy."

Son of a bitch. How long would it take to pull this guy's mustache out a single hair at a time? "Okay. Detective Sergeant Murphy."

"He's not here either."

Sam put her hand on my shoulder, the only thing that kept me from throwing my body against the plexiglass window. She said, "They must all be out dealing with the bomb threat. Do you know anyone else?"

"Mullarkey. But he's completely useless. And I doubt he'll talk to me. We didn't exactly leave things friendly the last time I was here."

"What about Harry?"

"Good idea."

I turned back to O'Fenton "Is Harry Dick here?"

"We have no Harry Dicks here." It took him a moment to realize what he'd said, then his face reddened.

I smirked. Harry Dick was the gift that keeps on giving.

"Chief Inspector Dick. The guy from Northern Ireland."

"Can I ask what this is regarding?"

"You can ask." He scowled. Point to me.

"What is this regarding?"

"I said you could ask. I didn't say I'd tell you." *Try to mess with me, motherfucker, and see what happens.*

He frowned sourly. "Is he expecting you? If you haven't noticed, we're a little busy at the moment."

"Look, counter boy, tell him Jesse O'Hara has information for him about a very large drug operation. He'll want to talk to me. And if you don't tell him, and your bosses find out I had this information and you kept it from them, you're going to be spending the rest of your career behind this little window, dealing with people like me."

He reluctantly picked up his phone, spoke for a few moments, and put it down. "Chief Inspector Dick will see you shortly."

"Thank you," I said with as much unappreciation as I could muster.

Sam and I waited, standing against the wall to be out of the way of the stream of officers still leaving the station.

Sam looked toward the exit. "Why would someone want to blow up the Abbey?"

"No idea. Let's hope it's just a threat. That place is over eight hundred years old."

We weren't waiting long before the door to the back opened and Harry gestured us in. We followed him through the main office to one of the hallways. The open area was almost empty of gardaí, all of them presumably out dealing with the bomb threat. The only one remaining in the room was Mullarkey. He'd been left to man the phones, probably as punishment for losing the CCTV video at the bus station and generally fucking up the investigation into Cait's disappearance. Or being drunk on the job. Or being all together massively incompetent. He stared at us as we walked through the main office and into a hallway.

Harry motioned us into one of the rooms. The small room had a desk covered with folders and papers, a few file cabinets, and some chairs. He followed us in and closed the door, sat down behind the desk, and gestured for us to sit in the two chairs on the other side without speaking a word.

"Thanks for seeing us. We—"

"I told you to stay away from any investigating for a few days. What part of that was unclear?"

I'd had about all I could take of officious officers. "Do you have any actual jurisdiction here? I don't think we're under any obligation to follow your orders."

Sam nudged me with her knee, a gentle reminder that now

might not be the opportune time to do the "you're not the boss of me" thing with Harry Dick.

I got a handle on my anger and tried again. "Um, yes, but we've uncovered something important. We believe that Danny Ryan is in the process of consolidating the drug business on the island and that in a day or two there will be a large shipment of drugs coming in somewhere along the coast near Sligo, or possibly Donegal."

"Well, that narrows it down to Sligo and the Irish county with the most coastline of any on the island. Thanks for that critical piece of unactionable intel." He was completely unimpressed with my information. They must have already known that much. If so, it confirmed my suspicions.

I tried to stay calm and ignore his sarcasm. "We believe Ryan is behind the murders of Kevin Larkin and Ciaran Beamish."

"How did you come across *this* information?" That didn't seem to surprise him either. He was more interested in how I knew it than what I knew.

"We also know that Liam Gilmartin is with the IRA, and he's working with Ryan on this operation. And that he's the one who gave the order to kidnap Cait."

He frowned and leaned forward slightly. "How do you know *that*?"

Okay, making progress. This clearly was new information to him. "Does it matter? You can pick him up and get him to tell you where Cait is."

"Have you talked with anyone else about this?" He looked down at his desk and shuffled some folders nervously.

"No." He was rattled. Why?

Harry frowned. "Why didn't you come to us earlier with this?"

"We just found out about Liam being with the IRA."

Harry raised his eyebrows at my familiar use of his first name.

"And that reminds me, we're also going to need protection until you catch him."

"Protection? Why?"

"We...uh...left a message with him."

"Who?"

"Liam. We told him we'd go to the gardaí and tell them everything we knew about him and Ryan's operation unless he told us where Cait was. He hasn't called back, so we assume he's not interested in telling us. And that we might be in a little bit of danger."

"You *threatened* him? A man you believe is with the IRA?" Harry was looking at us now in disbelief.

"Well, when you say it like that, it does sound like that might not have been the best decision."

He looked up at the ceiling. "Come with me." He got up and moved swiftly from around the desk.

Now we were getting somewhere. Harry was moving with purpose. We followed him back to the front reception.

Turning to O'Fenton, he said, "Under no circumstances allow these two back into the station. If they show up again, call me and I'll deal with them. If I'm not here, have them arrested."

"I guess this means protection is out of the question," I said to Harry's back as he walked through the door to the offices.

O'Fenton gave us a small wave. "Buh-bye."

"Is there anyone here you *haven't* antagonized?" Sam said once we were outside.

We both knew the answer to that, and I ignored the question. "Harry seemed to already know everything we were telling him."

"Well, the gardaí know something. The last time you were here he did tell you to stay out of things for a few days."

"I know. I was just hoping we'd found something they could use." There was nothing left to do now.

"Where are we going now?" asked Sam.

"I don't know. We can't go to the shebeen." Even I wasn't stupid enough to head back there and into the arms of the guy who might be interested in killing us. "Let's go back to the Gallaghers." Maybe Rose's magical tea could help us out again.

Two news vans were parked on the sidewalk in front of the Abbey Street barricade, reporters standing in front of cameras talking into microphones. We walked back to our car, fighting crowds along the way. I got behind the wheel and tried to leave. We had to wait over ten minutes for a space to form in the crowds that were in the street.

We finally made it out of the area around the Abbey, and I took the road to the Gallaghers. After a few blocks, I turned around, and started driving in the opposite direction.

"This isn't the way to their house," Sam said.

"I know. But someone's following us."

TWENTY-NINE

"We can't go back to the Gallaghers. If someone's tailing us, we don't want to drag whoever it is back to their house. They've got enough trouble in their lives."

I'd seen and read enough spy shit to have an idea of how to elude a tail. I drove around for twenty minutes, waiting at lights and then going just before they turned, turning down alleys, backtracking. Eventually, I made it to the Sligo Racecourse. There were no races today, and the parking lot gate was closed, so I stopped the car on the side of the road in front of it.

There was one street that ran alongside the facility and an empty field across the street. No one would be able to get too close without us seeing them.

After several minutes, I said, "I think I lost him."

I was relieved we'd lost the tail, but worried. Who was following us? Liam? One of Ryan's guys? Either way, it wasn't a promising development.

"Sam, we need to leave."

"Leave Sligo?"

"No, the Gallaghers. If whoever was following us is going to do something violent, I don't want it anywhere near the family." I unbuckled my seatbelt and leaned back in the seat. "Let's wait a few minutes to be sure we lost him, then go back there and get our stuff."

The fact that we were being followed meant we were getting close. But close to what? I had a familiar nagging feeling. I was missing something.

Liam had sent me to Galway to get me out of the way while he worked on his fuel laundering and the operation with Ryan. It made sense that he hadn't wanted me poking around in his business. And he hadn't wanted Cait poking around either, so he'd either had her picked up and stashed somewhere, or he'd killed her. I was pretty sure he hadn't killed her. He just didn't strike me as a violent man. Or maybe he had, and it had been an accident. That wasn't a useful train of thought, so I let it go. The thing that was nagging at me was why he had been running a fuel laundering operation at all.

"Sam, why do you think Liam was involved in fuel laundering?"

She'd been looking out the window, lost in her own thoughts. "What? To make money."

"I know, but why *now*? Ryan's drug deal has had to be in the works for some time. Why would Liam risk getting caught for something that amounted to chump change when he had something much bigger in the works?"

"I don't know. Maybe he likes to keep busy."

"What if he did it to get close to Ryan?"

She turned to me. "I don't think so. You saw Ryan's reaction when he heard Teagan was skimming money from them. And that Quinn and his boys were working on that instead of his business. Ryan's not a fan of the small shite."

"No, I mean, what are the chances that someone could work an operation like that in Sligo without Teagan finding out about it?"

"Close to zero, I'd imagine."

"Exactly. Anyone in this town who's met Teagan knows she'd be all over that shit in a minute. So what if Liam set it up for that reason, to get her attention? Maybe she was his way to get in with Ryan?"

I'd been operating under the assumption that Liam knew Ryan first and then met Teagan. But what if it was the other way around? Dating the boss's daughter was one way to get in his good graces. And we knew Liam was a ladder climber. It was no secret that Ryan had been working on something big. Even the gardaí knew about it. Liam probably did too, and wanted in on the action.

The other thing that was bugging me was Jarlath. What the fuck was up with him? He clammed up the minute I mentioned Liam. "And what about Jarlath? He—"

My train of thought was cut off by the sound of a gunshot. We both jumped at the sound of a bullet hitting stone, a sound I was quite familiar with by now. Out of the corner of my eye, I saw chips flying off of the wall next to the racecourse gate. We both ducked down low in the front seat. Another shot rang out, this one hitting the stone wall on the other side of the gate.

"I guess we didn't lose him," I said.

"Yes. What a surprise that the IRA and a drug lord would want to retaliate for us interfering in their business."

We were leaning down in the front seat, our faces inches from each other, and I was surprised to see she looked angry. "Are you mad?"

I'd rarely seen her mad, and never at me. Surprised, mildly annoyed, dismayed, sometimes appalled, often mortified, and frequently embarrassed, but never mad.

"Mad doesn't *begin* to cover it. What are we doing, Jesse?" she said in a vehement, angry whisper. "It was one thing to do your tunnel vision, Tommy Lee Jones federal marshal thing when you were going after crooked businessmen and their accounting fraud. It's a completely different matter when you're dealing with murderers."

"Nice *Fugitive* reference."

She glared at me. "We've been warned by *everyone* we've met to stay out of this, that it's way over our heads, and it's dangerous.

And guess what? They were right. Now we're going to be executed next to the Sligo Racecourse. *Happy?*" She was almost yelling.

I was speechless and could feel tears welling up. Being insulted, threatened, beaten, lit on fire, and shot at were nothing compared to enduring the wrath of Sam. I resisted the urge to get out of the car and take a bullet in the heart. It would have felt better than this.

A few more shots slammed into the walls on either side of us. Then I heard the sound of tires squealing. I raised my head over the dash, then dropped back down.

"At least whoever it was is a really bad shot. That stone wall is at least fifteen feet away from us."

She looked up but didn't say anything, her lips pursed. She wasn't ready to stop being mad at me yet.

"It must have been a warning." I sat up slowly and looked around. "Which begs the question, wouldn't you think by now they'd be trying to take us out for real?"

"You sound disappointed," she said, still under the dash.

"No, it's just that, like you said, we've been getting warnings since we've been here. There was the note on the car, and we got some pretty explicit 'get out of town' messaging from Ryan and Liam. If it was one of them, do you think by now we'd be getting warning shots? I mean, these were the same guys who probably put two bodies in the bog."

I'd been annoying the hell out of them for days. There was no way they could be that patient. Unless...

"Sam, why do we think it is that Cait was kidnapped?"

She finally sat up. "Because she did the same thing you did. She stumbled upon Liam's fuel laundering operation." Her voice had lost its edge. Apparently, I'd been forgiven. I felt a wave of relief.

"Exactly. But they didn't take her then. They didn't even know she was there. She went back to school and wasn't picked up by Liam's guys until she came back to Sligo."

"Yes, so?"

"So...how did Liam even know she found the fuel laundering site?"

Sam's eye widened. "She changed her major. We were wondering why. She must have told Jarlath about what she'd seen."

I nodded. "Yeah. Jarlath told Liam. It's the only thing that makes sense. And it explains why Jarlath looked so sick when we met with him. He realized he was the one who set her kidnapping in motion."

"But why? Why would he? Do you think he's working with the IRA?"

"No, of course not. He—" *Holy shit.* I put the key in the ignition. "Let's go."

"Are you crazy? Whoever it is could still be out there."

"He left. And we're fine." I started up the car, smiling. "Really, I don't think we're in any danger."

She crossed her arms and leaned back. "You'll understand if I don't entirely believe you."

"No, really, I'm sure of it."

She looked skeptical.

"Look, I know I put us in a lot of bad spots, and I'm really sorry. But I won't do that again." She raised her eyebrows.

"At least not in this case. Really."

We both knew I would do it again, but she let it go, and asked, "Where are we going?"

"To the shebeen. We need to find Liam."

"*What?* He might be the one who was just shooting at us. And I thought we were avoiding him."

"He wasn't, and we were." I put the car into gear and pulled out onto the road.

"Jesse, are you sure this is the right thing to do?"

"Trust me."

"Okay." She buckled her seatbelt. That was it. Her trust in me was absolute. Sometimes to her detriment. But not this time. "Are you going to tell me what this is about?"

"Sligo is a small town."

THIRTY

We drove to the shebeen and waited outside a few houses down. We didn't have to wait long. Ten minutes after we arrived, Liam walked out with Irish Kenny, Lurch, and Firbis. The three men got into a small truck and drove off. I waited until they were out of sight, then got out of my car and walked toward Liam as he was opening the door to his car.

He saw me and pulled out his phone. He was hanging up when I made it over to him. He looked at me and didn't say anything.

"You have some explaining to do."

"I don't owe you anything. You've no idea what's going on."

"I think I do."

He closed his door. "Not here."

Sam and I followed him as he walked across the lawn to the side of the house. He stopped and leaned against the wall, crossing his arms.

"She saw you, didn't she?"

"Who?"

"Cait. Give it up Liam, or whatever your name is."

He stared at me for a moment. Then he said, "Liam is fine for now."

"But it is detective, isn't it?"

Sam's head whipped around and looked at me, then at Liam.

He nodded. "I work for the GNDOCB, the Garda National Drugs and Organised Crime Bureau. Our job is to proactively dismantle organized crime groups, particularly as they relate to drugs."

"And you're working on Danny Ryan's drugs now, aren't you?"

"Yes, for two years." Liam cocked his head. "We've kept this quiet the whole time. Even the Sligo gardaí don't know about it. How did you figure it out?"

"Lots of little pieces. Your fast climb up the crime ladder, seemingly out of nowhere, in Belfast crime circles. The shooting at us today. If you were really working with Ryan, whoever was shooting at us wouldn't have missed by that much. The kicker was realizing that Jarlath has been feeding you information and let you know about Cait finding the fuel laundering operation. He's not a criminal, and there's no way he would have told you that if he thought it would put Cait in danger."

"She's not in danger. But I couldn't let her destroy two years of undercover work."

"Whatever. Where is she?"

"I honestly don't know. But once this is over, we'll take her back to her family."

"You don't know? Bullshit."

"Firbis and Quinn picked her up and were told to put her somewhere for safekeeping. They were given strict instructions to make sure she stayed safe."

"And you trust them?"

"They're not going to do anything without me telling them to."

"I don't care. You need to return her *now*. Her family is devastated."

"I can't. Not right now. Soon."

My face was set in a Teagan-esque mask of anger.

"Look, Jesse, this operation is huge. We're less than twelve hours away from taking down the biggest crime boss in the entire island. Daniel Ryan has been operating in Ireland for over twenty years. He's responsible for the deaths of hundreds of people, thousands if you count the lives he's ruined with drugs. And it's not just drugs. He murders anyone who gets in his way or he perceives as a threat. He's amassed enough money that he can buy gardaí, judges, elected officials. He's an existential threat to this country."

"So *arrest* him already."

"We've tried. But he's extremely careful, and we've not been able to get anywhere close to him. All of his top people are relatives, and he never does the dirty work himself. We catch them, but when we do, they won't speak against him. Not one. People will rot in prison before they grass him out."

"How does a man like Ryan garner so much loyalty?"

"It's not loyalty as much as fear. The last man who was going to testify against him came home to find his family murdered. And then he was beaten to death."

"So what is this big operation he's got going?" I didn't think Liam would tell me, but my curiosity was overcoming my anger.

He surprised me by saying, "There are three major players in Ireland related to drugs. They've operated for years alongside each other. Every now and then one of them gets out of line, an underling tries to take out a rival, and it causes a series of tit-for-tat murders. Then things calm down. About two years ago, we saw signs that Ryan was trying to expand his operations. And not just here but over the whole island, including the north. He's been steadily consolidating power, quietly undermining the other families with targeted assassinations that can't be traced back to him or his people. At the same time, he's been strong-arming the regional dealers to work with him only, or else. Anyone who tries to use other suppliers is threatened. Some have been kneecapped, some killed, some just...disappeared."

We'd been right about what Ryan was doing. It was a small consolation at this point.

"Eighteen months ago, his oldest son, Daniel Jr., was killed by the Bolan crime family. Daniel Jr. was in charge of the western region, Sligo, Galway, everything northwest of Limerick. When he died, Daniel Ryan put his daughter Teagan in charge of that region. You've met her."

"Yeah...my doppelganger."

He nodded. "A year ago, I was sent to Sligo, undercover, to see if I could get close to her and get actionable intelligence on his operations. She's young and relatively inexperienced but aggressive and eager to show that she's up to the task. And she's one hundred percent loyal to her father. In order to gain her trust, she had to view me as a real part of the underworld. I'd been undercover in Belfast for a year before I came down here to set up the fuel laundering operation and get her attention. I started hanging out at the shebeen, mingling with IRA supporters. That's where I met Quinn. I threw some money around and intimated I was tied into one of the new IRA splinter groups. They're so fractured at this point, it wasn't a hard sell."

"So I've heard."

"Quinn had been working fuel laundering and other smuggling operations, primarily cigarettes, for one of the IRA factions in Belfast. The PSNI was getting on to him, so he came down to Sligo to lay low for a while. He didn't have any particular loyalty to his own IRA faction. For most of these guys, they don't give a whit about politics, or a united Ireland, or anything else other than lining their own pockets. It was easy to recruit him to work for what he thought was my own IRA cell. It worked like a charm. Quinn brought a couple of his mates from Belfast and found Firbis in Sligo. We set up the fuel laundering operation, and within a short period of time, we had Teagan's goons coming around demanding protection money. She couldn't let us do that kind of business under her nose without taking a cut, that would make her look weak. The fact that I was tied into Quinn gave me instant credibility as a criminal. Eventually, she demanded a meet.

Since I was running an apparently successful operation, she viewed me as a valuable asset in the region. From there we developed a...relationship."

"You mean you've been boning her."

He hesitated, then, "Yes. And she's come to trust me. It was through the course of our...interactions...that I found out about the details of Ryan's operation. And she gave me an in to him."

"It looks like she gave you an *in* to her too."

He rolled his eyes. "Teagan's eager to prove herself. She's been aggressive and is trying to show her father she has the chops to take over the family business when it comes time."

"So the idea of bringing his drugs through this region was her idea?" said Sam.

"Yes. It's actually a pretty good plan. For a long time, most of the drugs coming into the country came through Dublin and then Cork. But the gardaí have been successful at stopping a lot of that smuggling and those areas are well covered now with law enforcement. But out here, it's much easier to stash a shipment offshore until the time is right, then bring it over. Ryan's shipment is sitting out there right now, just off the coast a little northwest of Sligo town. When the tides go low, he's bringing it ashore on the beach at Streedagh Point, then taking it all to a rendezvous spot near Benbulbin Forest. It's secluded, and there won't be any gardaí around."

"Why are you so sure? It's not that far from Sligo. Won't a bunch of guys in vans or trucks or whatever going to that place be suspicious?"

"Did you happen to notice the bomb threat at the Abbey?"

I nodded.

"There's no bomb. But every garda in the area will be looking for one."

Damn. Ryan was thorough.

"This will be the largest amount of coke ever to be brought into Ireland. Once he gets it ashore, he'll hand it out at the rendezvous point to his lieutenants of each of his regions and a few distributors in the north. The IRA—"

"You mean you."

"Yes. And the UDF. After it gets distributed and goes on the road, we lose the chance to implicate Ryan. But I've got men surrounding the Benbulbin Forest, ready to move in on my signal as soon as Ryan, his lieutenants, and his drugs are there." Liam's eyes sparkled. "We're going to take down the entire family and distribution network in one fell swoop."

I wasn't happy with what had happened with Cait, but this plan made sense. It was a great opportunity. "Is Harry in on all of this?"

"Harry?"

"Inspector Dick."

Liam nodded. "He is now. But not at first. We were a little too successful with the fuel laundering, and the Sligo garda contacted the PSNI through the Cross Border Policing Strategy to bring him down and help them eliminate the operation. It was a hassle...we had to keep moving the location of it. But in a way it was successful—"

"The fact that the PSNI and the gardaí were working together to shut you down made Teagan trust you even more."

"Exactly. But he was getting too close, so I had to bring him in on the operation. Up to then, we'd also kept the Sligo garda completely in the dark. I didn't know who I could trust. Given the amount of money the Ryan family throws around, it was a safe bet that someone in the garda was in their pockets."

"Like Mullarkey?"

He frowned. "No. Why do you think that?"

"Because he screwed up the investigation into Cait's disappearance. He lost the CCTV tapes, for one thing."

Liam shook his head. "You've got it all wrong. Through the course of his investigation into Cait's disappearance, Mullarkey came across the fuel laundering site and then the tapes that showed her being taken at the bus station. I had to bring him in on our plans so he would stop digging. He knows we were the ones who took Cait."

"Wait...you're telling me that he voluntarily took the rap for pretending to lose the CCTV tapes? And basically advertised to everyone he works with that he's completely incompetent? Why would he do that?"

Liam shifted his feet and looked down. "We...uh...gave him an incentive. But—"

"What kind of incentive?"

"You have to understand. We needed him to step into line or he would have blown the whole thing up. I couldn't let that happen. The national office told him if he didn't suspend his investigation and keep quiet about our work, he would be fired and lose his pension and possibly be locked up for interfering with a national investigation."

So Mullarkey wasn't a bad guy after all. They'd offered to let him keep his career, his income, and support his family as long as he would let himself look completely incompetent and deal with Cait's grief-stricken family. No wonder he'd been drinking. I could feel the weight of Sam's "I told you so" stare. She'd been right about Mullarkey. It wasn't much of a surprise. While I was unerringly right in knowing when people were lying to or hiding something from me, I couldn't see into their souls the way she could.

I'd need to work on that. At some later date.

"Why did you have to kidnap Cait?" I thought I knew the answer, but wanted to hear it from him.

"Cait stumbled upon our fuel laundering site back in November. She went back to her professor to talk about it."

"Jarlath."

"Yes, he's an expert on the intersection between gangs and paramilitaries. He's been working with us for years and is one of the only civilians who knows about me and this operation. He called me after Cait came to see him. She was getting ready to go to the gardaí. I told Quinn and Firbis to pick her up when she came back for the holiday. They went to Paddy to get information about when she'd be back and where to pick her up."

I thought back to Firbis leering at me in the warehouse and his excitement at the prospect of doing the same thing to me as the other "hoor." I shuddered. Then I had an even worse thought. "What about Paddy? Did you have him killed?"

"Paddy wasn't supposed to die." Liam looked genuinely remorseful. "Quinn's guys were only supposed to rough him up a bit, to make sure he didn't talk to the gardaí. It got out of hand."

I realized with horror that it was because of me that they'd gone to Paddy to shut him up. I was the one who'd told Liam that Paddy could identify the guys who took Cait.

Liam saw my look and raised his palms. "It's not that big of a loss, is it? Paddy was a whinging little drug addict who sold out his girlfriend to pay off a drug debt. Nobody's loss."

Jesus. "What kind of man *are* you?"

His mouth was set in a grim line. "The kind who cares deeply about his country. Do you know how many people are killed in the drug trade in Ireland every year? How many lives are ruined because of drug addiction? If this shipment comes in and gets distributed the way Ryan intends, he's set up to flood the island with cocaine. Not only that, but he'll make himself truly untouchable. The amount of money and power he'll gain by this...if this goes down, he'll rise to unassailable levels. He'll be able to buy off any judge, pay for any assassination. This goes way beyond a few lowlifes getting knocked off or one missing girl. We know that once this deal is done and he's set up, he'll retire to Spain. We're never going to have a chance like this again.

"Think of it, Jesse. If all of the drugs are consolidated into one man's organization and we get that man, it will cripple the drug industry in Ireland for years, maybe decades. This is our chance to roll up the biggest drug gang in Ireland, all of his distribution channels, and all of his top men."

"And women, right?" I was referring to Teagan.

Liam looked uncomfortable. "Aye, her too." He looked at his watch.

It was great that he was telling me all of this, really filling in the blanks. I wondered why, though. Guilt, maybe? For having Cait taken in the first place? Or maybe he was just really impressed with how we'd figured everything out and was finally treating us with the respect we deserved. It was about damn time.

While we were talking, an old blue sedan pulled up to the curb. It was the same one that had been following us earlier. Mullarkey got out of the car and walked over to us.

"I'm sorry, Jesse, Sam. I have a job to do. And you're in my way," Liam said.

"What the hell is this?"

Mullarkey approached us with two pairs of handcuffs dangling from his hand. "We can do this the hard way or the easy way."

That was why Liam had been standing there talking to us, telling us all about his operation. To give time for Mullarkey to pick us up.

Mullarkey handcuffed me and then did the same to Sam. As far as I knew, she'd never been handcuffed before. I'd no doubt get an earful about it later.

"Do we really need these?" I asked Mullarkey.

He looked at Liam.

"Keep them cuffed until they're in a locked room at the station."

Mullarkey nodded and led us to his car, putting us in the back seat.

I watched Liam get into his car as we drove away.

THIRTY-ONE

Mullarkey walked us in through a side door to the station. I wasn't sure why he didn't use the front entrance, but was relieved I wouldn't have to be exposed to O'Fenton's gloating smirk. He ushered us into the back, past the main area, and to one of the interrogation rooms I'd been in before.

When he turned to leave, I called out, "Hey. Do we really need these on now?"

"No, of course not." He took out his keys and unlocked the cuffs.

As he was walking out the door, he turned and said quietly, "I'm sorry about this."

He really did look sorry. Now that I felt like we were going to get Cait back, I let myself consider Mullarkey's position. He'd basically been blackmailed to drop an investigation, lose evidence, and be made to look like an incompetent fool in front of his boss and his colleagues. He really hadn't had a choice. It was either that or lose his job.

"That's okay, Calbach," I said.

He gave a weak grateful smile and left the room. I heard it lock behind him.

"Now what?" Sam said. "I know you're used to being hand-cuffed and locked up, but this is new for me." I was relieved she didn't seem angry. Likely because we were safely inside a police station.

"Now? I think we just wait." I took one of the seats on the police side of the table. "Liam—or whoever he is—is going to make the bust, roll up all of the bad guys, and then he'll find out where Cait is and bring her back."

"Do you trust him? He didn't seem to be too concerned about her."

"No, but it won't cost him anything. And as mercenary as he is, I doubt he wants the unnecessary death of a young woman on his conscious. What little of one he might have."

Sam looked uncertain, but sat down in one of seats on the perp side of the table.

I leaned back in my chair, folded my arms stiffly across my chest, and lowered my voice as deep as it would go. "So, we hear you've had recent dealings with known horse jerkers. Can you explain yourself?" We needed to do something to pass the time. Might as well play cops and perps, we had the venue free of charge.

"You'll get nothing out of me, copper. I'm no rat," Sam said in a pretty good imitation of James Cagney.

"You're a sucker, mugs."

"All right, it's my rap and I'll take it. But—" Her phone buzzed and she picked it up. "Hello?"

"*Hello?* Who is this?

"*Hello?*" She frowned, listening. Then she put the phone on the table and set it to speaker.

"Who is it?" I said.

She used her hand to shush me and pointed to the phone.

"...the new plan, then?" It was Liam's voice. But he wasn't talking to us.

We heard scraping sounds and a muffled voice. Then Liam's again. "I need to let Quinn and the boys know. Where are we going?"

"They've been told." The second voice was clearer now. It was Teagan.

I reached down and muted the phone. "He must have butt dialed us." We heard a horn. "They're in the car. Probably on their way to the rendezvous point in Benbulbin."

They didn't talk for a while. Then, "Why move the site?" asked Liam.

"He always does this. He sets everything to change at the last minute. Prevents problems." She said something else that we couldn't hear.

"What's wrong, baby?" I recognized Liam's flirty voice. "This is our big score. You should be happy."

"Nothing."

This was cool. We had a live audio link to the biggest drug bust in Irish history. I looked up at Sam, smiling. I hoped they wouldn't stop for a shag. I definitely didn't need to hear that.

She frowned back at me. "Jesse...Liam was setting up for the drug bust. He thought it was going to be at one place and Ryan's moved it. Obviously without telling him."

My smile faded when I realized the implications. "He's got no way to alert his support units that the site's been moved. He's on his own."

"Maybe he called us on purpose. To let us know. So we could tell someone."

She was right. He kept his phone in his pocket and had discretely redialed the most recent number to call for help.

"We need to let Calbach know," Sam said.

"Right." I went over to the door and started banging on it. I kept it up for a solid minute.

I turned to Sam. "I don't think he can hear us. We're way in the back."

"We can't call him...we don't want to hang up on Liam. We may be his only way to communicate."

"Okay. Keep listening, see if you can find out where she's going." I pulled my compact Dangerfield lockpick set out of my boot and went to work on the door.

The concept of lockpicking was simple, but really more art than science. It took years of practice to actually be able to open anything other than the most basic lock. I had that practice, having taken it up as a kid. Then, like now, I'd hated locked doors and the secrets they held.

Even though the garda station had been renovated, they hadn't gone to the trouble of retrofitting interrogation rooms with keycards or number pads. I opened the door in under a minute. We walked out, Sam holding the phone in front of her so we could continue to listen.

The station was almost empty, virtually everyone out dealing with the bomb threat. As far as I could tell, the only people left were Calbach and Harry. We came out of the hallway and into the main room.

Calbach was behind his desk, staring blankly at a bottle and a glass in front of him. The poor guy wasn't even trying to hide it at this point. He saw us and stood up quickly. "You need to go back to the room. I haven't formally arrested you yet, but I will."

"Calbach, stop. You need to hear this."

Sam put the phone down on his desk. There was no conversation coming through at the moment.

He frowned.

"The drug rendezvous site has been moved. Liam didn't know about it. He called us in secret."

He stared at me blankly.

"That means all of the setup he's done, any support he's got planned to move in when the drugs show up, they're at the wrong place. Liam's alone."

His eyes grew wide with understanding. "Where is the new site?"

"We don't know yet. He's in the car with Teagan. We're hoping he can get her to say it." We all stared at the phone. "Who should we tell?"

"I...I don't know. This wasn't a Sligo garda operation. Liam's with the national service. He's working with his own people. Normally, for something like this, he would use the Armed

Support Unit in this region. But this deal is so big, he might have called in the National Emergency Response Unit. The national groups don't keep us in the loop." He said the last part bitterly.

As we were talking, Harry came around the corner and waved at Calbach, then did a double take when he saw us. Calbach motioned him over.

Harry was frowning. "I told you to—"

I cut him off. "Liam's drug rendezvous point has been moved. He's being driven to the new site by Teagan. He's on his own and has no way to contact whoever he's been working with. He called us secretly, I think as a way to contact someone who could send help."

To his credit, Harry adjusted quickly to the situation. "Do you think he's been blown?"

That was a chilling thought. I had no doubt that if Ryan had found out about Liam, his retribution would be horrific. The cost for disloyalty to Danny Ryan was worse than death.

"We don't know. But whoever it was that was going to help him make the bust—"

"Western Region Armed Support Unit."

"They're at the wrong site."

Harry nodded grimly. "They're all gathering around Benbulbin Mountain. They're there, waiting for his signal."

"They're going to be waiting a long time. Is there any way to get word to them?"

Harry looked down at the floor. "Yes, I can go through my contacts at the PSNI. But it will take a while. I have to go to my own service, get it up the chain there, and then they'll reach out to Liam's group in Dublin. But what do we tell them? We don't know where he's going."

"Liam's doing everything he can to get Teagan to say it. We'll know as soon as he does." I turned to Calbach. "Can you get a hold of Murphy—?"

"Which one?"

"The older one. Tell him what's happening and that we might need the Sligo gardaí to help make a drug bust."

"They're busy with the bomb threat."

"It's a fake."

"Are you sure?"

"Yes, one hundred percent positive. Liam told me Ryan did it to make sure the garda would be preoccupied while this was going down."

Calbach nodded, all business now and eager to do something other than be a blackmailed stooge. "I'll tell O'Fenton. He can do a general dispatch. That will be the quickest way."

"Good. Uh...don't tell O'Fenton I'm involved. I don't think it will help."

He nodded and left his desk for the reception area.

"I'll get going with my contacts," Harry said. "And I'm going to drive to Benbulbin on the off chance the support unit will take my word for it." By the way he said it, I didn't think that was likely. He wasn't in the chain of command. "You two stay here, keep monitoring the call, and let me know the minute you hear anything about where they're going." He handed me his card. "Use the cell number. Once we know where the new site is, we'll pass that along to Liam's service so his forces can go to the new rendezvous point."

Harry turned to go to his office. He grabbed his coat and keys and left.

I picked up Sam's phone and walked away from Calbach's desk.

"What are you doing?" Sam asked.

"You didn't think we were going to stay here and wait, did you?"

THIRTY-TWO

e left the station through the side door and walked quickly to our car. Sam buckled in on the driver's side while I held the phone up between us. Liam and Teagan had been silent for a while.

She started the car and pulled out of the parking lot. "Okay. Where do you want me to go?"

I pulled a map of Ireland out of the pocket on the door and opened it. "The original site was at Benbulbin. Ryan's likely moved it somewhere else near the coast. Head toward Benbulbin. Hopefully, Liam will be able to pull more information out of Teagan as we get closer."

Sam turned north and toward the N15. "So we're going to the rendezvous site? What is it you think we're going to do when we get there? We're not exactly equipped to make a drug bust."

"Between Harry and Calbach, we're going to have either the Armed Support Unit or the Sligo gardaí, or both, coming to the rescue. Wherever it is, they're going to be coming in blind. Don't you think it will help them to have some eyes on the site? To let them know what they're dropping into?"

Her brow was furrowed. She usually trusted me, but getting shot at had altered her attitude.

"Don't worry. There are loads of forests and hills all over the place here. We'll stay out of sight."

She nodded, and we drove out of town, heading for Benbulbin. We stayed silent, waiting for more conversation between Liam and Teagan. It didn't take long.

"Isn't it risky, moving the distribution closer to the landing site?" Liam asked.

It was obvious he didn't want to seem too interested in or dismayed by the change in venue. But he was doing everything he could to give us information. He'd just told us we were on the right track and that the new site was closer to the coast than Benbulbin.

Teagan's voice was faint but clear. "If it were risky, he wouldn't have moved it."

A few minutes later, I heard Liam say, "So, what, we're going all the way to Northern Ireland?"

Good job, Liam. I looked at the map, then opened up another one on the phone. "Turn right just past Henry's Bar and Restaurant."

"Really?"

"Yes, really. I can't find any street names."

We drove for a few minutes. Sure enough, there was Henry's on a street corner. Thankfully, it was a large place with an extensive parking lot, almost impossible to miss.

"Well, I'm glad we're not doing this in a cemetery." Liam laughed.

It sounded forced, and I hoped Teagan didn't notice. I did a Google search for cemeteries near us.

Fifteen kilometers from us on the same road we were on was Keelogues Cemetery. "We're on the right track. Keep on this road."

Sam nodded.

I texted Harry where Teagan and Liam were headed. Shortly thereafter, he got back with, ***Having trouble getting through the layers. Still working.***

"Harry's not having a lot of success yet getting to the Support

Unit. Hopefully, Calbach can get the Sligo gardaí in gear."

We drove for another ten minutes. Then we heard Liam say, "Finally. But what are we doing at Brennan's place?"

Teagan's reply was too muffled to hear, but it didn't matter. Hopefully, Harry or Calbach would know where Brennan's place was.

I hung up on Liam and called Calbach.

"Calbach, it looks like their new rendezvous point is somewhere called Brennan's place, north of Benbulbin, past Keelogues Cemetery. Do you know where that is?"

"Aye, the only Brennan up that way is Charlie Brennan. He died last year."

"So the house is empty?"

"Aye. And no other houses around that way." That would make it a perfect spot to transfer drugs.

"The gardaí are wrapping things up here at the Abbey. You were right, Jesse, there are no signs of explosives. They should be able to get mobilized soon."

"Okay. We'll call you back if we learn anything else." I hung up and called Harry, giving him the same info I'd given Calbach. "Any luck yet with the armed services?" I asked.

"We're getting close. At least—is that a horn honking?"

Uh-oh. "I was blowing my nose."

"Jesse, are you in a car?" When I didn't answer, he said, "Where are you? You're not following them, are you?"

"Your guys are going to need eyes on the ground before they get there. We can do that."

"Absolutely not. You need to let law enforcement deal with this. You've done a great job up to now, but it's time to step back and let us handle things."

"In case it wasn't clear before, Harry, you're not the boss of me. We're doing it."

There was a pause, and then a long, heavy sigh. "Are you sure I can't talk you out of this?"

"Nope."

"Okay. Do you have a map?"

"Yep."

"Ryan will have lookouts posted up the main road from Brennan's place. You won't get within a mile of them if you drive up that way. There is another road that runs parallel to the one you're on, about a quarter mile north of you. Take the next through street north to that road and then turn right. The very last road before you hit the Leitrim County line cuts through to Brennan's place. Park your car at that intersection and wait for us. I'll let you know when we're on our way."

"I don't see a street there on the map."

He laughed. "It doesn't have a name. It's about a half mile past Tieve Báun Cottage."

This was sounding an awful lot like, "Take the road up a ways, then turn right at the blooming chuckanut tree, go past where Old Man Steven's dog peed on the lamppost in 1960, and then look for it over the next four miles after you pass the large bush." But Harry was right, going up the main road to their rendezvous was a dumb idea.

We cut over to the road parallel to the one we'd been on and continued to drive east. After passing the cottage he'd referenced, we found the through street. *Street* in this case was an exaggeration—it was a narrow asphalt path, slightly wider than one lane. We would have missed it without Harry's directions.

When Sam pulled over and parked, I opened my door to get out. "Are you coming?"

She was sitting in her seat with the seatbelt still fastened. "This is not a good idea. Harry's right, we should wait here."

"It will be fine. We're not going to get too close. Besides, we can't see anything from up here."

She sighed, but got out of the car to join me.

We walked south down the lane toward Brennan's place. The road was lined on one side by a single row of spindly trees and by low grass on the other. We walked for about a quarter mile. As we neared the T at the end of the road, we could make out the soft glow of lights from the left side. To the right and across the street was a house. There were no lights on inside or out and no cars in the driveway. As we got closer, we could see that the glow was coming from the headlights of six vehicles. Five vans and one black SUV were parked closely together on a large square of flattened grass that sat next to the main road. Two sides of the square were bordered by large black containers, like big fat oil drums. A line of blackberry bushes ran across the side of the square nearest to us.

"This must be it," I said.

Twenty feet from the line of bushes was a small copse of trees. We fast-walked low to the trees and hid behind them. From there we could see people standing on the pad. They were talking, but I couldn't make out what they were saying.

"I want to get closer. We can't hear anything."

"They might have guns. And when Harry's men get here, they will too. They're called Armed Support Units for a reason. And it means they expect a gunfight. It doesn't seem like a good idea to be anywhere near that."

"I'm not going to do anything. I just want to get close enough to see who's here and hear what they're saying. It might help Harry's guys and the gardaí if they know where Liam is. We don't want him to get shot by accident." That was true, but mostly I was just really curious. We'd come this far and I wanted to see it through. "You stay here." I emerged from behind the trees and walked low to the hedge next to the pad, then knelt down.

Five groups of two men were standing uncomfortably around their vans. They looked at each other warily. Three of the men were Ryan's lieutenants, his sons. Next to one of the vans was a large car with blacked-out windows. Likely Ryan himself and his crew of goons from Limerick. One of the other vans was flanked by Liam's fuel laundering crew, Firbis, Irish Kenny, and Lurch. Sitting next to it was another one sporting a Northern Ireland license plate. Those guys were some mix of the UDA, the UVF, and the LVF, presumably whoever was getting along with each other at the moment. I could see bulges under their jackets. They were carrying guns.

Ten minutes later, I heard a low rumble. Two large trucks

rolled into the clearing, followed by a car. All three vehicles parked on the pad. Teagan and Liam stepped out of the car. They each moved to the rear of the trucks and opened them.

The trucks were full of coke bales. I counted three hundred bales between the two trucks. With thirty-five kilos to a bale, there was something on the order of ten thousand kilograms of coke, over $250 million dollars' worth of drugs, headed for Northern Ireland and distribution around the Irish Republic. No wonder Liam had taken the risk of going undercover. This was enough to flood the entire island and then some.

Men from each group began to unload the bales from the trucks and distribute them among the vans. Teagan stood next to the trucks, a clipboard in her hand, keeping track of the amounts.

I pulled out the phone and texted Harry. *They're across the street from Brennan's. At the intersection, in a flat grassy area. The coke is here, and it looks like at least twelve people. They're carrying guns. Tell Calbach.*

He got back to me quickly. *Okay. Still working on armed services. Are you near them? If so, GET OUT OF THERE NOW.*

Okay, I replied, adding a smiley emoji.

Just on the other side of the hedges from me, Firbis was loading coke bales into his van. It was gratifying to see that his eyebrows had been completely singed off from our confrontation the other night. Irish Kenny was standing next to the van, his gun out now, pointed lazily at the ground. The van next to theirs was being loaded by a guy I didn't recognize. Another guy with a gun was standing next to it, eyeing Irish Kenny suspiciously.

The doors to the black SUV were still closed. I was surprised Ryan would take the risk of showing up at a drug transfer. But maybe it made sense because this was going to be his defining achievement, the start to taking over all of the drug business in Ireland. And maybe he wanted to get one look at the impressive amount of coke he'd bought while it was still all in one place.

There was no talking now, as the operation ran efficient and smooth. It was quiet, other than the sounds of exertion coming from the men carrying and stacking the bales.

I texted Harry again. **Loading almost done. Where are you?**

I didn't wait for his answer and put the phone back in my pocket. Maybe it was time to get out of—

"Enjoying the view?"

I looked up to see the wrong end of a rifle barrel pointed at my head.

THIRTY-THREE

The man holding the gun on me was one of Ryan's personal protection goons from the restaurant in Limerick. He motioned with the gun for me to stand up, then marched me into the clearing.

"Hands on your head now, nice and easy."

All eyes were on me as I entered the clearing. Liam was glaring at me. The man stopped me next to Firbis's van.

The front door of the black SUV opened, and another one of Ryan's goons got out and opened the door to the back seat.

Danny Ryan stepped out into the light. "Jesse, Jesse," he said, shaking his head. "I'm so sorry you could make it."

"I wouldn't miss it for the world."

He looked over the hedge. "Are you alone?"

"Yep."

"Hmmm. I don't think so. What I know is, wherever you are, your beautiful friend is not far behind." He raised his voice. "Miss Hernandez? I know you're out there. I suggest you come and join us."

Please don't come out. Please don't come out.

Ryan nodded to the man who had gotten out of the car with him. One of the guys from the restaurant, who still hadn't found a coat that fit him. He walked over to me and put his gun up to my face.

Ryan called out, "Miss Hernandez? You have five seconds to show yourself before I ensure that your dear friend ends up as fertilizer."

"One, two—"

"Hold on. I'm coming."

Damn. But cool. I wasn't ready to be fertilizer yet.

They all watched Sam walk from behind the copse of trees and to the grass pad. Ryan's guy gestured to her with his gun to stand beside me.

"Is there anyone else with you?"

"No. Just us."

"I hope that's the case. Because we wouldn't want anything to get in the way of our big day, would we, Teagan?"

"No, we wouldn't." She smirked at me. She was happy, clearly in Daddy's good favor.

Sam nudged me with her elbow and hissed at me under her breath. "I'll never put us in this spot again, you said. Trust me, you said. Sound familiar?"

"I know, I know. I'm sorry. But don't worry." Harry was probably on his way. At least, I hoped he was. They were almost done loading the vans and would be leaving soon.

Maybe I could drag this out. I raised my voice. "Why Sligo, Ryan?"

"That was Teagan's idea, and it's turned out to be a good one." He rewarded her with a smile and a nod.

She practically swooned.

"Really a perfect spot, despite it requiring me to come to this backwater bog."

He really hated Sligo. Having developed an affinity for the place and its people, I was offended on their behalf.

He continued, "The west coast of Ireland has far fewer eyes on it than the east side. And Cork is becoming difficult as well. The gardaí are everywhere, it seems. But here, it's almost a cakewalk to bring drugs ashore. We just had to have our trawler drop anchor and slip around the other side of Inishmurray Island, then wait for a low tide evening."

"Sure, Ryan, but why bring everyone to one place? Isn't that risky, to have your whole operation here at one time?"

He was smug. "It's not my first rodeo, as they say out your way. It might be for someone else. But over the years I've come to realize that the most important thing in my business transactions is to limit the number of people involved and the amount of time you spend on the exchange. The total time to get the drugs ashore, bring them here, load them, and get them on five different highways will be less than two hours. You see, these are my family." He waved at his sons. "And these other men, I've worked with them for years. It's not like they're going to want to tell on us. Not to mention that they all know the penalty for going against me."

It occurred to me then that the fact that he was telling me all of this meant it was unlikely he'd be letting us go. Or maybe he thought he'd be untouchable. I hoped that was the case.

He nodded to everyone else. "Keep going. We need to get out of here."

Liam looked sick. He wasn't aware that we had help coming. At least, I hoped they were coming. But they were sure taking their sweet time about it.

"You're not going to get away with this, Ryan." God, I sounded like a bad TV show.

He laughed. "The gardaí are busy making sure their precious Abbey doesn't get blown up. So, no, I don't think the calvary is coming over the bend. We'll be long gone before they figure out where we are." He was gloating. "Which by, the way, begs the question. How did you find us?"

Liam shot a quick glance at me.

"You know me. Very nosy, and very good at finding things out. Besides, it's not like you're all that good at keeping things secret. You're an open book, man. I'm surprised they haven't caught you already."

He frowned. I could see his eyes start to shimmer. "They

haven't caught me because I'm careful. And much, much smarter than they are."

This was good. Keep him talking. "Sure," I said sarcastically. "You're about as clever as a box of hair. Just because you've had your way up to now doesn't mean it's going to last."

Sam dug her elbow into me again.

"What, do you think I'm going to incent him to kill us *more*?" I whispered to her.

Making him mad might help. Maybe it would make him stick around a little longer. And I was really good at making people mad.

I turned back to Ryan. "You're a two-bit thug, Ryan, and for the record, you don't know anything about wine, or food, or whiskey. That stuff you served? It was garbage." That was a lie, but I knew he was proud of his personal label whiskey. "Seriously, what a nob. It's hysterical when guys like you try to pretend you're sophisticated."

The smug smile he'd worn up to now disappeared. "To be clear, the only reason you're still alive is because we might need a hostage at some point," he said evenly.

Damn. He was way too disciplined to be provoked. But his daughter probably wasn't.

"And your daughter? What a piece of work. A real chip off the old block. What did you do, Ryan, ask Satan for a loaner?"

Teagan put down her clipboard, balling up her fists.

I turned to her. "Are you even his daughter? More likely the love child of Cersei Lannister and Machete. And there aren't enough therapy dollars in the universe to fix your damage. Seriously, I'll bet that—"

"You little bitch. I'll show you what I can do."

She started to come toward me, but Ryan grabbed her by the arm and pushed her roughly back to the truck. "Get back over there. She's just trying to rile us up." He turned to me. "You're trying to stall. But it doesn't matter. No one knows where we are. And even if they did, I've got men all up the road. They'll let us know long before anyone can drop by."

Sam looked over at me, glaring. Man, this trip was really bringing out her other side. I guess I couldn't blame her. We were likely going to die here.

The trucks were almost empty, when another car drove up. All of the guns trained on it until Ryan waved them off with his hand. The car pulled up on the side of the road, and Quinn stepped out. He walked over to Ryan and leaned over, whispering something in his ear. He leaned back, looking smug.

Ryan nodded.

They finished unloading the vans and the trucks were closed up. Everyone was standing around, waiting for Ryan to give the signal to take off.

"One more piece of business before we leave. As you know, the most important thing to me is loyalty. Those who are loyal get rewarded. Those who aren't, well, here is your chance to see what happens to those people. Quinn informs me that the original site where we were to meet, Benbulbin, was swarming with Armed Support Units this evening. Before today, only five of you knew where we were going to have the original rendezvous tonight. My three sons, Teagan"—he turned his head to face Liam—"and you." He walked over and stood in front of Liam.

"I know my children wouldn't have called them in." He leaned forward, his nose inches from Liam's face. "That leaves you, Liam Gilmartin."

Liam shook his head. "No way. I've been working with you for two years. You know what I've done."

Ryan stepped back and turned to Quinn. "Search him."

Quinn walked over to Liam and patted him down. He pulled Liam's burner phone out of his pocket.

"Look what I found."

"It's just a phone, wanker," said Liam.

Ryan's face darkened. "Bring it here."

Quinn brought the phone over to Ryan. He scrolled through it for a second. Then hit a button.

Redial, as it turned out. Sam's phone started ringing in my pocket. I saw Liam roll his eyes.

Ryan said, "That's an interesting connection. But not a useful one, it seems. And that explains how you found us."

Liam was still trying to play it off like he was innocent. "I've got her phone number because I was trying to send her in another direction. And I don't know what he told you, but he's a lying piece of shit."

Quinn took two quick steps over to Liam and punched him hard in the mouth. Liam wasn't expecting it and fell to the ground, then stood up slowly, rubbing his jaw.

"I've known Quinn for over a decade. He knows better." Ryan shook his head in mock sadness. "I'm very disappointed. I had big plans for you. As did my daughter," he said, turning his head briefly to her.

Teagan looked like a deer caught in headlights. It was obvious she hadn't had a clue about Liam. A testament to his undercover skills, at least.

"Normally, your punishment would be long lasting and painful. As a demonstration to anyone who crosses me. But we have to assume that, eventually, law enforcement will figure things out. Time to get on the road."

One of his guys drew his gun and started to walk over to Liam.

Ryan waved him back. "I think this is a job for Teagan, wouldn't you say, dear?" He pulled a handgun out of the back of his pants and held it out to her.

Teagan looked like she was going to be sick. She definitely had feelings for Liam. On the other hand, this was her chance to prove herself in front of her father. And even if not, there was no telling what he'd do if she refused. I wasn't one hundred percent sure Ryan wouldn't kill his own daughter to make an example of her. She walked over to Ryan and took his gun. Liam had been a good lay, but she had Daddy issues to resolve. She brought the gun and pointed it at Liam's face.

"*Wait!*" I yelled.

Everyone looked at me.

"Uh, isn't this a little hasty? I mean, you have your drugs, you can take off. No one's going to catch you."

"That isn't the point. There's a price for disloyalty," Ryan growled.

"You know, it's one thing to kill drug dealers. It's another to murder a garda."

Liam groaned and rolled his eyes. I'd confirmed Ryan's suspicion, and apparently Liam was under the impression that he could still talk his way out of things. But I didn't think that was going to happen. Ryan had made up his mind.

Ryan shook his head in mild disgust. "You know I only need one hostage, right?" He looked at his daughter. "Get this over with."

Irish Kenny had been standing next to Liam, but moved away, probably to avoid having to wash brains out of his clothes.

Ryan nodded to Teagan. She brought the gun up again to Liam's face, her hand shaking slightly. I wondered what she was thinking, having to blow the brains out of the guy she'd been sleeping with.

Liam smiled at her, the same flirty smile he'd shown to me. "C'mon now, darlin'."

Her eyes narrowed. "You fucking bastard."

I closed my eyes. I had no desire to see Liam's face blown away. But I could still hear the shot.

THIRTY-FOUR

I opened my eyes and looked over to where Liam had been standing.

He was there, still vertical, and apparently bullet-free.

Everyone was looking toward the road. Flashing blue lights were coming from garda vehicles pulling up around the site. Doors opened and men got out of the cars, using the doors for cover.

Teagan turned from Liam and fired a couple of shots toward the gardaí. She received more shots in return and ran to duck down behind the SUV, joining Ryan and two of his men. The others ran behind their vans, then started shooting.

My exhilaration that the gardaí had arrived faded quickly when I realized the disparity in gunpower. There were a handful of Sligo gardaí on the street taking shots with pistols. Most of Ryan's guys had submachine guns. A storm of bullets flew toward the road. For every shot that came from the gardaí, a hundred came back at them. They hadn't been there more than a minute when I heard one of them yell. He'd been hit. One down and only a handful of lightly armed, albeit brave, gardaí to go. This would be over soon.

As if they were thinking the same thing, all of Ryan's men

except the ones with him by his car came out from behind their vans and started making their way toward the gardaí.

Sam, Liam, and I were kneeling behind Irish Kenny's van. He'd joined the others in slowly walking and shooting. Moving between vehicles, providing cover for each other, they walked methodically to the road, continuing to spray the cars and any exposed gardaí with gunfire.

Liam was peeking out from behind the van. I grabbed him and pulled him back.

"What the hell are you doing?" I said.

Huh. That felt funny coming out of my mouth. I was way more used to hearing that than saying it.

"I'm not letting him get away." He shrugged off my hand and leaned back around the back of the car, and I peeked over his head.

Ryan and his men had moved up toward the doors of his SUV. One of them opened the front door for cover, then the back door. As he was doing this, a bullet caught him in the back. He fell to the ground and lay there, unmoving.

Ryan rushed into the back seat of the SUV and closed it, while another of his men got into the driver's side and started up the engine.

Liam pulled away from me and ran toward the SUV. He grabbed the door to the back and started to pull.

Teagan stepped out from behind the car and, without hesitation, shot Liam. He let go of the door and dropped to his knees, blood pouring from his shoulder. She walked up right next to him and put the gun up to his head.

The SUV peeled out, running through a low decrepit wire fence and onto the road toward Leitrim.

Ryan had left Teagan behind. This was going to take her Daddy issues to a whole new level.

She watched the SUV drive down the road until it was out of site. Then she looked at Liam, who by now was sitting on the ground, holding his bleeding shoulder. She hit him over the head with the butt of her gun and stepped over him, moving to the front of the skirmish and joining the other drug runners. She wasn't bothering to take cover, just standing straight up, firing shot after shot in the direction of the gardaí. When her clip emptied, she threw her gun to the side and grabbed the gun from one of the UDA guys next to her. He tried to pull it back toward him, and she used it to butt him in the face. He fell to the ground. She took the gun and continued firing.

I got up from behind the van and walked over to Liam. He was laying on his back, trying and failing to stop the bleeding.

Sam joined us and waved me away. She leaned over and put pressure on his wound with both hands. "Can you find me some cloth?"

I looked around. There was nothing. I opened the nearest van. Bales of coke filled the back. I looked in the front and found some towels and a jacket. I opened one of the coke bales and took out a kilo. I brought the rags, jacket, and the kilo of coke to Sam.

"I'm not really in the mood to get high right now," she said, taking the towels.

"Isn't this an anesthetic?"

"Oh, yes, of course. Can you open it up?"

I pulled out my knife and cut into the package. Sam reached in and pulled out a small amount, then spread it on Liam's wound before wadding up the towels and pressing them on top.

"Now what?" I asked.

"I guess we just wait," she said. "And keep our heads down."

It wouldn't be long now, and it was a moot point, anyway. The shots from the gardaí were now few and far between. They'd either all been shot or were running out of bullets, or both. It didn't matter. However much ammo they had wouldn't be enough.

THIRTY-FIVE

"Oh shit!" I heard Firbis yell. He dropped his gun and came running back toward us.

Beyond him, I saw a line of new headlights coming down the road.

Six SUVs screeched to a halt near the garda cars. Doors opened, and I heard a fresh volley of gunshots, many from submachine guns. The Armed Support Unit was here and, true to their name, they were armed to the teeth.

Some of their shots made it past Ryan's men and were flying around us. Sam and I grabbed Liam and dragged him behind the van. Firbis was still running, but all of a sudden fell to the ground. He didn't get back up.

The others tried to hold their ground, but it was clear they were outmatched. A few of them dropped their guns and put their hands up. Unfortunately for those guys, they were standing in a group and some of the others were still shooting. The gardaí continued to fire on them until they were all on the ground or standing with their hands up.

The gunfire finally stopped, and then it was quiet. Armed gardaí were yelling at the drug runners to lay on the ground. One by one their hands were cuffed or zip tied behind them, and they were led to the road, left to sit on the side with an armed officer standing guard.

"Over here! We need an ambulance," I yelled.

A garda walked toward us, pointing his gun. I put my hands up. Sam kept hers pressed on Liam's wound.

"It's Liam Gilmartin. He's your undercover guy. He needs medical attention."

When he got close to us, the garda lowered his gun and spoke into the microphone on his vest. "We're not with them." I pointed to the criminals. "Jesse O'Hara and Sam Hernandez." He kept his gun trained on us.

We waited, Sam keeping pressure on Liam's wound until ambulances started to arrive. They hadn't been far behind the support unit. One of them drove onto the clearing and stopped next to us. Two medics jumped out of the back and took over from Sam, tending to Liam on the ground.

Sam and I sat there, our hands in the air, and waited while uniformed gardaí and men in suits walked through the site, opening up the backs of the vans and taking men into custody.

The medics put Liam on a stretcher, then put him into the ambulance and drove off, joining others in which injured gardaí had been placed. There were injured drug runners, but they would have to wait their turn until the good guys were taken care of.

One of the guys in suits walked into the clearing. It was Harry.

"They're with us," he said to the garda who'd been training his gun on us. He lowered it and walked away.

"Are you okay?" Harry said.

I looked at Sam, who nodded. "We're fine," I replied.

"How about Liam? How bad is it?"

"I think he'll be okay. He took a bullet in the shoulder." I stood up. "Ryan is headed north in a black SUV."

"We know. We've got a car going that way."

Harry reached his hand down to help Sam up. "I hate to say this, but you'll have to go to the station to give a statement."

I was exhausted. "I can give you a statement right now. F—"

"Please, Jesse, I'll make sure you get in and out as quickly as possible. It will really help us if you can tell us what happened." He looked around the site. "I need a few minutes here, but then you can ride back with me."

"Okay." I needed to talk to Liam anyway and find out where Cait was.

We walked back out through the grass to the road. Several of the gardaí had been shot. No one killed, thankfully. Uniformed gardaí were taking the remaining thugs into custody, and the injured were taken away by ambulance.

Teagan was one of the few bad guys who was uninjured. As one garda tried to put her in handcuffs, she yelled insults and struggled, and he was taking a face full of punches and kicks to his shins. He called for help, and eventually three of them got her cuffed. They led her to the road and into the back of a car. I could still hear her yelling after they closed the door and left her to wait.

Harry led us to his car, and we got in the back. "I'll be right back," he said, closing the door.

I watched him walk back toward grass pad, talk to the different groups of gardaí who had taken over the site, and inspect all of the vans and the trucks.

Forty minutes later, he made it back to the car. As we drove off, I looked back at the site. Six of the gangsters were lying unmoving on the ground: two of the UDF guys, Ryan's oldest son, one of his personal protection goons, and Quinn. And they'd killed Irish Kenny.

THIRTY-SIX

News vans were parked in front of the Sligo garda station. A group of reporters were in front, all circled around and holding microphones in front of someone at the center. As we got closer, I could see it was Liam.

No great surprise there. He was at the center of the largest drug bust in the history of Ireland. Not only that, his stint as an undercover agent was great copy. He was savoring the moment too. Two years of undercover work had paid off. He was trying but failing to control an exultant smile as he answered their questions. His arm was in a sling, but other than that he looked fine.

We pushed through them and walked through the doorway, into the station. It was a madhouse. Even though it was ten at night, it looked like the entire station was on duty, uniformed and suited gardaí alike rushing in and out of the front entrance. O'Fenton was doing his best at triage, managing reporters, family members of those involved in the shootout, and gardaí requests all at once.

The drug runners were trickling in one at a time, all in hand-cuffs or zip ties, escorted by a uniformed officer. They would be placed in cells until they could be charged and moved to more secure locations.

"Can you two wait here for a moment? I'll find out who's ready to take your statement." Harry maneuvered his way through the crowded reception area and went into the back.

Sam and I found a spot against the wall and leaned against it. I started to close my eyes, but opened them when I heard yelling and a familiar voice.

"Get your hands off me, you cunts!" It was Teagan, being escorted in by two officers. She was kicking and thrashing wildly, no mean feat with her hands cuffed behind her back. One of the officers had bleeding scratches on his face, and the other was limping.

She broke away for a moment and started to run back out the front door. The officer with the bleeding face grabbed her around the neck and dragged her to the ground. They wrestled with each other until the other officer pulled something from his belt.

"Taser!" the officer yelled out.

The garda on the floor scrambled away from Teagan, and as she was starting to stand up, the other one let her have it with the taser.

She screamed and went rigid, falling back down to the ground from her knees. She laid still for a few seconds, and the two men moved over to her and picked her up. They half dragged/half carried her through the door to the back.

As they lifted her up, I saw something fall to the floor. It was her locket. I picked it up and put it in my pocket. She was a real bitch, but I didn't begrudge anyone a gift from their mother.

A moment later, Liam came through the entrance.

I moved away from the wall to stand in front of him, blocking his way to the back. "Congratulations. Now it's time to find Cait. Where is she?"

"Listen, Jesse, this needs to wait. I have things to do." He moved around me and left for the back, shutting the door behind him.

Damnit. So close. I was getting antsy to wrap things up.

It surprised me a few minutes later when a garda came

through the front entrance, escorting Irish Kenny. I looked at Sam. "I thought he was dead."

She shrugged and shook her head.

Shortly thereafter, Harry poked his head in from the back room. "We're ready. C'mon in."

He opened the door and I brushed past him, making a beeline into the office area.

Liam was standing near the center of desks, smiling broadly, groups of admiring gardaí standing around him.

"*Hey!*" I yelled. "Haven't you forgotten something?" I wasn't going to let him stand there and wallow in glory while Cait was still missing.

He looked over at me and frowned, then came over and grabbed my arm. "Not here," he whispered sharply.

He led Sam and I into one of the offices that ringed the room and then closed the door.

"Look, Jesse—"

"No, *you* look. I've waited long enough. *Where* is Cait? Have you talked to Firbis?"

He looked away, uncomfortable. "Firbis is dead."

"Okay, who else knows where she is?"

"Uh, no one."

"What?"

"I told Firbis to put her somewhere safe and not to tell anyone."

I thought he'd been lying when he told me that earlier. "Are you fucking kidding me? What about Irish Kenny?"

"Who?"

"The little red-haired guy with Firbis and Quinn."

"You can ask him, but I don't think so. The only one Firbis told was Quinn. And he's dead, too."

"And no one else knows where she is? Really?"

He shook his head. Taking my hands in his, he said, "Look, Jesse, you helped us make the biggest drug bust in the history of this island. Danny Ryan will never recover from this. Not being able to sell all of that coke means he will be too busy avoiding his creditors to keep running his business as usual. We did a lot of good. Thousands, tens of thousands, of people's lives will be saved because of what we did today. Cait didn't—"

"Die in vain? Is that what you were going to say? Do you know for sure that she's dead?"

He put up his hands. "No, no, of course not." He tried to put his hand on my arm, but I shrugged it off. "There's always collateral damage in war. And make no mistake, this is a war. Many people have died because of Danny Ryan. We've changed that today."

"Wait...Firbis wasn't at the pasture. That means he left alive in an ambulance and died later. Did you go to the hospital? Did you try to talk to him?" I already knew the answer. "You were too busy doing your public relations news tour with the reporters, weren't you? Nothing was going to get in the way of your big shining moment, was it?" I spat the words at him.

He not only didn't know where Cait was, he'd let the only guy who did die before even bothering to ask him. All so he could have his time in the limelight in front of reporters. I tensed up, ready to let him have it with both barrels. "You *arrogant, shitty*—"

Sam put her hand on my arm. She normally did this to keep me from attacking someone. It wouldn't work this time. But as I looked over at her, I saw something I'd never seen before in my life.

Fury.

Sam's eyes were blazing. I'd known her for years and had never seen that look on her. Not even when she'd chewed me out in the car. Then she'd been scared. Now she was enraged.

"You *bastard*," she said, low and venomous, moving to stand in front of him. "All you had to do was ask Firbis where he put her. Even when you *knew* things were coming to an end. A short conversation, that's all it would have taken."

Liam looked like he'd been slapped, and I didn't blame him. Seeing Sam this angry was like being struck by lightning. Rare and devastating. I took a step back.

"You *knew* it was going to be dangerous. You *knew* there

would be a shootout. That's why you called in the Armed Support. You *knew* there was a good chance he and the others might be killed. All you were thinking about was your precious undercover operation. Did you enjoy your time in front of the cameras today? I hope so. Because by the time we're done, you'll be lucky if you ever get a job in law enforcement again. Those reporters out there will be very interested to know that you were the one who had Cait kidnapped in the first place. They're going to *love* that story, the shining law enforcement officer who turns out to be a glory hunting wanker."

"I'm really sorry. I—"

"Do you realize that if it hadn't been for Jesse, Ryan's drugs would be on their way all over the island and you would be lying dead in that pasture?"

"Yes, thank you. Look, I'll make sure to give you credit for—"

Sam's hand flew out and slapped him hard across the face. "Don't you *dare*." She turned and stalked out of the office.

I trailed after her, slamming the door behind me. Usually, I was the one to go off, but Sam had done it for me. I was seeing a whole other side to her on this trip.

Harry had been waiting for us outside of the office. "What's happened?"

"All of the men who know where Cait is are dead."

"Oh no. Jesse, I'm so sorry." He put his hand on my shoulder. "Look, if you're not up to this right now, we can wait until tomorrow."

I shook my head. "No. I'm up to it. But can we take a detour? Irish Kenny—the little red-haired guy—may be able to tell us something. Do you know where they put him?"

"Follow me."

Harry led us down the hallway to the back of the station, where groups of men were sectioned off into two large cells.

Irish Kenny was sitting on the floor, leaning against the wall.

"You, over here." Harry pointed to him.

He got up slowly and walked over to the bars.

Harry turned to me. "Go ahead."

"Do you know where Firbis took Cait?"

I thought by now I might have picked up some of the accent, but his answer was indecipherable. I turned to Harry, "What the hell did he say?"

Harry translated. "He doesn't know who that is."

"Yes, you do. The woman who found the fuel laundering operation, the one Liam told Firbis to stash for a little while."

Angry mumbling.

"He says—"

"Never mind. I got the gist." He'd been expressing his displeasure about Liam. "Whatever. Do you know where Firbis took her?"

Calmer mumbling.

"He says he has no idea."

"Do we believe him?"

"Yes, I think so. If he did know, he'd use it to bargain for a lighter sentence. He's no dummy."

Irish Kenny smiled, then mumbled something again.

Harry started to turn away. "Uh, are you ready to go?"

"No, wait, what did he say just then."

"It's not relevant."

I stood, not moving.

Harry sighed and said, "He wants to know if you or your friend fancy a ride." His face reddened.

"No, thanks. Sam?"

"I'm good, thank you."

"Enjoy prison, asshole." I turned and walked out of the room.

Harry led us to one of the small interrogation rooms. "I'm sorry about this, all of the interview rooms are full. But I thought you'd want to get this over with as quickly as possible."

"It's fine, thanks." It didn't matter anyway. All I had to look forward to now was going back to the Gallaghers and destroying their lives with the worst news possible. Sam and I sat down.

"Are you sure you two are up to this?"

I looked at Sam and she nodded, and I sighed heavily. "Let's just get it over with."

Harry took both of our statements. We signed them and got up to leave.

"Thank you again, Jesse and Sam, for all you've done. I know this isn't the outcome you wanted, but we really did do something important today. And I'm so, so sorry about Cait."

"It's not your fault."

He reached into his pocket and handed me some car keys. "Your car is in the lot. I had one of the officers drive it back here."

"Thanks, Harry." That was really thoughtful. It wasn't like he didn't have a thousand other things to deal with.

"And, uh, Jesse, one more thing." He stood up and smiled. "My name is Aiden."

I tried to smile back but it wouldn't come. I was too devastated about Cait. It was really, finally the end of the line.

He walked us back out to the reception area. As I started out the door, I remembered something and turned back to him.

Pulling Teagan's locket out of my pocket, I said, "This is Teagan's. It broke off when they were bringing her in. I think it's from her mother." Before I handed it to him, I opened the locket latch and pulled it apart, looking at the picture inside.

You've got to be kidding me.

I couldn't believe this day could get any worse, but it just had.

THIRTY-SEVEN

I was frozen, and had no idea how long I'd been staring at the locket. "Harry—uh, Aiden, can you do me one favor?"

He nodded.

"I need five minutes with Teagan."

He started to shake his head. "You may have noticed, she's quite volatile. They've had to put her in a room by herself. I can't let you in with her."

"If it weren't for us, Liam would be dead and Ryan's drugs would be flooding the island. You owe me."

He sighed. "Okay. Five minutes. But you aren't to get too close."

Sam looked at me for an explanation.

"I'll be right back."

I followed Aiden to the back of the station again, and he showed me to a small room with a door. He motioned to the uniformed garda standing outside of it to open it up. He put in his key and unlocked the door.

I stepped in, Aiden close on my heels, and stood on the opposite side of the table Teagan was sitting at. Both of her hands and her legs were chained to thick metal fixtures on the floor and the table. She stared at both of us malevolently. I couldn't believe that much vitriol could come out of one person's eyes. I hated that she had my face. I'd been despondent at losing Cait, but seeing that smirk sent me right back to Angry Town.

"Can we be alone?" I asked Aiden.

He looked skeptical, but Teagan was completely chained up. He walked out and closed the door.

I sat down across the table from her.

"What do you want, you fucking bitch?"

"I see getting tased didn't affect your jaw muscles."

"Fuck you."

"I thought maybe all that electricity would wipe that stupid look off your face, but it looks like it didn't help."

She tried to raise her hands up, but the chains prevented her from moving them any more than a few inches.

"Get out, you bitch."

"Hey, guess what? You're not the boss of me. Maybe I'll stick around for a while." I put my boots up on the table. "I'm really looking forward to walking out of here. That is, when I'm good and ready." I leaned back in the chair and stared at her.

She stared back.

We sat there for several minutes, staring at each other.

Finally, I said, "I have your locket." I pulled it out to show it to her.

"Give it here."

"I will. After we have a little talk." I put it on the table, just out of her reach.

"I've nothin' to say to the likes of you. Me da owns enough judges and lawyers, I just need to wait for him to get me out," she sneered at me, leaning back in her chair as far as she could.

"Your dad is halfway to Spain right now. You think he's coming for you? All I can say is, don't wait up."

I realized I didn't need to strong arm her into talking to me. She hadn't taken her eyes off of the locket since I showed it to her. She wanted it. That's all I needed.

I nodded at her. "Okay. Bye." I stood up, collecting the locket in my hand.

"*Argh.* Wait."

I sat back down and put the locket back on the table.

"What do you want?"

"Who is the woman in the picture?" I opened it up and pointed to the picture. It was a photo of a woman standing in front of a small house, smiling. She was about twenty-five years old and pretty.

"It's me ma."

"Do you know when this was taken?"

"How the fuck—?"

I picked up the locket and stood up again to leave.

She added hurriedly, "Before I was born. I think the year before."

"This is your house, yeah? The one you're living in now?" I recognized it from the night we saw her and Liam together.

"Yeah. After me ma died, the house went to me."

"Not to your dad?"

She looked down. "Na. He and Ma lived there for a while, but he moved away when I was born. He doesn't like Sligo."

"When did you mother die?"

"Fifteen years ago. When I was ten. I went into care."

Care meant a home for orphans, or into whatever Ireland's foster system was. For some reason, Ryan had let her be taken there instead of watching over her himself.

She was slumped in her chair, her chin resting on her chest, trying to sound pathetic. Going for the pity move now.

No fucking way. I glared at her and said, "You think you have the monopoly on shitty childhoods, you fucking self-pitying bitch?"

"Don't come at me with that. I know you're a spoiled little bitch who had everything growing up in the States."

"*Oh yeah?* Did your dad kill *your* mother? At least he wasn't around to fuck up your life when you were a kid."

"Boo-fucking-hoo. And you, what are you, a lawyer? Fucking American know-it-all fuck'n bitch..."

I'd kept it together up to now, but I'd had it. I had reached my limits. I was exhausted, and I'd just found out that the young woman we'd been looking for over the last week was gone forever. All I had to look forward to now was telling her family that they'd never see her again. I'd been the hope crusher since I arrived and was finally going to put the nail in the Cait hope coffin that Rose carried around with her.

I stood up and leaned over Teagan and let every bit of grief and anger and sadness wash over me and onto her. "There isn't a sorrier piece of shit on the planet than you. I hope you enjoy spending the rest of your worthless life in prison, you unbelievably poor excuse for a human being."

"You're a fucking geebag."

What the hell is a geebag? "Oh yeah? At least my dad didn't just drive off and leave me to get shot."

Her face reddened further; I could tell I scored with that one.

"At least I don't have a face like a smacked arse."

"Hello, Einstein, in case you haven't noticed, whatever's going on with my face is going on with yours too."

"Sure, you're all brave with me tied up. Fucking pox bottle cunt."

It was hard to stay focused while wondering what all of these insults were and trying to commit them to memory so I could look them up later and potentially add to my repertoire. But I called her every name I could think of. And even though she couldn't stand because of the chains, her mouth was free and she matched me insult for insult. It was like arguing with a mirror image. My vocabulary of verbal abuse was extensive, and it appeared hers was a match. We were going to be there for a while.

The volume was ratcheting up, and after a particularly loud exchange, the door opened and the garda who had been outside peeked in.

"Everything okay in here, ladies?"

"*It's fine,*" we both yelled at once. He quickly closed the door.

All of a sudden, I was exhausted. This was too much. I sat back down.

Teagan's face was flushed. The same as mine, I supposed.

"Why are ye so damned interested in me locket? Give it here."

I closed the locket and placed it on the table in front of her. I didn't need to look at the picture anymore. I already knew it well.

I'd seen it before. In my parent's house.

I was five when my mom and dad went to visit our relatives in Sligo. I still remembered the bitter arguments when they got back. I was too young at the time to understand what they were talking about. But I knew now.

After my mother died and Dad went to prison, I'd gone through the house and removed anything that would remind me of him. Among other things, I'd cleaned out his sock drawer. Hidden underneath the socks in the back of the drawer had been a picture of a woman. The only reason he would hide a picture of a woman was if he were hiding his relationship with her. In this case, the same woman in Teagan's locket. Her mother. He'd cheated on my mom on their trip. With Teagan's mom.

It was no coincidence that we were dead ringers for each other. We were half-sisters.

I pushed away and got up to leave the room.

"Wait, what the fuck is all this about?"

She was a cold, ruthless killer, but I felt a small wave of pity for her. Maybe because she looked like me. That definitely made it easier to empathize. And it was no wonder she had Daddy issues. Ryan had probably suspected the whole time that she wasn't his and treated her like it.

I'd seen how hard she'd tried to curry favor with him and the way he looked at her. The chance that he was going to swoop in and save her with his army of lawyers was nonexistent, even if he wasn't running for his life.

I stood up numbly. "Goodbye, Teagan. Good luck in prison."

She'd probably be running the place in no time flat. Her combination of rage and crazy would serve her well there.

I walked out of the room and back to the reception area in a fog.

Sam stood up when she saw me, concern written on her face. "You're white. What's going on?"

"It's no coincidence that Teagan looks like me."

"What do you mean?"

"My dad used to come over to Ireland to visit family when I was a kid."

Sam's eyes got wide.

I didn't need to say the words. She knew where this was going.

"You're kidding."

"Nope."

"Are you okay? How do you feel?"

That was a loaded question. Cait was gone, and I had a crazy half-sister I'd never known about. I was feeling a lot of things. Surprise, disgust, grief. Anger, as always. But now, mostly sadness. I hated sadness.

"I knew he ran around on my mother. I just hadn't counted on him doing it on other continents. And who knows how many other siblings I have out there?"

Sam stood speechless, staring wide-eyed at me.

I couldn't blame her. I wouldn't know what to say either to someone who had just learned that their dad had cheated with a drug lord's wife and spawned a hell baby.

Whatever. The discomfort I was feeling would pale in comparison to what the Gallaghers would experience when I told them the investigation was dead and we'd likely never find Cait. We now had the delightful task of ripping the guts out of her family.

I wasn't used to failing. And in this case, failing meant destroying a family I'd come to care about. I started to fantasize about buying another case of whiskey and just losing myself for a few days.

The lobby was still busy. Now, instead of officers bringing in drug dealers, it was family members being escorted in and out. Some were looking for information on their incarcerated sons and some were finding out their child had been killed. The men at the drug bust were criminals and drug dealers, but every one of them had a mom and a dad who would feel the loss.

Soon, the Gallaghers would be experiencing the same thing. I walked out slowly. No need to rush the news.

We were almost out the door when a uniformed officer and another set of parents, a middle-aged couple, came out from the back. The woman was crying.

"Mr. and Mrs. Firbis, let me just say again how sorry we all are about your son. Someone will contact you when we're able to release the body."

I stopped and stood there while the couple walked past us and out of the station. I recognized the woman. She was the lady who'd booted us off the property at Carrowmore when we'd visited before opening hours.

I grabbed the keys out of Sam's hand and rushed out the door. "C'mon." I ran across the street to our car, Sam keeping pace with me. "I'll drive." I got in and started up the car.

"What's going on?"

"I'll tell you on the way. Right now, I need you to call Brian. Tell him to meet us at Carrowmore. And to bring Fergus."

Thirty-Eight

"Sam, do you remember Jarlath's article about tiger kidnappings?" I was speeding along one of the small roads leading west out of town, not worried about getting pulled over. The Sligo gardaí were all busy with the aftermath of the drug bust.

"No. You're the article reader."

"His research showed that tiger kidnappers don't generally stash people very far away from where they're abducted."

"Okay. So?"

"Quinn, Lurch, and Irish Kenny are from Belfast. But Firbis was from around here. He's the one who stashed Cait."

"Yes, I know. He's dead and didn't tell anyone where."

"Jarlath's research also shows that they keep kidnap victims in places that are familiar, places that are comfortable to them.

"I'm not following you. What does this have to do with Cait?"

"That couple that was just leaving. They're Firbis's mother and father."

Sam nodded slowly. "She's the woman who asked us to leave Carrowmore when we showed up too early the other day."

I rounded a corner, screeching tires letting me know I took it a little too fast. "Yeah. And that visitor center...it looked like it might double as their house. And even if not, it's likely Firbis spent a ton of time there. What could be more comfortable to him than that?"

"You think Cait's in the center?"

"Probably not. It's too small. But I think she could be near it."

I made record time to Carrowmore and parked in the lot. Seconds later, another car pulled in behind us. It was Brian. He opened the back door and helped Fergus get out of the back seat and onto the pavement. Wee Petey busted out of the car around them and started running circles in the parking lot.

Brian walked toward us, Fergus walking stiffly beside him. "What's going on, Jesse?"

I didn't want to get his hopes up, but didn't know what to say other than the truth. "There's a small chance that the men who took Cait stashed her here."

"Here? Carrowmore?"

I gave him the short version of tiger kidnapping, leaving out the part about not having any other options at this point and that our only other leads were dead. I avoided looking at his face and the hopeful look that I knew would be there.

The front door to the visitor center opened as we approached, and a young man who looked a lot like Firbis came out. "No dogs allowed."

"This is official garda business. We're coming in."

He made a feeble attempt to block the doorway as we pushed past him.

"You're not the gardaí. I'm calling the station."

"Good luck with that." The last thing on their minds right now would be dealing with fucking dogs.

I didn't think Cait would be in the building. Firbis wouldn't have wanted to take the risk that his family would find out he'd kidnapped someone. But it was worth checking out. And there might be something of Cait's still around that could give us a clue.

I guided Fergus into each room and closet in the building, letting him sniff around. He didn't react to anything, so we walked out the back door. I led him around the house, looking for a shed or any signs of a cellar door.

After we'd circled the building twice. I led him onto the main area of the site. I took off his leash, and we watched him wander around the grassy field, sniffing, occasionally peeing on small bushes. Wee Petey was going nuts, doing larger and larger circles around us and darting off into small stands of brush and trees. Off in the distance, I could see Knocknarea and Queen Maeve's tomb at the top.

We walked in silence, watching Fergus.

After fifteen minutes we were reaching the end of the major portion of the site, and I knew this was a bust.

"This is our last chance, isn't it?" Brian had been watching my face.

"I'm sorry, Brian. I must have been wrong." *The hope crusher strikes again.*

He nodded and turned around. "C'mon, Fergus."

Fergus was at the far southern end of the site. Brian walked over to him and put on his leash. He turned to walk back to the car, but Fergus stopped. He was facing away from the parking lot, staring into the other direction.

Brian was pulling on the leash, but Fergus didn't move. "What is it, boy?"

"Can you let him off of it?" I said, trying not to sound too excited.

Brian unhooked the leash, and Fergus ambled away.

I couldn't see what he was going for. There was nothing at that end of the site, just more grass and a few trees. It was technically part of the cemetery, but not where anyone would go to look at anything. The map of the site didn't include anything of interest in this area.

Since he'd arrived, Fergus had been slowly wandering around the site on his arthritic legs. But now he was trotting. He ran for another twenty yards, then came to a stop, barking wildly at something in the trees. I hoped to God he hadn't found remains.

As I got closer, I could see near the trees was a slight overgrowth of grass and some bushes that almost completely covered a short set of stone stairs going down. They were surrounded on each side by the remnants of a stone wall. At the bottom of the stairs was a large slab, leaning against an opening into some kind of underground space. It was winter, and this part of the site was far away from anything interesting. There was no reason anyone would come here.

I'd told Sam that ancient ringforts were often accompanied by the underground souterrains. I'd seen lots of pictures of them, and this stone entrance looked a lot like those. And while the identified Carrowmore ringfort was at the other end of the site, I also knew that often there was little remaining of them and we might be near another one that had disappeared over time.

We'd found an unexplored souterrain. In another context, I'd have been thrilled to make that discovery.

Fergus was barking madly, up on his back legs, scratching at the stone slab in front of the opening. The slab was slightly ajar, leaving a two-inch opening into the dark cave.

"Sam, can you take Fergus?"

She put him on his leash and struggled to move him away from the opening.

Brian and I grabbed the stone and tried to move it to the side. It wouldn't budge.

He leaned over and yelled into the open gap between the slab and the frame. "*Cait!* Are you in there?"

We heard nothing.

I didn't say what we were all thinking. If she'd been in this hole the whole time, it wasn't likely we were going to find her alive.

"We need something to move this stone," I said.

"I've got something in the car." Brian ran to the parking lot and came back shortly with a tire iron.

Brian wedged the iron between the slab and the frame, and we each grabbed it and pulled.

At first nothing happened. We kept at it, and after a minute, I could feel the stone move. We increased our pressure and were rewarded with the scraping sound of stone on stone. This thing had to weigh at least half a ton. Thank God for levers. Eventually, we were able to move the stone almost a foot away from the frame. Wee Petey darted around us and ran through it. We continued working to increase the gap, while Wee Petey barked excitedly from inside. Fergus busted free of Sam and bounded into the opening as we continued to enlarge it. We heard him whining.

Finally, we moved the stone enough that I was able to slip in and join the dogs.

The crack of light from the opening illuminated a small room. Fergus was standing next to a blanket on the floor against the back wall. He was whining and licking the blanket.

Brian ran past me and over to the blanket, pulling it back. "Cait!"

She was laying on her side, the blanket wrapped around her. It was freezing in there and damp. There was a small empty bowl next to her, and the floor was littered with plastic water bottles. A bucket sat in the corner.

"Oh, Cait, Cait..." Brian knelt on the floor beside her, picking up her shoulders gently and bringing her face close to his.

Her eyes fluttered open. "Brian?" she croaked.

"Don't speak." He picked her up with the blanket, and we followed him out of the tomb.

The car was a million miles away.

"Sam, call an ambulance," I said.

"No, it will be quicker if I take her," Brian said as he fast walked to his car.

I fished into his pockets for the keys and then opened the back door. He gently laid Cait down in the back and covered her with the filthy blanket.

"I'll come with." Sam went around to the other side and slid in next to Cait, putting her arm around her.

"Jesse, can ye take Fergus and Petey back to the house." He closed the door and got into the front.

I could see Brian open his phone as he peeled out of the parking lot, no doubt calling Rose and Mik to tell them the news. I drove back to the Gallaghers with the two dogs.

THIRTY-NINE

Cait stayed at the hospital until the next morning. The doctors wanted to keep her for a few days for observation, but she would have none of it, and once she warmed up and got some food in her, she demanded to leave. She was tired, dehydrated, and hungry, but she'd been gone long enough. It was time to go home.

Sam and I were waiting at the house with the dogs when Rose, Mik, and the boys brought her into the house. Fergus was beside himself, wagging his tail like a puppy and walking in tight circles next to her.

Cait had bags under her eyes but looked happy. The underground stone room had been cold, and she was still struggling to warm up. Rose yelled at Brian to bring hot tea while they set her up on the living room couch, swaddling her in blankets. Rose and Mik flanked her on the couch, the boys standing behind it, their hands resting lightly on her shoulders. Wee Petey jumped onto the couch and curled up on her lap.

I didn't think she'd want to talk about the ordeal, but she brought it up on her own.

"I was waiting for Paddy at the bus station. I saw his car and started to get in when I realized it wasn't him. I recognized the two men I'd seen at the fuel laundering site. I tried to get away, but they grabbed me and pulled me into the car. They put a hood over my head and drove me to Carrowmore. I tried to get out, but the stone was too heavy. And at first, Firbis came by every day with food and water."

Colin was balling up his fists. "If that wanker wasn't already dead, I'd go kill him meself."

Cait looked up at him and patted his arm. "He didn't touch me, Colin."

He leaned down and kissed her on the cheek.

"But then he missed a day, and that turned into another day, and another. That's when I started to worry."

"To be fair, he had a good excuse for yesterday, being dead and all," I said.

Cait reached for my hand and gave it a squeeze. "I don't know how long I would have lasted there, Jesse. Thank you for finding me."

I looked at Sam. "It was a team effort."

We stayed the night, joining the family around the dinner table and then the next morning for one of Rose's massive breakfasts. Then it was time to clear up a few things.

Sam and I headed back to Murphy's pub where I'd insulted the entire country in an attempt to distract Liam. I wanted to be able to come back to Sligo at some point and didn't want the pub to be off limits in perpetuity.

When I walked in the door, the regulars at the bar stood up and started toward me.

The bartender said, "No, get out. You're not welcome here."

The pub was almost full, and I was receiving glowering looks from every person in the place. Fortunately, I'd brought a secret weapon.

Rose walked in from behind me and strode into the pub. "Now you listen te me, Sean Murphy," she said loudly, standing in the middle of the room with her hands on her hips. "This lass saved my girl Cait, and I'll not be havin' ye turn her away from yer bar. Everything she did was for Cait. She's risked her life for my girl, and she'll be welcome here and everywhere else in this town from now on." Rose stared daggers at Murphy.

He nodded, saying politely to me, "May I pour you a Guinness, Dr. O'Hara?"

"Yes, thanks very much."

Brian, Sam, and I sat down at a table. Once it was clear that I was no longer to be persona non grata, Rose left to go back and be with her daughter. I suspected she wouldn't be leaving her side for some time.

Even though we'd been officially rehabilitated by Rose, I still felt the need to apologize and make amends to the bar patrons, many of whom were still staring at me with unfriendly eyes. Receiving forgiveness from the group required buying four rounds for the entire pub and a lengthy apology speech, in which I shared my deep and abiding love for Ireland, its history, its heroes, actors, and singers. I threw in my mother's devotion to Enya and committed to name my first child Michael James. That seemed to do it, and I was rewarded with slaps on the back and a series of return rounds from every group in the bar.

As closing time approached, the trad players put away their instruments and people started to file out. The bartender gave last call, but when he came to our table to collect our glasses, he leaned over and whispered something to Brian before he walked away.

"Are you up for a lock in?"

"What's that?"

"We stay past the time when the pub is closed. But once it's locked, you're committed to stay here a while. No leaving during a lock in. It's not really legal, so people can't be filing in and out after hours."

Being forced to stay in a pub? The more I learned about the country, the more I liked it. "Count me in." I looked at Sam.

"Sure." She was smiling, and I felt a wave of relief. Angry Sam would hopefully not make another appearance any time soon.

Once the last non-lock in patron left the pub, the bartender locked the door and closed the blinds on the windows. He dimmed the lights, and we continued to drink and talk. The trad players stayed too, singing without instruments to keep the noise down.

"Isn't this risky, doing it right down the street from the garda station?" I said, putting away my umpteenth shot of Redbreast.

"Normally, yeah. But Sean's got it sorted with them."

The lock in lasted a few hours. It was probably a good thing when it ended, as by this time I was barely functioning, although still managing to tell the trad players that they needed more cowbell and urging them to play "Free Bird."

Brian had stopped drinking earlier in the night and drove us back to the house. We said good night to Sam and he walked me to his room, my room for the night. With Cait back he was sleeping on the couch. He tried to say good night, but I grabbed his hands, backing into the room. "Don't you want a nightcap?"

I didn't have any whiskey in the room, but it didn't matter. We didn't need it.

———

The next day was our last with the Gallaghers. I slept in late, with only a little bit of a hangover. Sam busied herself in the pasture with the twins and the horses, and Brian drove me over to the Athru distillery. It was beautiful, situated on the Lough Gill peninsula on a three-hundred-year-old Palladian estate. There was nothing to taste yet, but I made Brian promise to let me know when their whiskey would be ready. I'd make a trip back. And not just for the whiskey.

Leo had driven up from Galway, and Cait finally introduced him to her family. They didn't seem to mind his family connections. Almost losing their daughter had put some perspective on that, and we made sure to build up his part in helping find her.

Cait had recovered quickly, and invited Sam and me for an afternoon hike at Knocknarea. The sky was clear, and it was a far more pleasant experience than my previous trip. She regaled us with tales of Queen Maeve and the local history.

When we got back, Rose had prepared a lavish meal for our last night with them. The only negative was the final toast, which Rose insisted be done with her poteen. I resisted the urge to ask for a bleach chaser.

We said goodbye, which included long hugs from every member of the family and an extra-long one from Brian.

Sam and I stopped by the garda station to say goodbye to Calbach. He'd been promoted as a result of his role in the drug bust. He looked happy, and for the first time since I'd met him, didn't reek of whiskey. He filled us in on the aftermath of the operation.

They hadn't caught Ryan yet, but it was only a matter of time. Ireland's Criminal Assets Bureau had frozen all of his accounts, and now the only question was whether or not the gardaí would catch him before his drug suppliers did.

"Where's Liam?" I asked. I realized I never knew his real name.

Calbach shook his head. "He was called back to Dublin."

Someone had sent an anonymous note to the national An Garda Síochána, letting them know about Liam's behavior. And even though he'd orchestrated the largest drug bust in the history of the island, it was clear that without considerable outside help, he would have failed completely. And his superiors were less than thrilled about his cavalier attitude toward collateral damage. I suspected Liam would be working a desk in Donegal for the remainder of his career.

When it was time to leave, Chief Superintendent Murphy walked us out. Reaching out to shake my hand, he said, "There are many other lovely spots in Ireland. You'll be visiting them, yes?"

"I'm not sure. I'm thinking about sticking around Sligo for a while." I winked at him to let him know I was just kidding.

Sort of.

FORTY

Finding Cait had taken longer than we'd planned, so Sam rescheduled our flight to give us a few more days in Ireland. We spent as much time as we could in the Sligo area, visiting the beaches, doing the Benbulbin Forest Walk, and taking a tour of the Abbey. We visited my relatives, the O'Haras and the Boyles.

We drove the Wild Atlantic Way and then on to Cork, where we took a tour of the Middleton Distillery that housed the Jameson, and my new favorite, Redbreast labels. Then it was on to Dublin for the Guinness tour, trips to the Whiskey Museum, and Sam's selected art galleries and museums.

It wasn't enough time. I felt like I could live the rest of my life here and never get tired of what the country had to offer. As our flight to Chicago lifted off, I watched the green island fade away and knew I'd be back.

We both slept for most of the flight, and once we landed in Chicago, Sam and I split up. She went home and I took a cab from the airport to my house. Now that Svetlana knew where I lived, it was time to think about giving it up. In the meantime, I'd be living at Sam's. But I didn't know how long I'd be staying there, and thought one more night in my own bed couldn't hurt. And I wanted to stop by anyway to pick up a few things.

It was dark when the cabbie dropped me off in front of my house. I had some jet lag, and while the trip had been great, I was looking forward to hitting the sack.

I pulled my suitcase up the stoop and reached for the door, pulling out my key. I reached for the handle and saw the door was cracked open.

Shit. Had Gideon left it unlocked? Good thing I had nothing worth stealing. I wondered if whoever had broken in was still here.

I put the suitcase softly on the ground and pulled out my boot knife. I gently pushed the door open and stepped inside. I could see a light from the kitchen and heard scuffling sounds. Someone was in here.

Goddamnit. I wasn't in the mood to deal with this shit. Normally, I might have backed out and called the police. But I was tired and mad.

I walked to my kitchen and found a man bent over, looking into the refrigerator. "Who the fuck are you, and what are you doing in my house?" I yelled, waving at him with my tiny knife.

He stood up and turned around. He had a drink in his hand. "You really don't believe in keeping any food in the house, do you? At least I knew where you kept the whiskey." He raised his glass in a toast and drank.

I put my knife back into my boot and leaned against the wall.

"Hi, Dad."

NOTES AND ACKNOWLEDGMENTS

This story and all of the characters in it are fictional, although many of the elements are real. In particular, the whiskey. More on that later.

The Sligo Abbey and the garda station are real, but for hopefully obvious reasons (i.e., I've never been arrested in Sligo) the description of the inside of the station is fictional. The Limerick restaurant *Fómhar* is also a figment of my imagination, although it's inspired by the many very fine chefs and restaurants in Ireland. All of the wonderful monuments and megaliths around Sligo, such as Queen Maeve's tomb, and Carrowmore, are real, although I've taken a few liberties with some of the landscape details.

I'm very grateful to the Midelton Distillery for making such great whiskey. Part of me is sad that my personal search for my favorite whiskey in the world is concluded. Redbreast PX Edition is it. And this is after considerable testing. Unfortunately, PX is a limited edition, so here's hoping they'll reprise it, and in the meantime I'll make due with the Redbreast Lustau, which is also very delicious. Speaking of whiskey tasting, I would be remiss in not appreciating the people who joined me on this journey of exploration. Many thanks to the Happy Hour Ladies and Gentlemen for your help in sampling the finest Irish whiskeys. Also Ciara and Brian, my brother Cam, Jonathan, Kathryn, Robbie, and Dave the Neighbor.

Thanks to Jason Pinter and Polis Books for putting Jesse O'Hara out into the world, again.

Ciara, thank you for going over this so carefully and bringing your Irish perspective. I appreciate you, and your friendship. That goes for you too, Brian.

My beta readers, Mark Patterson, Barbara and Cindy Gaines, Anna, Suz, Kaveri Hurwitz and Jennifer Schulz, you always bring it. Debra Hartman (theprobookeditor.com), you're wonderful to work with. I look forward to the next project.

Kristen, I'm lucky to have you in my life.

Pat Knauss, my godmother, I feel your incredible support from a thousand miles away.

Trace, "good attitude" is a great addition to the family lexicon, which not only appears in the book, but I use often in my everyday life. Mom, thanks, I think, for "your face will freeze like that," although I'm not sure how I feel about the years of worry that it caused me as a child, along with a fair number of my adult ones. If I'm being completely honest, I still make a point to change my facial expression regularly, just in case it might freeze like that.

Last and the opposite of least, I wouldn't be able to do any of this if it wasn't for you, Anna. And it wouldn't be nearly as fun.

About the Author

Wendy Church has been a bartender, tennis instructor, semiconductor engineer, group facilitator, nonprofit CEO, teacher, PhD researcher, and dive bar cleaner. She is the author of *Murder on the Spanish Seas*, the first Jesse O'Hara novel, which is set on a luxury cruise in the Iberian peninsula, and introduces smart-mouthed amateur sleuth Jesse O'Hara, whose adventures are partly informed by Wendy's expertise and international travels. She lives in Seattle, WA.